JUSTIFY MY THUG

WAHIDA CLARK

A NOVEL

CASH MONEY CONTENT

First Trade Paperback Edition: April 2011

Book Layout: Peng Olaguera/ISPN

Cover Design: Oddball Dsgn

For further information log onto www.CashMoneyContent.com

Library of Congress Control Number: 2010942562

ISBN: 978-1-4516-1709-2   pbk
ISBN: 978-1-4516-1711-5   ebook

15

Printed in the United States

Dedicated to all of my readers, all over the world.

ACKNOWLEDGMENTS

All praise is due to the creator. I thank him for Yah Yah, my consultant and the most gifted visionary I know. My staff and Street Team who has sacrificed and will sacrifice at the drop of a dime. Lil' Wahida, Hasana, Al-Nisa, Rachman, Omar, Kisha, Wanda, Sabir, Dewey, Hadiyah and Jimil. The extended Street Team and staff, Hakim (Silver Stars) Al-baeth, Sherry, Razzaq, Aminah, Lindsey, Marie and Samad.

Karen Thomas, my editor since my first publishing deal. Thank you so much for sticking by me. Latoya Smith thank you. From The Agency Group Molly Derse, Sasha Raskin and everyone else behind the scenes. Intelligent Allah, (Lickin' License) I told you that you are a blessing and a very thorough editor. Buckey Fields, (The Ultimate Sacrifice) thank you for reading and sifting through everything I send you and a super big thanks for your feedback with Justify.

Marc Gerald thanks for introducing me to Cash Money Content. Slim, Baby and Vernon, let's do this. Let's show them how this is supposed to be done, how we do it!

To my family, moms, Aunt Ann, Aunt Marva, Aunt Ginger, dad, lil' brother Jabree. Melvin, dude, finish your book!

To the WCP Team, those here and those to come, y'all picked a winning Team. Take advantage of it.

JUSTIFY MY THUG

ONE

TASHA

I desperately wanted to scream, click my heels together and make myself disappear. I felt him. I could always feel his presence and I tried to tell Trina's ass that he was coming.

"Girl, chill and let me get this dick," she whined.

Well I listened to her and now look what the fuck chillin' got me. When I saw Trae I wanted to shit on myself. Thanks to her I'm now in a standoff between my husband and my possible baby daddy. Things were about to go from bad to some CSI shit. If Kaylin wouldn't have slammed the door and locked it I'm positive that Trae would have started blasting. I couldn't prepare my mind to get into argument mode because my missing niece Aisha called. I was hoping that it was some kind of a sick joke, but deep down inside I knew it wasn't. That was definitely Aisha calling her Auntie Tasha. She knew my cell number by heart because she used to always call to ask if she could come over to spend the night. I dialed the number back and somebody answered the phone and then immediately hung up. I called again but it went straight to voicemail.

That's when I panicked, rushed to the door and snatched it open. Trae was pacing back and forth, looking like a pit bull, but I didn't give a shit. I said, "Trae, I just got a call from Aisha. She wants me to come and get her. When I asked her where her mother was she said she thinks she's dead." He looked at me as if he didn't know who I was.

"Trae, did you hear what I just said to you? Our neice Aisha was just on the phone. I called the number back and the first time someone answered and hung up. The last time it went straight to voicemail. Call from your phone to see if you can get through. Maybe Marvin will talk to you. Something isn't right, Trae." I held up my cell phone displaying the number that Aisha had just called me from. What I had just told him must have finally registered. He snatched the cell phone from me and came into the apartment. Before he could hit the redial button on the phone, he looked up at Kyron. Everybody got quiet and we all held our breath as Trae and Kyron stared each other down. They stood not even ten feet from one another. The tension between them was suffocating. The silence had grown loud and I exhaled a sigh of relief when Kaylin spoke.

"Kyron, let me holla at you in the back," he said.

"Kay, not now," Kyron snapped, never taking his eyes off of Trae.

Kaylin, just like me, knew exactly what was about to happen. Somebody was getting ready to die.

"Nigga, I said, let me talk to you in the back for a minute." Kaylin gritted.

"Naw, baby boy. I ain't tryna talk right now. I got a plane

to catch. Kendrick, let's bounce, son!" Kyron said, nixing his brother off.

Kendrick went and grabbed his belongings out of Trina's bedroom and then walked over to Kyron. They both headed for the door. When they got close to Trae, Trae swung and hit Kyron in the face. I thought I heard Kyron's jaw crack. Trae followed up with another punch but this time Kyron weaved out of the way. He countered with a few punches of his own and the next thing I knew, they were all over the apartment tearing shit up. Kay and Kendrick struggled to break the two of them apart. Since Trina was screaming at the top of her lungs about them fucking up her apartment, I didn't hear my phone ringing. I happened to glance at the caller ID and I saw that same *859* number. It had to be Aisha again and thanks to these niggas fighting over pussy I missed her call. At that moment I was like, "Fuck both of them niggas," and I lost it.

"Stop it! Stop it!" I screamed, "Kyron you get the fuck out!" I went over to him and pushed him towards the door. "Get out Kyron!" I then pushed him out the door and Trina got rid of Kendrick. My niece and sister are missing and y'all acting like bitches." I then turned to Trae. "Trae, I need you to call Marvin and get me some answers." By that time I was so mad I started crying. Thankfully the phone rang again and thank God it was Aisha.

ANGEL

Leave it to the Queen of Drama and my best friend since the seventh grade, Tasha Macklin, to wreak havoc on everyone's lives, especially her own. I usually don't mind her antics because, they keep me entertained and rarely does she do shit on a small scale.

Now don't get me wrong, I love my girl to death and it's one thing when it's her and Trae's bullshit, but when it starts to spill over to me and my husband Kaylin, I'll be damned if I'll let her fuck up me and mines.

My circle is real small. It's just me and my three girls, Tasha, Kyra and Jaz all from Jersey. Each of us ended up with hustlers, Kyra with Marvin and Jaz with Faheem. Kaylin and Trae, who are like brothers, are from New York. They wasn't no block niggas either. They hustled hard, moved up the food chain, got money, and went legit. Me and Kaylin remained in New York while for the last few years Tasha and Trae have been living in California. I didn't want Trae to drag her clean across the country, that's where all this damn drama stemmed from. If they would have kept their asses in New York with me and Kaylin, they wouldn't be ready for Divorce Court. From what I was able to piece together, Trae allegedly got caught cheating with some Asian bitch named Charli Li. When Tasha found out, being the Queen of Drama that she is, she went ballistic and obviously went for revenge. But this bitch didn't go for subtle revenge. You know, sleep with another nigga and keep the shit to herself and move on with her life, type revenge. She didn't just fuck with some random nigga, she kept it close to the family and hooked up with Kyron, Kaylin's brother. Then to add insult to injury she gets pregnant. *Drama.*

I had no idea Tasha was going to sleep with Kyron. But you can't convince Kaylin of that since he knows that Tasha and me have always been thick as thieves and we tell each other everything. *Newsflash.* The ho ain't tell me shit and now my man is threatening divorce because he has it in his big ass head that I kept this from him. I'm like what . . . the . . . fuck? And then the next thing I know Trae leaves Cali and shows up at our home in New York to fill Kaylin in on their drama. Oh, the plot thickens. While he was here, he somehow found out that Kyron had just left for Cali and before I know it, him and Kaylin are off on the first thing smoking to catch up with Kyron and to do God knows what.

KAYLIN

Shit was crazy. I still can't believe it. Hearing from Trae about Kyron and Tasha creeping was one thing, but to actually catch them together was a beast of a different kind. It was like watching the *Animal Kingdom* on TV and knowing that the gazelle was not supposed to hang out with the lions.

I still asked myself, *how did this shit happen right under my nose? And why didn't I see it coming?* Even though I asked the questions, deep down inside I already knew the answers.

I knew all about the problems Trae and Tasha were having. They were the same problems that many married couples go through. So when Tasha told me that she needed a little space and wanted to crash at my spot for a little while, I had no problem with that. Shit, after all, we are family. Having my brother Kyron, who had recently come home from Upstate, in my house as well, I never thought it would be a potential disaster waiting to happen.

Kyron knew that Tasha was taken. I told him that she was Trae's wife the day we picked her up from the airport. It never crossed my mind that he would disrespect the game and not treat her as if she was off limits. And I damn sure didn't expect Tasha to cross that line. I thought he'd be content with Mari, the lawyer chick he bagged while Upstate. We all know talked about how she did the last seven years of his bid with him. I never thought that he'd shit on Mari and Trae like that. All I know now is that I really don't know my brother anymore. Years in the bing done put Kyron on some real grimy shit.

Kyron would always tell us to never shit where you eat and family first. If somebody would've asked me about a month ago, what were the odds of Tasha and Kyron fucking, I would have said a million to one. And I'm glad that no one ever asked and I never put money on those odds because I'd be a broke muthafucka right about now. I feel totally disrespected.

The whole situation is a bitch slap in the face to me. Why? Because it appears that I had a hand in it but I didn't. But wait a minute. Now that I think about it, that shit may have been brewing at my record label's anniversary party. Hell yeah. I had Kyron escort my artist Lil' E to the event. I didn't want to do it but I did. The first time she saw him she started drooling at the mouth, so I made it happen. Especially since she kept sweatin' me about him. I told her she couldn't handle Kyron, but she didn't want to listen. Her snow white ass is no doubt a nigga lover.

I had the event at this major spot, Cipriani's on 42nd street, New York. When we do it, we do it big. Just call me the black Donald Trump. Niggas ain't used to doing things of this caliber. Shit, show me a man with money as long as mine and I'll buy his out. Tonight was about making a statement and as soon as niggas stepped through the door, that statement was made.

I had my girls Tasha and Trina with me and since there had been so much drama going on, it was good to see Tasha smiling again. From time to time I had noticed Kyron checking Tasha out but I ain't sweat it, plus Lil' E wasn't letting that nigga out her sight.

KYRON

Fuck all the bullshit, let me tell y'all how it really went down. My brother wanted me to escort his artist Lil' E to the label's anniversary party. He told me that she wanted to meet me. I was like, meet me? A white bitch of her caliber can only suck my dick. Her money wasn't long enough for me. So I wasn't trying to hear that shit, I was too busy chasing behind Shorty. So when Kendrick told me that Shorty and her sister would be at the party, I said, "Bet I can kill two birds with one stone," especially since me and Shorty had to sneak around anyways. So fuck it, I got dressed and went and picked up Lil' E.

I pulled up to her condo around nine and had to admit that she was official for a white chick. She had ass, hips and lips. The ass and hips she had squeezed into some little black dress and her tiny pedicured toes were sitting in a pair of fuck-me stilettos. I was feelin' her outfit. We smoked a blunt and made no conversation as we rode in back of the limo to the spot.

We pulled up on 42nd and I was like damn, "Lil' Bro doin' it up." When I stepped inside the Italian Renaissance my thoughts immediately drifted to the dons. I had some work to do for them that I needed to get ready within the next couple of days.

Lil' E squeezed my hand, bringing me back to the here and now. I scanned the room and saw that everybody who was anybody was up in here. When I finally spotted my brother he was standing on the red carpet and surrounded by flashing lights and the press. He had on a white Saratoria Domenico Caraceni white suit with a Cuban cigar dangling from his mouth. The media was eatin' that shit up. And here this nigga made everyone else wear black and he had on white.

"Hey brother in law," Angel said as she came over and gave me a hug. "Look at you Miss Lily. Girl, you better watch him."

"Oh I plan to." Lil' E responded and then I watched as the two of them exchanged some phony air kisses and E went to the bathroom.

"You must going to be lookin' up."

"Yeah, I'ma be lookin' up and using no hands."

"Well damn. It's like that?" Angel interrupted.

"Girl, let me go to the ladies room before I get myself in trouble."

I laughed and as soon as she stepped off I said to Angel, "You lookin' good tonight. Does my brother know how lucky he was that he saw you first?"

"What's that supposed to mean?"

"You know what it means."

"No, I don't. Why don't you explain yourself?"

I was getting ready to but then I saw *her*. Tasha came through the door, looking good enough to eat, hanging on the arm of some nigga. When I saw some of the press move towards them it dawned on me that dude was one of the artists on Kaylin's label.

"Damn, my brother pimpin' everybody out tonight. What's up with that?"

"Kaylin pimps everybody out every night and every day," Angel said. "He's not going to be satisfied until he owns New York. I just hope that he doesn't kill himself in the process. The nigga is going crazy with it."

"Damn it's like that?"

"I'm his attorney and his wife. Trust me when I say, yes, it is like that."

Just then my brother motioned for his wife to come over to where he was.

"Excuse me Kaylin, God is calling me," Angel said and walked off.

Shorty had my undivided attention. She was wearing the shit out of this long black Tom Ford dress that I bought her. Her abs, arms and back were out. Her breasts were damn near exposed. Son had his hand resting on her ass as they posed for the camera. My dick tried to get hard as I fantasized about me sucking on her nipples until she came and then yanking the dress up over that phat ass and hittin' it doggy style . . . raw dog.

Lil' E eased up next to me and slid her hand into mine. "That's Explozive," she told me, apparently she thought I was looking at the rap nigga, but she had me fucked up. I was looking at Shorty and was wondering why Kay sent her with this fuckin' clown. I shrugged it off because E was pulling me towards the ballroom. When we stepped into the VIP area all I could say was, "Damn, I need to be robbin' all of these niggas up in here."

I recognized DJ Khalid's voice before I saw him. Niggas were on the dance floor and they had waiters passing out drinks. My brother had officially brought the hood to the burbs. Lil' E grabbed us both a drink and we went to our table and sat down. I took a sip and immediately started looking around for Tasha. I swear I couldn't get her off of my mind, even with E's hand resting on my thigh.

I leaned over to whisper in Lil' Mama's ear and my brother came walking over and was trailed by two bodyguards. He grabbed a seat next to me and his security guards stood behind us. He began to fill me in on tonight's agenda and then that's when Shorty and that rapper muthafucka came walking towards the table. He was all over Shorty as if he owned her.

Explozive came over to Kaylin and started running his mouth, but like me, my brother didn't hear shit. All we saw was this niggas hands all over Tasha.

"Muthafucka, you must be tired of livin'," Kaylin gritted.

"What? What I do?" Explozive slurred.

"I told you who you had on your arm and I told you how to act."

"C'mon boss man. I'm just a squirrel trying to bust a nut." Explosive smiled through a platinum grill as he held Tasha even tighter, obviously forgetting all about the instructions. "That's what escorts are for, right?" Explozive was drunk as shit.

"Tasha, come over her and sit next to Kyron," Kaylin ordered.

As she tried to walk away, Explozive grabbed her around the waist.

"Tone, get this nigga," my brother said as if he was reading my mind.

His bodyguard grabbed drunken-ass Explozive and put him in a chokehold. We watched as a stunned Explozive looked over at our table and started pleading his case.

"C'mon, Boss man. I thought we was here to have a good time?"

"Nigga, I told you that she was family and that she was only eye candy for tonight. You said you understood. But obviously you didn't. Either that or you just didn't give a fuck. So I'll see you when I see you."

I couldn't see the look on Tasha's face and I couldn't help but smile. It was saying, "Damn, Kaylin it was only an ass rub! You just fucked up my paper. That nigga had my purse a couple of Gs richer. I was planning on rapping his pockets and sending him home with a hard dick and a wet dream. Then to add injury to insult you going to sit me down like a child next to the nigga who has been giving me fever and this little white girl that apparently was planning on having him in her mouth before the night was over."

She shot us a few daggers as she plopped down in the seat next to me. But lady luck was in the muthafuckin' house. Kay sent Lil' E to sign some autographs and then when Slim and Baby of Cash Money came over he got up and they walked away.

"What's so funny?" Tasha asked me with a slight attitude. "And why is Kaylin trippin'? I'm grown."

I wasted no time moving closer to her, not caring about my brother or anyone else. "You wear my money well," I said referring to her dress that was showing off her beautiful legs. I couldn't help but think if I had my way, right now I would be bending her over one of these chairs and she would be yelling out my name.

I sat there looking at Shorty. "Damn, you look good enough to eat," I told her as I continued to take her all in.

"You look good . . . enough," she teased.

I grabbed her hand and pulled her to me, "Let's get out of here."

"And go where? I thought you are here to assist your brother. As a matter of fact, why aren't you entertaining your little snow bunny?"

"Because I would rather entertain you."

"Whatever. You don't want to entertain me because you too scared of your little brother."

I chuckled, "Shorty, you be talking a lot of shit."

"And I can do that. Why? Because I can *back* up every word."

"Well, I got something for you to back up into."

Tasha looked at me and smiled. I could see her cheeks getting a little flush. I was getting ready to make my next move when Lil' E emerged from signing autographs. "You ready Kyron? I have something I *want to show* you."

I looked up at lil' Mama, then back at Shorty, and for the first time a brotha was stuck. I was grateful for Angel, who came rushing over to where we were.

"Tasha, come here Kaylin wants you to be in these pictures. We gonna be on the cover of Black Enterprise."

As she pulled Tasha to her feet she looked back at me and said, "I hope you save some." I looked at Angel to see if she had heard what Shorty had just said. Shorty had just raised the stakes to our dangerous game. Angel didn't appear to have heard her because she yanked Tasha away from me.

"Save some of what?" Lil' E asked playfully.

I stood up and took lil' Mama by the hand, "Don't even worry about it. Come show me that no hands thing." Sheeit chasing Shorty had me all worked up. I was now good and ready to get a nut off my back.

She looked at me with a big ass Kool-Aid smile and said, "Follow me. I found the perfect spot."

When I emerged from a small room in the back I could see the party was getting livelier by the minute. I looked down at lil' Mama who was apparently disappointed that she couldn't get me to slide up in that, but shit I can only give a bitch of her caliber what she asks for and nothing more. My philosophy is, when a bitch tells you she wants to suck your dick you let her, and then you make her pay for the rest. Plus, the only pussy I was trying to slide up into was Shorty's.

I scanned the room and saw that a small line of cats wanting to holla at my brother was beginning to form, then I found

Tasha talking to Angel at the bar. I quickly dismissed lil' Mama and headed over to where they were. Fate had to be on my side because just as I approached them, one of the staff members came over to Angel and needed her assistance giving me another opportunity to snatch up Shorty.

I slid up behind her, positioning myself up against her soft ass and whispered in her ear, "I saved the best part for you."

She quickly turned around and we were face-to-face and I wasn't backing down. "What are you doing?" She tried to look around me to see if anybody was watching us.

"What? You scared of my little brother?" I said with a smirk on my face.

"No . . . like I said, 'I'm a grown ass woman.' I can do whatever and whoever I want." She answered me as she looked me up and down. "I was just making sure your little girlfriend didn't catch you all up in my face. I don't want to have to fuck her up."

"Aiight then, since you so grown, you can leave with me right now."

"And go where?"

"Don't worry about it." On instinct my hand went to her nipple. And since lil' Mama had just taken care of the foreplay, I was ready for the main course.

"Nigga, we ain't fuckin', I already told you that."

"You said we can play. I'm ready to play." She gently grabbed my hand to move it from her nipple. I held on to it and took it down to my dick. When she squeezed it I knew I had her.

"You ain't ready to play," she told me as her fingers glided across the head. "I'm disappointed, you ain't even hard."

"Look in the dictionary under play and my picture is right

there. I just need you to fill in the definition on what you con-
sider as *play*."

She smiled and squeezed my dick again. "I already told you
my definition. A nigga who eats and swallows everything on the
menu. That's it, that's all. No strings attached."

"And I already told you. I can handle that. The dick ain't got
to be hard to eat and swallow."

"It's the principle, Kyron, you not being rock hard tells me
that I ain't doing my job."

"Trust me. You doin' your job. A nigga just has a little more
control than what you used to."

She smiled at me. "Let's go then."

Me and Shorty headed for the nearest exit.

KAYLIN

I remember wondering why both of them niggas were ghost for
the rest of the evening. Now I know.

And even though Trae never said it, I know that in the back
of his mind he thinks that I know. But what's in the back of
mine is my wife *had* to know about this shit. She and Tasha go
back to Reeboks, shit they like Oprah and Gail. Ain't no way in
hell Angel didn't know anything.

When Trae came to my house and told me what was going
on it was like a hand grenade being tossed in my lap. When he
told me that Tasha was pregnant and didn't know if the baby was
his or Kyron's . . . *BOOM!* . . . that grenade exploded in my face.

Brother or no brother, hands down, Kyron was in violation.
And I planned to tell him that as soon as I saw him. I *wanted*
answers and Trae *needed* answers.

So, he ended up talking me into flying to California with him to confirm everything that he had just told me. And when I walked into Trina's apartment and Kyron came walking out of the bathroom, I knew right then that it was all true. I also knew that shit was about to go from bad to worse in zero to 60 seconds flat.

Glancing over my shoulder, I saw that Trae was still standing in the doorway. The look on his face was one that I had seen many times. It was the look that signaled he was ready to kill.

KYRON

When I was Upstate on lock, I read a book by some D.C. cat called *The Ultimate Sacrifice*. In the book, the main character went home from prison and fucked his man's woman. I remember thinking to myself that son was crazy foul for crossing the line like that. I also can remember an old timer telling me that sometimes art imitated life. I knew that, but it had nothing to do with me. I wasn't imitating shit, as far as I was concerned I'm always gonna do me and be me. But then I became like the main character of that novel and I crossed those same lines. But fuck it, I'ma thug and thugs ain't gotta justify themselves to no one.

From the moment I saw Shorty at the airport, I knew I had to have her. I knew Tasha was Trae's wife, Kay told me that the moment he saw the spark in my eye...

"*That's Trae's wife, nigga.*"

"*Kaylin, all I said was shorty is fine.*"

"*You heard what I said,*" my brother warned me.

And he was right. I did hear what he said, but after doing all those years Up Top, my urges wasn't tryna hear that shit. At first, I was able to control myself around her, but once I talked myself up on that first kiss, it was on. I decided right then and there that I wanted Shorty and I wasn't taking no for an answer. My inner voice said, "You foul for this." But my outer voice said, "Fall back son, I got this." Shorty said that she and Trae was getting a divorce, so she's fair game."

Tasha is such a bad bitch, that in a few days she made me forget Mari doing the last of my bid with me. I knew that eventually I'd have to deal with Trae and my brother, and that almost changed my mind about the moves I was making. But I was so caught up in the moment that I went bare back and once I got that gushy, that shit went out the door. Her pussy was so warm and tight that I came so hard that day I swear I heard fireworks going off inside my head. It was some shit that ain't never happen to a nigga before.

When I heard that Tasha was supposed to be pregnant, there was no doubt in my mind that she was carrying my seed. I wanted to see her and talk with her. A nigga needed to find out where her head was at. So me and my cousin Kendrick shot out to Cali.

I came prepared, pregnancy test in hand. Shorty was scared to take it but I made it known that she didn't have any choice in the matter. When she went into the bathroom, I can't front, those few minutes felt like hours. When she came out stone faced I knew what it was. So I went into the bathroom and confirmed what I already knew, that it was positive. I came out ready to celebrate, looked up and my brother Kay was walking into the apartment and Trae was standing in the doorway. I knew what they were there for, but I wasn't trying to hear that shit. The positive test was me and Shorty's moment. I wasn't being denied that for nobody. To keep it 100, I knew I should have left when Tasha had asked me to leave. Hell, she begged me to leave. But Shorty and her pussy is like a drug. I had to get high. So now I was busted, but fuck it. Me being in Cali already told whoever was paying attention that I didn't give a fuck. I had made up my mind and stuck to my guns, so the next move was Trae's.

TRAE

So many years in the drug game and killing field had taught me to always trust my gut instincts. So when I heard that Kyron's bitch ass was out of town, my instincts told me that he was on his way to the west coast to see *my* wife. And like always they were right.

"Yo, Trae, you buggin', son," Kay said when I told him what my gut was telling me.

"Bullshit," I replied. When he saw that look I get when I'm ready to body something it took no further convincing and we were on the plane to Cali.

Everybody, including my own mama, knows that Mama Santos is like a second mother to me. We family and when she heard what her bitch ass son did she began praying in Spanish for her son's safety. I love her to death, and for her I am going to give this nigga a pass. If he was anybody else she would be picking out a tombstone and a suit. I'm lying to myself; she may still have to depending on how this pussy nigga acts.

This punk came straight home and disrespected me. Him and everybody else know that I done killed niggas for lesser shit. That's how I know he did the shit on purpose. I just have yet to figure out why. He knew that Tasha was my wife. Shit, all of New York knew it. The nigga still said fuck me. It's obvious that he don't really know how much weight I carry. My name alone put the fear of God in niggas. He knows better than anybody that I ain't none of them fake ass gangstas he was locked up with. Again, so why? What did I do to this nigga?

Tasha was too blinded by my betrayal and hers to see that the nigga was just using her. While I can't forgive her, I'll be damned if I just step aside and let the next man have what's mine. I don't care who he is. It's the principle of the thing.

From the doorway of Trina's apartment, I saw Kyron coming out the bathroom holding a pregnancy test. My hand went immediately to the .45 Glock in the waist of my jeans.

Knowing me like he did, Kaylin turned around and barked, "Remember whose brother he is. Plus, you told me that you'd let me talk to him first." He slammed the door to the apartment in my face and locked it.

I paced back and forth in the small hallway like an animal trapped in a cage. My temper was trying to get the best of me as I tried to decide who I was gonna body first and how I was gonna clean up the mess. Then all of a sudden I got mad at Tasha all over again. What the fuck was she thinking? Why does she always have to go to the extreme? Always trying to prove some shit to me. Look at the position she done put everybody in.

Raised voices inside the apartment broke my reverie. Tasha was saying something to Kyron. I wanted to bust the door down and let everybody know how I was feeling, but then I remembered that I had too much to lose by getting loud and emotional. After all, I'ma bad boy and bad boys move in silence with violence.

TWO

I'm Jasmine Mujahid. I married the love of my life, Faheem. Faheem is considered the big daddy of the crew. You know, the level headed one, the one who keeps everyone on point. For example, when we lived in Jersey, everybody would call him for advice. Now don't get me wrong, we had our share of drama. Everyone recalls and still talks about how I wouldn't get with Faheem for the longest time. And I wouldn't. Hell, no. Not as long as he was in the game. So he eventually gets out and then he later discovers that I, Miss 'don't want to fuck with a drug dealer' Jaz, had my hands dirty cooking meth for the white boys. Man! You would have thought that I murdered the president! His family was mad and he was that much madder, more like . . . mad amplified by ten. I was called every hypocrite in the book. But to me I wasn't in the game . . . well not like he was. I wasn't flippin' birds or nothing like that. I would cook, get paid and keep it moving. Them white boys loved me. But then it all came tumbling down. Faheem would have never found out if I hadn't gotten busted in a meth lab, and he had to get me a lawyer, bail me out, make a witness disappear, the whole nine. All the shit you see in the movies. And to this day, I don't know what was worst—getting busted by the Feds or by Faheem. Thanks to Faheem, except for a couple of days in a holding facility, my ass walked.

To keep some of the heat off me, I had to remind him that he was no angel either. It wasn't as if he just quit hustling in one day. Hell no. That nigga hustled and stacked and hustled and stacked until he was *ready* to get out. It just so happened that I waited for him. I did my best not to give him that impression, but hell yeah, I waited. I wanted to be with him.

Anyways, that was then and we got through that and Faheem is still the love of my life. We've been happily married for almost five years and we have a seven year old daughter named Kaeerah Aaliyah. I was the first one in the crew to get pregnant. Then it was Kyra, Tasha and finally Angel. Me and Faheem relocated to Georgia where I enrolled at Spelman. School is kicking my ass as usual, but Faheem keeps pushing me, and seems more deter-mined than me that I finish. I think he just likes me out of the house so he can milk the stay-at-home dad role. Yes, he takes the daddy role very seriously. He has Kaeerah on a rigid schedule. She goes to dance class, takes piano lessons and is on her school's soccer team. He makes sure she stays involved in something all year round. I'm not surprised though, as bad as he wanted me to get pregnant, I knew that he would be a good father.

But our shit took a turn for the worse on the Saturday morn-ing that Faheem wanted to go to ghetto-ass South DeKalb Mall to check out his boy Jabree. Jabree just recently opened up a clothing store. He's from Jersey and also relocated to the ATL. We were chillin', strolling through the mall, mostly window shopping. I was munching on an almond pretzel from Auntie Anne's, and Kaeerah was begging her daddy to buy her everything she saw, when this little boy runs right pass us almost knocking Kaeerah over. I was getting ready to snatch his ass up but Faheem beat me to it.

FAHEEM

"Daddy, that little boy kicked me," Kaeerah whined.

"Lil' man. You gotta slow down. You can't be running and stepping on the ladies." Lil' man didn't say anything. *Why was he by himself?* I wondered. I looked around to see if someone may have been looking for him but there was no one in sight. So I walked over to him and kneeled down in front of him. The more I looked at him the more he reminded me of someone.

"I'm sorry," he finally said as he looked at Kaeerah and apologized.

"It's cool. Are you lost?" I asked him.

"Yes, I don't see my mommy," he responded with a low voice. I guess he knew that mama was going to beat that ass when she found him.

Then I heard a woman yelling out, "Faheem. Oh my God where is he? Faheem." I rose to my feet, turned around, and was face to face with Oni . . . my ex. And from the look on her face you would have thought that she saw a ghost. She reached out and grabbed lil' man's hand and put him behind her which said it all.

"So you named your son after me?" I asked with a smug grin.

She returned the same grin and then said with sarcasm dripping from her voice. "No I named *your son* Faheem." She then turned to walk away. I reached out and grabbed her by her shoulder, stopping her dead in her tracks.

"Come again. Did you say *my son?*" I was confused and was sure that this bitch was fuckin' with me.

Oni turned around and said, "Yes, Faheem. If you weren't being such a fucked up, self-centered person maybe you would have tried to find out." This bitch had the audacity to knock my hand off her shoulder.

"Fuck you mean, 'find out'? You was supposed to tell me!"

"Faheem, why don't you do what you do best, leave."

JAZ

Faheem? Faheem is not a common name. I looked at the little boy and my mouth hit the floor. And recognizing Oni it was obvious that I was seeing exactly what Faheem was seeing.

And before I knew it Faheem had his hands around her neck and was trying to choke her to death. Thank God we were in the hood, because instead of getting a whole bunch of white people screaming, the hood niggas simply gathered around and enjoyed the spectacle. The security guards came and managed to pull Faheem off of her. Little Faheem was crying while Kaeerah was holding on to me for dear life. She didn't know what was going on. I was only praying that the mall cops wouldn't try to play 'captain save a ho' because Faheem was seeing fire and I knew that he was packin' a burner.

"Nigga, if you don't get your fuckin' hands off of me," Faheem threatened the rent-a-cop.

Thank God the rent-a-cop was a little shook. He let Faheem

go and turned his attention to Oni, "Ma'am, are you okay? Do you want to press charges?" The mall cop asked as two other ones ran over.

Faheem was towering over her yelling, "Oni, how could you fuckin' do this? What the fuck is the matter with you?" he spat.

Like a bitch with some sense, she got the fuck away from a crazed Faheem and came over to where I was. "Here." She handed me her business card. Then she looked at Faheem and said, "When you calm down, call me."

"Call you? Bitch . . . call you? Calm . . . down?" Faheem was starting to stutter, which meant that shit was getting ready to get ugly . . . again.

Sure enough, no sooner than I thought it, he lunged for her ass again. She ducked, grabbed little Faheem and the bitch took off running. We both stood there looking at the little replica of Faheem. The same little boy who was the spittin' image of our daughter. I was at a loss for words.

FAHEEM

I took off my NY fitted and wiped the sweat off my forehead. A big nigga like me was actually feeling dizzy. Niggas were gathered around me as if I was a circus animal or some shit. I started walking and the people parted as if I was Moses and they were the Red Sea. There was no doubt in my mind that lil' man was my seed. *My son.* And here this bitch done robbed me of the most important years of his life. The years that I, the father, was supposed to do the molding and shaping. I should have snapped that bitch's neck right there on the spot.

Oni and I kicked it off and on back in Jersey. Mostly when

me and Jaz were fighting. Those other broads were too jealous and would come at me with all the bullshit that a real hustler didn't have the time or the patience for. They couldn't grasp that I just needed a jump-off for the moment. Oni understood and accepted that Jaz was wifey and a dog would always find his way home. That's the only reason I would always fuck with her. She knew her position and played it well.

From looking at my son . . . damn did I just say that? *My son?* He looks to be the same age as Kaeerah. This shit is crazy. That means that her and Jaz must have gotten pregnant at the same time. But why would she keep it from me? Most chicks would use that as leverage. But she just ups and disappears. Oh, this bitch *is* going to pay for this shit.

ONI

I first spotted *him* and Jaz strolling through the food court. At first I was telling myself, *that couldn't be.* I kept staring and following behind them. I was so focused on them that little Faheem took off running. When I finally realized that he was out of my sight, that's when I slipped up and called out his name and I knew, right then and there I was busted.

"Girl, what is the matter with you? Why are you crying? What happened? Are you and Faheem okay?" My mother Marie was obviously ready to call the police.

"No, Ma. I mean, we are fine." I made a feeble attempt to calm her down.

"Then why are you crying?"

"I just saw *him.*"

"Saw who?"

"Faheem's father."

My mother was quiet. But I knew she was trying to find the right way to say, *I told you so!* So, I waited patiently.

"Oni, I tried to tell you that one day whether it would be five, ten, fifteen years from now, a child always finds the way to their parents soul."

Here she goes with that tribal shit. I thought to myself.

"I told you that Georgia, Tennessee, Chicago . . . it didn't matter where you went, he was going to find out about his son because you was dead wrong. Wrong for not allowing him to be a part of that boy's life. You didn't even give the man a choice. The choice to be a man. So now what? There's nothing I can tell you. I knew this day was coming. What did he say?"

"He didn't say anything, mama. I gave him my number and left."

"What do you mean he didn't say *anything*? You didn't introduce him to his son?"

"Mom, no. I left. I gotta go. Bye." I hung up on her.

I wasn't expecting my mom to be sympathetic, so I don't even know why I called her. She has always been Faheem's number one cheerleader. I called four other people before I called her, but just my luck she was the only one who answered their phone.

JAZ

I didn't want to believe this shit. This bitch had a son? I had to admit, I was a little jealous. She gave *my man* a son. Faheem has been trying to get me to give him a son ever since Kaeerah was a year old. But I wasn't trying to have no more babies, especially not while I'm in school. Now look. And he looks just like his dad. I'm dying to know why she kept it from him. And of course

Faheem is so angry he can't even talk. So much for making it
to the grand opening of his boy's store. We came straight home
and he's been sitting in the backyard smoking blunts for hours.
After I put Kaeerah to bed I went outside to join him.

I sat down on his lap. "Are you ready to talk about this?"

"Get her on the phone."

"What?" I was not expecting that response.

"Get her on the phone." He glared at me as if I wasn't moving fast enough.

I stood up, looked at my husband and went in the house to
go get the business card that I had tucked under my jewelry box.
I lifted the jewelry box up and studied the business card. She
was CEO of some hotel chain. Oni Mason. This was the chick
who would always be there for Faheem when we would break
up. I never understood that shit. The bitch would sit and wait
patiently. It seemed to me that having his baby would have been
the trump card she needed. But instead she got ghost. I was not
looking forward to seeing how this plot would unravel.

I dialed the number that was scribbled on the back of the
card and it went straight to voicemail. "Oni, this is Jaz. Faheem
is trying to reach you. Call *us* back at this number." I ended
the call. She must have had the phone in her hand because she
called right back.

She said, "Hello. Jaz? Wait! Don't give Faheem the phone.
Take down my address, tell him to come by tomorrow. I can't
do this with him over the phone."

She gave me the address and I jotted it down. But I couldn't
resist. I had to make sure me and this sneaky bitch was on the
same page. So I said, "I don't know what type of slick shit or
trick shit you on, but I'm letting you know up front, in case you

even think about trying to fuck Faheem and bring us any drama. You don't want to try me."

She must have thought about what I said because she was quiet for a while. "Jaz, you got him. You are the victorious one. Don't allow little ole me make you feel insecure. I only gave birth to his son. You married him."

I had to laugh at that one. *No this bitch didn't go there.* "Insecure? I'm not the one who sat around waiting for another bitch's scraps to fall off the table. I'm not the one who went into hiding because you obviously thought he was going to reject you. Oh yeah, now that was real secure," I said with as much sarcasm as I could muster, and then I hung up. When I turned around Faheem was standing in the doorway.

"What was that all about? I just asked you to get her on the phone. Not to add more drama to this shit then there already is."

"Well, if you didn't want any more drama then you should have called her yourself," I snapped.

"Who the fuck you think you talking to, Jaz?" He glared at me and I shut the fuck up.

I handed him her address. "She said come by tomorrow."

He glanced at the address. "Fuck that. I'm going by there tonight." He was already headed downstairs for the kitchen.

"Bullshit," I spat. He looked at me as if I was crazy but I didn't care. "If you're going tonight I'm going with you," I told him.

"No you're not. Wait up for me and I'll see you when I get back." He snatched his keys off the counter and I followed behind him.

"Why can't I go Faheem?" I spoke to his back.

He stopped dead in his tracks and turned around. "Tell me why you want to go, Jaz? What do you think is going to happen?" When he saw that I was at a loss for words he said, "Now who's the one acting insecure? I said I'll talk to you when I get back."

I followed him to the front door, speechless as I watched him jump into his Escalade and drive off to go do God knows what. I went and peeked at our daughter sleeping and then went into my bedroom. I needed to talk to my girls.

The first person I decided to call was Kyra. The house phone kept ringing. I looked at my watch and wondered where in the hell could this girl be? I then dialed her cell and it said it was no longer in service. *Damn.* It hasn't been that long since I spoke to her. Or has it? She could have at least called and gave me the new number. I dialed Tasha's home number and cell. No answer. *Those bitches must be out running the streets together.*

I dialed Angel at home and she picked up on the first ring. "Hello."

She sounded like shit. Like she needed someone to talk to. "It's me, Jaz. What's the matter with you?"

"I know who it is. What's up? Why you sounding like you lost your best friend?"

"Well the shit must be contagious because you sound like you just lost yours. So spill your drama first. What's going on? You and Kaylin alright?" I asked her.

"Girl, I don't know where to start. Have you spoken to Tasha yet?"

"Oh God. Don't tell me this has something to do with her." Tasha's ass stayed into something.

"You don't know the half of it," Angel let out a huge sigh. The kind that says I don't even want to talk about it right now. I was like damn, but I still needed to get my venting off because I was about to blow. "Well, I got hit with a bombshell today."

"What? What happened? Everybody okay?" Angel asked me.

"You remember Faheem's jump-off? That chick named Oni?"

Angel snickered, "You mean your competition?"

"Whatever. Well, we saw her today."

"Oh really? Where? In Georgia? Who she know down there? What she say to y'all? That girl knows she was crazy over her some Faheem."

"Well, she got her own little Faheem."

"You mean a nigga that look like Fa? Damn, she still ain't over him, is she?" Angel apparently thought that was cute.

"No, Angel. She got a little son named Faheem."

You could hear a pin drop. She must have been trying to digest what I had just told her.

"I know you are not saying what I think you're saying."

"You're supposed to be the smart lawyer. What do you think I am saying?"

"She got a son by Faheem? Faheem was creeping with that bitch? He brought her to Georgia? What?" From her short breaths I could tell that Angel was up and pacing back and forth. "Don't have me guessing. What the fuck is up?"

"Apparently she didn't want Faheem to know she was pregnant, so she relocated down here, getting away. I thought the ho knew that we were already down here, but I think she was down here before us."

"Oh shit! She got a son and didn't tell him?"

"Nope."

"A son, Jaz? What did he do? What did he say?"

"Nothing. He just tried to strangle her to death right there in the mall. Security had to pull him up off of her."

"Oh my God! Where is he now? What else happened?"

"He just left to go see her."

"This time of night? That's some bullshit, Jaz. You should have gone with him."

"Angel, you are not helping. I'm trying to be mature about this whole . . . situation." I honestly didn't know what to call it. But I did know that since I had wanted to go and Faheem stopped me, Angel's last comment got under my skin. It was time to focus on her drama. "So what about you? Why are you so agitated?" I wanted to know what or who was crawling up her ass, hoping her drama wasn't worse than mine.

"Man, me and Kaylin is getting ready to go to war if we don't come to an understanding."

"Well, damn. What happened? And how is Tasha involved?" This was going to be good. Tasha never let us down. "No, wait. Let's get her on three way." I wanted to be thoroughly entertained.

"I just called up there. No one's answering. Not even Kaylin."

"Kaylin? What is he doing in Cali?"

"That's what I was trying to tell you. Major drama. Since Tasha found out that Trae fucked that Asian bitch, she decided she's gonna get some get-back by fucking Kyron. And guess what?"

"Tasha fucked somebody else? She cheated on Trae?" I gasped and grabbed at my heart. "Angel, you lyin'. Tell me you're lying. Kyron. Kyron? Why does that name sound familiar? Who is that?"

"You heard us mention Kyron. Kyron is Kaylin's brother. The one who was locked up."

"Oh snap." I needed some popcorn and a drink right about now. Angel was not lying when she said, 'major drama'. "So how does everyone seem to know that she fucked Kyron? How did she let her business get in the streets?"

"Kaylin's sister caught them."

"Shit, the one who don't like her because she snagged Trae?"

"Exactly."

This plot was definitely thickening.

"And that ain't all," Angel continued.

But at this point you could have stuck a fork in me because I was done. So I decided to crack a joke. "What else could there be? She pregnant?" I found myself laughing at my own joke. But Angel wasn't. I almost choked on my own spit. "Angel? Don't fuckin' play like that. Tell me you're lying."

"I wish I could."

At that moment, I saw that my own situation wasn't half as bad. "Angel, please don't tell me that Tasha is pregnant by some other nigga." My heart sank to my feet. I had so many questions. I didn't know where to start. What has my girl gotten herself into? "What is Trae saying? How did this happen? Kaylin let this go on? What the fuck was Tasha thinking?" I wouldn't let Angel get a word in. But I needed to hear the answers to my questions from the horse's mouth. "Let me see if I can get Tasha on a three way call," I told her and started dialing Tasha's cell before Angel could respond. As soon as it started ringing, I clicked Angel in.

"H-e-llo." The amount of strain in her voice made me know that shit was ugly, but what she told me floored me for the second time tonight.

"Tasha, it's me. I got Angel on the other line. We are worried about you. What the hell is going on? You or Kyra never answer the phone. Where y'all at? And why haven't I heard from either one of y'all?"

"I just got a call from Aisha. She said something about Kyra being dead." Tasha told us.

"What?" Me and Angel shrieked at the same time.

"Tasha what the fuck are you talking about?" Angel was on it. She and Kyra are first cousins.

Tasha started crying. "I kind of believe it because I haven't heard from Kyra in a while and that ain't like her. Marvin has been layin' low so we figured he and Kyra ran off some—"

"Tasha, Kyra would have told us if she was going away," Angel screamed at Tasha, cutting her off. "Why don't you know where she is? Especially if you hadn't heard from her in awhile, that didn't raise a red flag? And why didn't you call me?"

"Angel, I'm not in the mood for your bullshit. You could have just as easily picked up the phone and called me. Just like you, I had no control over the girl calling. And you know I've been back and forth to New York dealing with my own drama. The number Aisha called from, we called back but no one is answering. Trae has been trying to get through on his phone. He has numbers of folks that Marvin was running with. I'm telling y'all, it's some shiesty shit going on, we just don't know what. Marvin was back getting high, so it ain't no telling. I just know that Aisha told me that she thinks her mom is dead and for me to come and get her. Then somebody took the phone from her."

ONI

I put little Faheem to bed, went to my den and poured me a shot of Henny. I was both restless and tired. Hearing Jaz's voice over the phone was like déjà vu. I hated how she always reminded me of how I wished that I was in her shoes. I hated that she was the one that he always went home to. And this time would be no different. Well, there would be a difference. If he wants to be a part of his son's life then he would *have* to be a part of mine.

Seeing Faheem released so many suppressed emotions. Emotions that I had buried away very deep and never planned on digging up. I know I was wrong for not telling him about his son. But I knew that one day he would find him and it would hurt him. And I wanted him to hurt, too. I looked forward to the day when he would feel the same hurt that he left me with over and over. I poured another shot.

My doorbell rang and I decided to ignore it. It most likely was one of my brothers, but I was not in the mood for any company. I simply reclined back onto my favorite easy chair and closed my eyes. The bell rang again but I didn't care. I allowed the Hennessey to make me feel warm and fuzzy. The bell rang again and again and then my phone rang. I glanced over at the caller ID. It was *them*. When Jaz called me earlier I didn't know if it was from her cell phone, *their* house phone or *his* phone. I didn't want to know. What do they want this time? I answered it and she didn't even give me a chance to say hello.

"Faheem is at your front door. He said you won't open it."

I almost shit on myself. "He's at my door?"

"That's what I just said."

Oh Shit. I ended the call and looked around the room as if Faheem could see me. I literally couldn't move. The bell rang again and this time I jumped up. I ran to my purse, put on some lip gloss and dabbed on some Heat by Beyoncé. The Henny hit me hard. Somehow I made it to the mirror and fingered my hair. The bell rang again. My heart was pounding a mile a minute. I tightened up the belt to my robe and headed for the front door. He was now pounding on the window.

"Okay. Okay," I yelled before snatching the door open. "I told you tomorrow Faheem."

He looked at me as if to say, *bitch please* and brushed right past me.

"Come in, please." I was being sarcastic and I didn't mean to say that, but that's what came out.

"Who else is here with you?"

"Just me and your son." I stood there playing with the sash on my robe as he stared me down. I think he was waiting on me to say something. But I couldn't. All of those old feelings came back and the next thing you know, I stepped up to him and my lips found his.

THREE

KAYLIN

We were finally able to separate Trae and Kyron. It took a whole lot of begging from me and Tasha to get Trae to realize killing my brother was not something I could swallow. I left Tasha tending to Trae as I slipped out the door with my brother and cousin in tow. These two muthafuckas were partners in crime and the shit was eating me up. I was hoping to get to the bottom of the situation and put a stop to it before somebody got killed.

As soon as we got into the parking lot, Kyron got on some bullshit. "Yo, that nigga swung on me first, Kay. So don't start talking that bullshit to me, you saw that I was tryna bounce. You should have let us fight."

"Let you fight? Nigga, where you think you at? In a cell? In the day room up North? Nigga's ain't fighting no more, Ky, they killing."

"That nigga ain't the only one that kill—"

"That nigga? That nigga? Nigga, is you stupid? Because you actin' like a real bitch right now. You act like Trae ain't family, nigga. I don't believe this shit. That nigga, as you say, was the same nigga that touched two of your witnesses after you blew trial. That nigga, made sure that I was straight so that I could keep your books straight. All that fly shit you like to wear, all them fuck books and flicks, that nigga was in on that shit. Them bad dime bitches that hiked up North in the snow, nigga, he sent some of them too, remember? That nigga always loved you, and this is how you repay the man? C'mon Kyron, you fuckin' kidding me right? You fuckin' the man's wife, now he catches you with her and all you can say is, 'Yo, he swung on me first'?" I couldn't believe the stupid shit he was saying.

I walked up on my brother, put my finger in his face and said, "Him swinging on you was the least he could do. Be thankful that you still breathing."

"Thankful?"

"Yeah, nigga. Thankful. You know Trae, just like I know him. If it wasn't for ma, and Kyra's daughter calling Tasha's cell phone, you'd be dead, fool."

Kyron laughed. "Get the fuck outta here with that bullshit. Yeah, the nigga did some shit for me, but he ain't the only one. Shit, what I'm supposed to do? Suck his dick? Fuck that nigga! I don't owe him shit. I put y'all niggas on. He owes me and I'll take his bitch as a down payment. What the fuck is wrong with you? Got me out here explaining myself in the middle of the night."

"You fuckin' up, Kyron."

"Don't worry about me, Kay. Let me do me. And because I love you I'm gonna tell you one more time to mind your fuckin' business."

"Nigga, this family *is* my business." I looked him dead in the eye. "And watch your mouth."

Kyron hawked and spit out a wad of blood. He came up on

me as we stood nose to nose. Clenching his teeth he said, "This family may be your business, but I'm home now. So don't forget I'm in *charge* of this fuckin' family!" He pounded on his chest. "How the hell you gonna stand here and go against me? Trae is like family, no doubt. But that's Santos blood running in your veins. You never cross your blood. Don't you ever cross me, muthafucka. You know how I get when a muthafucka crosses me."

"Oh, you threatening me now?"

"C'mon y'all," Kendrick pleaded.

Here we were, eye to eye, neither one backing down. All I could think was *did this nigga, my brother, my own flesh and blood just threaten me?* Then he turned and walked away.

I yelled out, "You know what? You on your own nigga. When you get so deep that you can't get out, don't say that I didn't try to intervene. You playin' with fire nigga. And another man's wife *is* that fire."

KYRON

I left my brother standing there. Why? Because there wasn't shit left to say. I fucked Tasha, yes. But did I regret it? Hell no. I already knew I was playing with fire but I didn't give a shit. I do what the fuck I want. I stopped walking and turned around to look at my brother. I warned him again, "This ain't got nothin' to do with you."

He was just standing there looking at me and shaking his head. "Walk away now. If you don't, shit is going to get real ugly."

Kendrick hit the horn and I turned away from Kay. Kendrick was already in our rental and had it revved up. I knew that my cousin was heated and was going to be talking shit. He was deep in pussy all night, and was dog tired and all of this bullshit got him up out of his sleep. He was planning on laying up with Trina for another day. But now, thanks to me, his trip was cut short.

I jumped in the ride and took out my cell. I called Tasha and she picked up on the first ring. "Nigga, are you crazy?" She gritted on me.

"You were crying when I left. I need to know that you are alright. Go somewhere where you can talk. Or do you want me to come back?"

She was quiet. I guess she was weighing her options. She then had the nerve to hang up on me. I called her ass right back. "Tasha, talk to me. That test said positive."

"You don't have to remind me of that, Kyron. But now is not the time. I'm hanging up."

"Shoot back to the city as soon as you can," I told her. She hung up on me again. "Turn the car around Kendrick."

"What?" He looked over at me.

"Turn the car back around. I got something I need to do."

"Nigga, come on. I think you need to chalk up your loss and keep it movin' for right now. Your brother back there trippin', Trae back there itchin' to blow you the fuck away and you talkin' about turn the car back around."

"Nigga turn the car back around or let me out here." Yeah. I said it. All the while thinking, *Damn. Good pussy will get you hemmed up every time.*

TASHA

I had to control my shaking. When my cell rang and I saw that it was Kyron I'm sure the color drained from my skin. How was

this nigga going to call me at a time when I got grenades blowing up all around me? Lucky for me Trae was so caught up with
getting a hold to Marvin that he was not focused on me. So I
eased down the hallway and picked up the pregnancy test off the
floor. I was holding it when Kyron called. When he mentioned
coming back, I panicked and hung up on him. The second time
he called, Trae was coming down the hallway. I hung up and
went to give my phone to Trina. She was in her bedroom. I then
went back to deal with Trae. I turned around to face him. "What
did you find out? Did you talk to him or Aisha?"

"Sit down Tasha."

"What? Sit down? No Trae. Just tell me." This had to be bad.
My head was spinning. "Just tell me, don't sugarcoat it. Where
is Kyra?"

He led me to the extra bedroom and sat me down on the bed.
His phone rang. He looked at the caller ID and answered it. He
stepped out the room and closed the door. I jumped up and followed behind him. "Trae, no. I need to know what's going on."
He went into the bathroom, shut the door and locked it. I stood
by the bathroom door and tried to listen but he was talking low.
He finally came out and brushed past me. I followed him into
the living room. Kaylin was back, Trina had let him in and he
was sitting on the couch. "Talk to me Trae."

He sat next to Kaylin. "Yo." Trae ran both hands across his
face. "I don't know how all this went down without me knowing about it."

"What?" Me and Kaylin asked at the same time. I sat in the
chair across from Trae.

"Apparently, Marv jacked some nigga for his dope and cash
some years ago. That same nigga recruits Marv's own cousin to

jack Marv back and them niggas start bustin' right there on the block. Word is, Kyra was with them and so was Rick." He looked at his watch. "I'm supposed to meet with one of Marvin's cousins in about an hour. I hope to get more answers along with some addresses."

I was still stuck on the Rick part. "Rick?" I said.

"Yeah. Marv is the one who supposedly took him out. He was mad that him and Kyra was creepin' around." He let his words hang in the air as he glared at me as if his shit didn't stink. Then he got up to leave.

"So where is Kyra and Aisha? Where is Marvin? You talked to him?" I knew Trae and I knew where he was going. I called myself steering away from the 'creepin' around' subject. He wasn't going for it because he got up and came over to where I was.

He stood over me as I looked up at him and sneered, "What? Y'all bitches signed a pact? Y'all runnin' around here fuckin' all our friends and shit. Who is Angel fuckin'?" He turned to Kaylin. "And what about Jaz she got some side dick too?"

I couldn't believe he said that shit. "What the fuck ever, Trae. Mr. Dirty Dick ass nigga. All I want to know is about Aisha and Kyra. You mighty quick to point the finger. What about that rice eating bitch Charli Li? Isn't she pregnant because you fucked her? Instead of worrying about my fuckin' womb you need to make sure that baby she carrying don't come out twisted up. Only God knows what that rotten pussy bitch has. Didn't I tell you what I would do if I caught you cheating? But you thought that I was bluffing! I thought you knew me better than that, Trae. I told you what I would do!" I yelled. I couldn't help but let the tears flow. He made me so sick, and the sad part was, in spite of everything, I still loved him.

I wiped my tears away, "Look, I ain't tryna go through this shit with you right now. I'm trying to find out what's up with Kyra and my niece. Then I will set you free to fuck all the egg roll hos you want. I will even send you your fuckin' divorce papers. Just sign them muthafuckas as soon as they come and let's go our separate ways."

I was talking mad shit and spoke more bravely than I felt. With Kaylin sitting over there, somehow I felt safe. I saw Trae's nostrils flare up and I knew that he was beyond furious.

"Are you finished? You need to go ahead with all that drama bullshit. Sign the papers huh? Why? So that you can be with that nigga, have his baby and think that y'all just gonna live happily ever after with my sons as the step-brothers? Where you think you and that nigga gonna rest at but in a grave? Nah, I ain't going out like that. I don't give a fuck how you try to justify that bullshit you pulled fucking close to home. Tasha, I suggest that you stop while you're ahead. Kay, talk some sense into her, if you can."

He turned around, gave Kaylin some dap, and left. All I could do was cry.

KAYLIN

Shit had definitely turned ugly. I actually felt defeated. Usually I would be the voice of reason. Everybody would listen and then everything would go back to normal. There was no chance in hell that was going to be the case . . . not this time. In order to reason you have to talk. I couldn't even visualize Trae and Kyron talking. And him and Tasha were verbally fighting.

I looked over at Tasha and asked, "Why? I expected so much more out of you."

She stared at me for a while before she stood up, still crying. She came over to me, laid her head on my shoulder and cried long and hard. I let her get that off her chest as my thoughts drifted to my own issues. I heard Trae ask if they had a pact to each fuck a friend. That question now replaced the top issue on my list. Did Red know that Tasha and Kyron was creepin' around? If she did, she was getting her walking papers. If I couldn't trust her, then she had to go.

"Tasha, what were you thinking?" She wouldn't stop that crying shit. "Aiight then. Well tell me this, did Angel know?"

"I told you already. No. You need to believe and trust your wife."

"Well, Trae said he wasn't in a relationship with that Chinese chick. It was business. Nothing personal. Why don't you believe and trust your husband?"

"I did. But it's too late now. I'm pregnant, Kaylin."

"It's not too late. Get rid of the baby. I'ma tell you, just like I told my brother, somebody's going to get hurt. Did Kyron tell you about his girl, Mari?" She looked up at me, got up and stormed to the bathroom. I got the effect that I was looking for. When she came back she had regained her composure.

"Who is Mari?"

"His woman. She was doin' his last seven years holdin' him down. He never mentioned her to you?"

"No. He didn't."

"Well he should have. They've been together for years. She travels around the country a lot. You need to know that shit. You need to stop fuckin' with him and fix your marriage."

She turned around and headed for the kitchen. I heard her slamming shit around.

Trina appeared from the back. "Is she alright?"

I looked at this thirsty bitch and frowned. "Why you ain't have your sister's back? If you had her best interest in mind you wouldn't have let her fuck up her marriage like this. What was in it for you?" This bitch started pacing back and forth. Then she stopped in front of me.

"Shit was fine as long as it was Trae who was the one fuckin' up. All y'all hypocritical niggas is the same."

"I'm not talking about Trae or other niggas. I'm talking about you having your sister's back."

"Listen to me Kay, what started out innocent, spiraled out of control. At first Tasha was trying to hook *me* up with Kyron. But Kyron wasn't feelin' me like that. He was feelin' her. So he hooked me up with Kendrick. I didn't pay them much mind because I was sure that nothing was going to come out of it. I never thought that she would fuck him, Kay, and I damn sure ain't tell her to."

I could only shake my head in disbelief. I didn't know what the fuck was on Kyron's mind. "Well, if Tasha and Trae aren't able to get their shit back on track, you need to know that you played a big role in fuckin' up their family. I'm out." I got up and left.

TRINA

"Good riddance," I said as I slammed the door after Kaylin. Gonna come up in my house and look at me as if I was a piece of shit. Like I told him, I didn't know shit would get serious between Kyron and Tasha. Tasha is a grown ass woman and she had already told me that she wanted a divorce and was done with Trae. I didn't believe her until she started fucking Kyron.

And that shit happened so fast, just like he didn't see it coming, neither did I. I was so caught up with getting to know Kendrick that when I looked up, Trae and Kaylin were at my front door. Well, that last part ain't totally true. Kyron did call and tell me he and Kendrick were coming.

Thinking about Kendrick made me want to get a pulse on how serious shit was, so I grabbed my cell to call him when Tasha came rushing out of the kitchen like a maniac. She was peeking around, I guess to make sure that everyone was gone, then she started rippin' me a new asshole.

"Bitch, you know most of this shit is all your fault, don't you? If you wasn't so busy being sneaky, this shit would not have happened. You could have told me that Kyron and Kendrick were coming over. All of this here could have been avoided. Now look. How could you do this, to me, Trina? Next time mind your fucking business. Let me handle my own shit. Stay the fuck out of mine! I should put my foot in your ass!"

There was nothing I could say. I definitely wasn't about to tell her that Kyron gave me five hundred dollars to keep quiet and to make sure I kept her over at my apartment. She was getting ready to cuss me out some more, or like she said, whip my ass, when there was a knock at the door. She stood frozen in place. I was not moving to answer it. I simply sat back and did like she told me . . . mind my own fuckin' business.

TASHA

I was itchin' for Trina to say the wrong thing so that I could light that ass up. But when someone knocked on the door I panicked because the first person I thought of was Kyron. I made my way to the door and put the chain on it. I put my eye to the keyhole and didn't see anyone. I asked, or more like snapped, "Who is it?" When no one responded I cracked the door. When I saw it was Kyron I went to close it but he stopped the door with his foot.

"Tasha, wait." He grabbed my hand. "I just needed to know that you're alright. You were crying when I left. Did he put his hands on you?" He grabbed my chin and was trying to look over my face through the crack in the door.

"Now is not the time Kyron and don't come here anymore."

"Tasha, come on now. Bullshit aside. You carryin' my seed." He then had the nerve to tell me, "We in this shit together. So I think we need to talk. Come back to the city with me."

I almost lost it. All of this drama *I've* been through in the last forty eight hours and he's talking about we in this together? He got me twisted. "Kyron, I am not fucking with you like that anymore. As a matter of fact, go talk to Mari because me and you don't have shit to talk about."

"I don't mess with Mari anymore and we *do* have shit to talk about. You are carrying *my* seed, Tasha. Since we can't undo what went down between us we need to map things out. I'm not going to let you go through this alone. So, you either let me in and we talk now or pack your shit and come back with me."

I turned around and started towards the bedroom. I was not having this conversation with him. And then I heard *BOOM!* I turned around and this nigga had kicked the front door in. That little cheap ass chain didn't have a chance. Trina had the nerve to be sitting there on the couch trying not to laugh. I swear I was two seconds away from knocking out her front teeth.

"Tasha! Come here!" Kyron yelled as if he was my father. I closed the bedroom door and locked it.

"Kyron, get the fuck out of here. I am not opening the door." I rested my back against it and grabbed my head. I wanted to pull my hair out.

"You want me to kick it down?"

Damn. I thought about the front door and I snatched this one open. "Kyron, please. Not now. Trae could come back any minute."

"Then stop fuckin' around, get your shit and let's go."

"I can't Kyron. Not now." My heart rate was on speed dial. I had to get him out of there before Trae Macklin came back. But this nigga had the nerve to sit down on the bed and look as if he was going to get comfortable. "Kyron, please. Okay. I'll come to the city, but not today."

"Then when?"

"Give me a day or two."

He looked at me as if he didn't believe me.

"I need a little more time to sort some things out, Kyron." I grabbed his hand. "C'mon you need to go. I'll see you in a day or two."

He pulled me to him and gave me a hug. "I just need to be sure that you are going to be alright and don't do nothing stupid."

"What do you mean stupid?" I pulled back.

"Like get an abortion stupid."

I simply looked at him. I had already figured out that's the reason he was sweating me so hard. He wanted this baby. But at this moment I honestly had no idea what I was going to do. Hell, this shit happened so fast, I didn't have the chance to think about anything. "I need a day or two. We can talk then."

He took the bait and left.

FOUR

MARVIN

"... *if you want your wife, I suggest you give me my muthafuckin'*
dough right now."

I looked over at the driver's seat and saw that Mook now had a
gun pressed up against Kyra's head. I didn't know if this clown was
serious, so I had to roll the dice and call his bluff.

"Mook, get that fuckin' burner away from my wife."

"I'm telling you, Blue, he's going to split her wig, just give me my
dough. You owe me nigga," Junie spat.

"I don't owe you shit, nigga! That was years ago. And here you are
pressing me about some fuckin' chump change? Why you pressin' me
about that shit?" This muthafucka was starting to get under my skin.

"Stop haggling, Marvin. Just give the nigga the money," Kyra
blurted out as she slid me my piece.

"Listen to your wife," Junie said.

"Babygirl, these pussies ain't going to shoot nobody, not like I will."
Pow! I shot Junie in the stomach. "See. That's how you do that. I didn't

even have to get out. Put the car in reverse babygirl and let's get the fuck out of here."

As soon as I said that Fish jumped out of his ride and started waving at me. "Hold up babygirl," I said to Kyra and she stopped the car. I hopped out. Fish snatched the gun out of a frozen Mook's hand and put a bullet in his head.

"Pussy muthafucka." He clenched his teeth as he watched him slump to the ground.

I started laughing. "Fish, nigga, where did you get these pussy muthafuckas from?"

He shrugged. "That's what happens when you send a boy to do a man's job." Fish pointed his gun at Kyra and shot her in the head. Boom! . . .

"N-o-o-o-o-o!" I shot straight up in my bed and looked around the darkened bedroom. It took me a minute to regain my equilibrium and realize that I was having the same nightmare again. A nightmare that was also my reality. My chest was soaking wet with perspiration, my forehead, too. Rising from the bed, I walked into the bathroom and ran water in the sink. Then I splashed water all over my face. Looking in the mirror, I was ashamed at the person I was seeing. I am a man who abandoned his wife and left her for dead. My past had gotten her shot in the head and what did I do? I ran.

I ran and got high. Got high and ran. I ran all the way until I ended up in Kentucky. High off the heroin, my clouded mind convinced me that me and my daughter could just go on with our lives. Kyra was gone and there was nothing I could do about it. But then came the nightmares and the dream. Every night I had one or the other or both. In the dream, Kyra would be standing a few feet away holding Aisha's hand and staring at me. It was the stare mixed with the look of disappointment on her face that haunted me most. Aisha would be trying to tell me something, but I could never hear her. Then the sun would start shining so bright that I could no longer see either of them. I'd then hear Aisha's voice as I looked away from the overbearing sunlight. That's when I would wake up. I could never hear what my daughter was saying.

A few months after settling into Kentucky, I got a call from my cousin Lo, telling me that Junie, the dude that I shot in the stomach, was out of the hospital and hiding out. I left my daughter with a babysitter and headed for Cali. It took me two days to find June. He told me that Kyra was dead, then I killed him with my bare hands. His weakened condition made him no match for my strength. Then, like a thief in the night, I came back to Kentucky. I got high as a kite the night I returned and placed a call to Trae. I lied to him and told him that Kyra was okay and chillin'. I told him that we were in Florida while I rehabbed. But the entire conversation I could hear the doubt in his voice. For some reason I became very afraid. That fear in conjunction with my nightmares and dreams made me kick my dope habit. I was sure that it was the heroin that had me feeling like a pussy. So that very next night, I kicked it cold turkey. And when I did, I saw things for what they were—I had fucked up and I had fucked up bad. My wife was gone and now my daughter wanted to go.

I walked down the hall to Aisha's room and peeped in on her. She was all that I had left. I loved her with all my heart but everyday that passed, she was becoming more difficult to handle. Her questions were too complex for me to answer: "Daddy, why did we move here? Where is my mommy? Is she dead? Why was her head bleeding? Why did we leave her, daddy? Are you going to leave me too?" She always looked at me with disappointment on her face when my answers couldn't satisfy her.

Aisha, being the spittin' image of Kyra, didn't help my situation at all. Yesterday, I discovered that she snuck and called Tasha. I didn't know how many times she'd called. I was mad at her at first, but then I empathized with her. She missed her mother. She missed her Auntie Tasha and the rest of who she knows as her family. My gut was telling me that letting Tasha take her for a while would be the best thing. I needed to put her well-being first.

I had to make a difficult decision. I knew how close Kyra and her girls were. It's been months since they've talked to each other. Add the call that Aisha made, and I know that trouble is brewing on the horizon. The girls are going to press somebody and before long that somebody is going to come looking for me.

ONI

No . . . he did . . . not . . . just push me away! That little stunt sobered my ass right on up. I wanted to crawl under a rock. Then he added salt to the wound by yelling, "Get the fuck away from me! What the fuck makes you think I want to hug you?" His face was all contorted and he looked appalled.

I fell back and he came at me. I thought he was going to hit me, so I covered up my head with my arms. He stood over me and his raging anger was unmistakable. "Oni, tell me what the fuck was you thinking? What did I do to you to make you hide my son from me? That's some fuckin' bullshit! We had an understanding. You know damn well you didn't have to do that shit," he spat. The house felt as if it was shaking and the only sounds were his hard breathing. "Oni, you better fuckin' tell me something or I swear to God I'ma—"

"What you want me to say?" I yelled out. "Faheem, you should already know why. You always go back to *her*." I broke down crying. "Every . . . fuckin' . . . single . . . time and I always hurt. So I wanted you to hurt. It was always so easy for you to just walk in and out of my life. Did you ever stop to think how that made me feel? I just couldn't take it anymore." I ranted back with just as much rage. Then he slapped the shit out of me.

"Shut the fuck up with that bullshit. Bitch, this ain't about how you felt. We talking about my son! And Jaz was my woman. I was supposed to go back to her. You knew what it was."

"Faheem I was—"

"This ain't about you! This shit is about my son. How many years of his life did I miss? And for what? Why? You knew what was up." And then his voice lowered. "How old is he, Oni?"

"Seven," I sobbed, stuck on him slapping me and calling me a bitch.

"Seven fuckin' years. Ain't this some shit!" he barked. Then walked away from me and started pacing back and forth.

"Mommy." My . . . our son was now up and wiping sleep out of his eyes. "Why are you crying?" he asked as he looked over at Faheem.

"Say hi to your daddy, Faheem." He looked over at Faheem, came over to me and buried his face into my shoulder. "Say hi," I forced myself to utter and was sobbing at the same time.

"Hi." He kept his face on my shoulder but peeked up at the man I just said was his daddy.

"Faheem, I'm sorry."

Faheem walked away from the both of us.

"Go ahead!" I screamed. "Do what you do best, walk away," I yelled in anger, hoping he would come back. But all I heard was the door slam.

FAHEEM

Man, I can't lie. It took everything in me to not kill that girl. So I figured the best thing for me to do was leave. But not until after I snatched that bottle of Hennessey that was sitting on the counter. When my little man came downstairs I got all choked up. Seven years old? I missed his first seven years? I couldn't get past that. How the fuck can this bitch rob me of being a father to my son? I stood outside on the back porch, took the top off the Hennessy and sniffed it. I wasn't even a drinker but I took it to the head. I slammed the bottle up against the wall sending the glass everywhere. I then got into my truck.

By the time I pulled into the driveway, I didn't even remember driving home, my dick was hard and my vision was blurred.

JAZ

I heard Faheem's truck faintly in the background. The neighbor's annoying German shepherd was barking. It seems like he stands by the fence and waits for his truck. I looked at the clock on the nightstand. It was 3:17 a.m. I didn't know if I wanted to act as if I was asleep or go downstairs and start some drama. Coming in here at three in the damn morning. *He got me fucked up*. I turned over onto my stomach and decided to play sleep.

For some reason Faheem was taking his time coming up the steps. That could only mean the nigga was guilty and had something to hide. He came into the bedroom and sat on the bed. I smelled liquor. *Ohhkay.* That explains why he could barely make it up the steps. He took off his shirt and it sounded like he tossed it at the bedroom door. He then fumbled around with his Timbs. This nigga was obviously toasted because he was having a hard time getting them off. That shit was funny. He finally stood up, took off his jeans and boxers, almost tripping in the process. He then climbed into bed and shook me. *I know that his ass don't think he's getting some.* That's when I turned over and this nigga climbed on top of me, and the next thing you know his dick was at my pussy.

"Faheem, no." I struggled to push his heavy, liquored up, smelling ass off of me. "I'm not even wet."

"Why not? I told you to wait up for me," he slurred.

"Wait up? It's almost three in the morning. It took you that long to talk to her?" This nigga was still trying to put his dick in me. "So what happened? Y'all had drinks to catch up on old times?"

"Yeah, we did." He tore open my night shirt. I heard the buttons pop off. He started sloppily sucking on my breast.

"What did y'all talk about? Why did you have to drink with her? It wasn't a fuckin' social call." His responses or lack of, were starting to piss me off.

"Jaz, shut up. You killin' the moment." He went back to trying to put his dick in but I wasn't having it.

"Moment? You ain't having no moment with me Faheem. Why did you have to drink with her? You don't even drink. You were supposed to be finding out about your son, not having a social call." I was still struggling to get his heavy ass off of me. "So what happened?"

"We fucked."

I froze. Did I hear this nigga right? I was in shock and as I thought about what he had just said, he wasted no time to seize the moment and was down between my legs, fingers inside my pussy and was licking my clit. "What did you say?" I looked down at him as I felt my pussy tingle. I tried to fight the high that I was getting ready to embark upon. *He fucked that bitch and then came home to do me?* I spread my legs wider. Faheem was a pussy eatin' god. I went to heaven each and every time. I now had both hands on his head. "You fucked her . . . Faheem?" He could have told me that he married her and at that moment I would have said 'fine'. "Ohhhhh . . ." I moaned out. "Stop it Faheem and answer me. Oh shit, baby, right there." My back was arched and I was grinding into this nigga's face. Right when I was about to cum he stopped eating me and flipped me over onto my stomach. I assumed the position, putting my ass up into the air. He slapped my ass leaving it to sting, entered me and slapped me again. Damn, my baby got some good dick. As always, it seemed as if he was reading my mind.

"Whose dick is this?" He slapped my ass again. How did he expect me to answer when he was dickin' me down so good? He was giving me nice and slow strokes, pulling his dick all the way out, to rub up against my clit and then put it back in. That shit drives me crazy. He knows exactly how I like it. All I could do was grab onto the sheets, bite down on my lip, and throw my pussy back at him. We were fucking like we were trying to win a game of tug of war with *my* pussy. He slapped my ass again and it felt good. "Whose dick is this?"

I was ready to ride my dick. "This is . . . my . . . dick . . . nigga," I gasped.

"Well act like you know." He pulled out and assumed the position. His dick was standing straight up, veins popping and shiny from my juices. I like the taste of my juices on his dick and on his lips so I couldn't resist. I crawled between his legs and gently held his balls as I slurped them. I was making his dick even harder. He groaned. I moved to the base of his dick, licked some more before I got greedy and took him in my mouth. His breathing got sharper and I got greedier, sucking, sucking, slurping, teasing . . . sucking until my pussy was throbbing, I couldn't take no more. My nigga was trying to ram his dick down my throat and release his load, but it wasn't time to do that. I needed to get mine. So I eased his rod out of my mouth. He leaned up, looked at me with this wild look in his eyes that screamed, "Why the fuck did you stop?" I got in position to climb on top. He knew what time it was because he put one hand behind his head and fell back.

FAHEEM

My baby was sucking the shit out of my dick. I don't know if it was the alcohol or if she was just that good. I was so fucked up I couldn't decide. I watched as my sexy-ass wife assumed the position, grabbed my tool and slid down on it. She was wetter than the ocean. I swear I could hear the waves sloshing as she seductively rocked back and forth side to side. I slid my hands down to her hips and raised mine. Now we were fucking each other good. We both picked up the pace as our breathing got sharper . . . faster. She moaned. I grunted. I felt like I was going to cum first but she beat me to it and started shaking. Face twisting. Pussy clenching on my dick. I thrust harder. Wanting her to cum longer. This was my baby. Her pussy belonged to me. I could hold it no longer. I released my load into her.

"Nigga, this dick belongs to me." She gasped as she fell onto my chest.

FIVE

CHARLI LI

"Ms. Li, I have the specs you requested for the property in Japan. I believe that the Kumano Kado region would be a great place to build your hotel. It is a mountainous resort region. For centuries the Japanese and foreigners alike have come to the area to purify their minds, bodies and souls in the Kumano luxurious countryside. According to our research, thousands make the trek to Kumano to visit its various blessed shrines and to bask in the scenic luxuries. Kumano Kado literally translates to "old passage." It is recognized by the UNESCO World Heritage for its pilgrimages and spiritual history. The three main Shrines—"

"Hon, please do not bore me with the religious details. Proceed with the financial group you have assembled and do whatever necessary to procure access to the land and go from there. Just keep me posted. You may go now. Thank you."

I sat at my desk and watched Hon Wu leave my office. I'm in a terrible mood and this pregnancy is making it worse. This is my first one and I promise it will be my last. Usually I'm pretty good with using protection and making sure I don't get caught up. Doctors have always told me that since my uterus is slightly out of position it would be hard, better yet, damn near impossible to get pregnant. I guess that's why I let my guard down when it came to Trae Macklin. Being a woman of power who jet sets all over the globe, I've had my fair share of men in every country in the world. Men of all different nationalities, religious backgrounds, tax brackets, you name it. I could kiss and tell about the powerful men I've bedded and create global scandals.

And for the most part, I've toyed with them all. But Mr. Trae Macklin? To this day, I don't understand how I allowed myself to lose control with . . . a . . . low life . . . drug dealer. A gorgeous, sexy, thug that probably doesn't even have a high school diploma. Somehow I allowed myself to lose my power and now I feel as if he's in control.

Maybe it was the way he treated me that turned me on. Before him, I had never met a man who didn't want me. To be constantly denied and turned away by a man that I felt was beneath me became arousing. It turned into a game of hide and seek. Trae Macklin forced me to become a hunter, when I'm usually the hunted. I recall that day in his office inside the club when I forced myself on him and sucked his manhood. I was confident that my fellatio game would make him act right, but I was mistaken. Then the night I went to the condo where he was staying to give him a check, he made me feel like a two dollar whore. He fucked me, threatened me and sent me on my way. Nobody, and I mean *nobody* had ever treated me that way before. I was so aroused that I went outside to my limo and played with my pussy all the way home. I had entered new territory.

Weeks later I'm nauseous and throwing up at least twice a day. A quick visit to my doctor revealed that Charli Li, the least likely to ever get pregnant, was indeed pregnant. My initial reaction was disbelief and shock, then stunned silence and acceptance. It was meant to be. Aborting the pregnancy wasn't even an option for me. The child growing inside of me was mine and my father would be pleased to have another Li heir.

I had mixed emotions when I thought about whether or not to tell Mr. Macklin that I was pregnant. But eventually I decided that it was only fair to let him know. So I called him and gave him the good news. His reaction was one that I never expected. He laughed and hung up the phone. However, I managed to get his attention when I sent him a copy of the pregnancy test results. He called me shortly thereafter.

"How did you let this happen?" he asked me.

"You attacked me," I replied. "Or have you forgotten?"

"How do you know it's mine?"

When he asked me that, I exploded. And then he exploded. The conversation ended with him threatening me. I told him that I was leaving the country for a while and that I needed some time to think and decide my next move. After that conversation, I flew to Seoul, South Korea, where I am now. But now that my work is done, I'm heading back to the states, back to California and back into the arms of my child's father.

I laughed to myself as I thought about how my decision to have the baby probably wouldn't sit well with Trae and undoubtedly he'd start again with the threats. Trae Macklin was a lot of things, but wise wasn't one of them. All sex appeal, brawn, business-sense and hardly any brains. He had no clue that he was completely out of my league. Being the only child of one of the world's most feared mob leaders, makes me a dangerous bitch. And with one phone call, Trae Macklin and his whole family would cease to exist. I silently prayed that he wouldn't force me to make that call. Just thinking about him makes me weak in the knees. So, I'm now looking forward to paying Mr. Macklin a visit. After all, I do miss him and with what I have for him, I think he'll be very glad to see me.

Leaning forward, I hit the button on the desk phone. "Yes, Ms. Li?" my receptionist and cousin Sue Li responded.

"If my father calls, please put him through to my cell. Call Captain Cheng and have him prepare the plane. I'll be ready in precisely thirty minutes. Then page my assistant and tell him that I am ready to go home."

"Right away, Ms. Li."

TRAE

I was sitting in the car trying to see where this nigga Lo was going. I needed to know where he rested so that I could put the other half of this puzzle together. At first I got the impression that Marv's cousin Isis was loyal. But obviously it don't take much for a friend to start flapping the gums. I tossed her a C-note and she began singing like a bird, as if she had a catalog as thick as the O'Jays. She was going non-stop. She told me how Marv was back in the game . . . and deep. And on top of that he was selling hammers, robbin' and leanin' on niggas. She was talkin' like he was on some Omar bullshit like from *The Wire*! No wonder the club was on the radar. Here I was walking around as if my shit was squeaky clean, and this nigga had me dirtier than a muthafucka. From all the shit she told me, there was no

doubt in my mind that many niggas was out to get at Marvin.
I just had to find him first.

When I caught up with Lo, he wasn't as generous as Isis was
with the info. I could tell that he was only giving me bits and
pieces. I also sensed that he knew where Marvin was rested at.
Lucky for him that at the time we were in a public spot. Not so
lucky for me because then I had to follow his ass around. But I
did get out of him that Kyra was shot in the head and he had
to make Marv leave her because the police was coming and they
were mad dirty. I asked him where the body was. He said he
didn't know and that I had to talk to Marv about that. He said
he left him to go and handle the police nigga they had stuffed
in the trunk and all of the work they had on them. So you see
why I needed to talk to this nigga some more. I knew that he
had all the answers I needed. I was very glad for the thrill and
excitement because it took my mind off of Tasha. I was ready to
release some tension . . . in a violent way.

ANGEL

Kaylin was obviously on his way home when his ass finally
decided to call me. "Red, baby, I'm just checkin' in. What's going
on? Are you and my baby alright?"

I sucked my teeth, looked at the clock and saw that it was
almost midnight and then decided against cussing him out.
Instead I said, "Just checking in? It's damn near two days later.
Why couldn't you answer your phone? I called you several times."

"Why do you think I didn't answer the phone? And it hasn't
been two days."

"What did you say?" My blood pressure was almost at its

boiling point. I know this nigga was not disrespecting me like this and on top of that, some asshole was laying on my doorbell. They wouldn't stop ringing it. I was giving him one more chance. "Why haven't you answered my calls, Kay?" Whoever was on my bell wouldn't let up.

"What nigga you got ringing my bell at midnight? And don't be questioning me. Looks like I need to be the one doing the questioning."

I jumped up off the sofa trying to decide who's going to receive a royal ass whipping, my husband or the fool that was laying on my doorbell. Since whoever was laying on my doorbell was closest, I went for it. I'd get with Kaylin later.

"Answer the door and let your nigga in. I'll talk to you later." He had the nerve to hang up on me.

Now I had smoke coming out of my ears. Later for who was at the door. It was on. I dialed Kaylin back and it went straight to voicemail. I stomped in place and threw the phone at the sofa. Since he wouldn't answer, that meant the fool that was still laying on my doorbell was getting ready to feel my wrath.

KAYLIN

I ended the call with Angel and hit my camera button on my cell. As soon as I did, she snatched the door open with this crazed look on her face and I got my picture. She didn't know how to react.

"Oooh, I hate you," she gritted. "Why you gotta do shit like that Kaylin?"

"To get you all riled up, that's why."

I put the phone away, stepped inside the doorway, dropped my bag and rushed her. I smashed her up against the wall, ran both hands up under her robe, rubbing her thighs before grabbing me two handfuls of her luscious ass. She roughly grabbed my face and kissed me. Her kiss was soft and long. I lifted her up and she wrapped both of her legs around my waist.

"I missed you," she told me and I could tell.

"I missed you more."

"I was worried about you. I don't like it when you don't answer my calls. I always start thinking the worst has happened." She kissed me again and now my dick was talking shit saying, "Yo nigga, we gonna do this or what?"

I held her up with one arm, fumbled with my jeans and grabbed my joint. The head found her opening and she was already wet. I slid up in her right there up against the wall. The pussy received me well. I had her back smashed up against the wall and since she couldn't move I fucked her as if I was gone for a couple of years instead of days. She held on tight and the seductive whimpers that escaped from her throat were letting me know that my dick game was on point. I got in as deep as I could; she grabbed me tighter and started whispering shit in my ear.

"I'ma patent this big, brown dick. No nigga ever fucked me as good as you do." She moaned as she nibbled on my ear. "This is my dick and this is your pussy. I'll never give your pussy away." That's when I tried to tear the bottom out. She started yelling, "My spot babeee . . . aww shit you on . . . my spot," she groaned. I was beatin' it up.

Her pussy started squeezing my dick as I stroked in and out, long and deep. She was cumming and I wanted to fuck her a little longer but I couldn't hold back. That shit drove me over the wall. My dick started releasing a river load. We held onto each other as we rested against the wall. We were breathing as if we had just run a marathon. I raised her a little and carried her to the sofa. I eased down with her still straddling my lap.

"I love you," she told me.

"I love you more."

ANGEL

I can never stay mad at Kaylin for too long. Well, that's not totally true. I remember when he called off our wedding. I was not letting him go, in other words, no matter what, we would be walking down that aisle. And we did. We tied the knot right here in the living room around three in the morning. Nevertheless, I stayed mad at him for a long time. It's a damn shame that once I get the dick all is forgiven. This time was no different. I ran my fingers across my husband's handsome face. He was only gone for a couple of days but I swear it seemed like forever. I missed him lying in the bed next to me.

"So, are you still mad at me? You still want your divorce?" I kissed him softly on the lips. "And do you still think I wouldn't have told you about Tasha and Kyron if I knew?" I looked in his eyes for his answer.

"Nah. I'm not mad at you anymore." He pressed his lips against mine and slipped his tongue in my mouth. We tangled our tongues until I came up for air. "I thought you said you missed me?" my baby teased.

"I do but let's save some for our bedroom. And don't try to get off the subject. Answer me, Kaylin."

"Why we got to save some good fuckin' for the bedroom? We got enough to go around."

"Boy, stop being so greedy. Answer me and tell me about the trip."

"No, I don't want a divorce. And I won't answer the other question. I gotta hold something over your head."

"Stop playin' with me Kaylin. Now tell me about the trip." As soon as I said that, his forehead wrinkled up. "Was it that bad?" My heart rate sped up.

"What part of the bad news you want first?"

"Oh shit." I put my hands over both of my ears. "None of it. I don't want to know none of it." And I didn't. Tasha and her drama, I could deal with. But the possibility of my cousin being dead, that was just . . . unfathomable.

He gently moved my hands away from my ears. "Well, I think you need to hear this."

I damn near held my breath because I knew that what I was getting ready to hear was not going to make me feel good.

KAYLIN

I swear I didn't want to be the bearer of bad news to my baby. Kyra and Angel were not only first cousins but they were like best friends.

"Trae went snooping around Marvin's old hangout, talking to his cousins. They told him that Marvin was gettin' jacked while Kyra and Aisha were in the car and that niggas was blastin'." Angel gasped and covered her mouth with both hands. I gently removed them and held her hands into mine. "Baby, don't go jumping to conclusions because no bodies were found and Trae is looking into that."

"Then why haven't we heard from her? And what about Aisha talking about her mother is dead?" Red got choked up.

"I don't know baby. It's possible that some foul shit went down, we just don't know what. But like I said, no bodies have turned up."

"Kaylin, we talkin' about the streets. We talkin' about Marvin. A body may never turn up. And speaking of Marvin, where is he? Why hasn't anyone heard from him? What did he do to my cousin?" Angel burst into tears.

"We don't know what's up yet, baby. Hope to have some answers for you soon."

That's all I could say at the moment. I hugged my wife as she sobbed quietly in my chest. I kept thinking about Trae. I couldn't shake my thoughts of him. This nigga was a walking powder keg. I know him. I just hoped he wouldn't do anything that I wouldn't be able to get him out of.

ANGEL

As I sat up in bed staring down at my husband sleeping peacefully, I couldn't shake the haunting thought that Kyra may be dead. *Damn. Were we so caught up in our own bullshit that we ignored the signs? Why didn't I hear her cry for help? What kind of cousin am I that I didn't even check on her or wonder why I hadn't heard from her in months?* I covered my mouth as the tears rolled down my cheeks. I feared the worst, and the sad part is we couldn't place all of the blame on Marvin. We all could share the blame equally. Each and every one of us was so caught up in our own separate little worlds. We were so disillusioned by the notion that we had gotten ourselves together, that in reality we have damn near been fucking up more than cleaning up.

I had to do something. But what? Where would I start to

look? Then it hit me. There was one lawyer out west who owed me favors. Favors as in more than one. It was time for me to cash in on them.

TRAE

It took me three days to finally catch Lo like I wanted to. The way I was moving I felt like a certified bounty hunter. I found out that he had a house on LaBrea Avenue in the Jungle section of LA that was a Blood stronghold. Breaking into the house, I discovered that he lived with his woman. Climbing the stairs quickly and quietly, I found her asleep in a bed in one of the bedrooms. Since I was tired from chasing this nigga for the past three days, and the fact that I didn't feel like the whole screaming, tying her up, and crying bullshit, I smothered her until she went limp. I then checked her pulse. She was gone. I went downstairs, grabbed a seat and then waited patiently for Lo.

There is nothing like the element of surprise. About an hour and a half later, he came strolling into the house and I caught his ass totally off guard. He tried to put up a fight because I was sure that he was using them hard drugs just like Marv. I was able to subdue him quickly, knocking him the fuck out. I then dragged his unconscious form to the back of the house. I found some table linen in a closet in the hallway. Using a kitchen knife, I shredded the table cloth and used it to tie him up and with the remaining pieces I gagged him. Once he was in the helpless position that I wanted him in, I grabbed a chair and sat so that I was facing him. I poured a big cup of cold water, and threw it in his face and smacked him. His eyes opened and settled right on me.

"It's me again, son. Remember the other day when we talked?

I didn't feel that you were keepin' it 100 with me. You were giving me bits and pieces and not the whole shit." I pulled my .45 out of my waist and pressed it up against his temple. "I think we need to talk again. But this time, I'm gonna need you to fill in the blanks. You think you can do that for me? If so, nod your head."

When Lo didn't nod his head, I smiled. "So you think I'm bullshittin' huh? I can respect that." I left him on the floor and stood up to look for the kitchen knife. It was right there on the table where I had left it. I took the knife and stabbed him in the shoulder. I stuck the blade as far as it would go, twisting it before I yanked it out. For several minutes I watched the dripping blood. His muffled scream didn't faze me at all. I stood and walked over to the cabinet on the wall. Opening a couple of drawers, I found exactly what I was looking for. I grabbed the Morton's salt box and went back to my victim. Adjusting the spout so that most of the salt poured out, I began dumping it into the gaping shoulder wound. He began to yelp like a dog does when you step on his tail.

He started screaming again as I took my finger and gathered the salt around the wound. I then took my finger and the salt and stuffed it inside the wound. He screamed out again, but the gag was doing its job of muffling the sounds.

Satisfied with the result I was getting, I said, "Shhhhhh! Gangstas don't scream, Lo. That's what you are, right? A 'G'. And you're trying to prove to me how gangsta you are, right? Well, I don't believe you, son. I think another couple of pokes with this knife will break that gangsta shit down."

I pulled him over until he was on his back with his hands under him. I stabbed him in his other shoulder and repeated my salt routine with that wound. The nigga had the nerve to pass out. I got up to get more water and splashed him again.

"Wake up, you muthafuckin' gangsta. What the fuck are you doing? You giving real gangstas a bad look, fainting and shit. I need you to stay with me now. If you tell me what I wanna know, I'ma let you live. If you wanna be gangsta and keep quiet I'ma put you in that gangsta lean, feel me? Now, I'ma take that rag out of your mouth. If you try anything other than telling me what I want to hear, I'ma blow your head into this wooden floor. Closed casket. But not before stabbing your legs and doin' our little salt thing, since you seem to like it so much. If you understand me nod."

Lo nodded his head as tears ran down his cheeks. I pulled the gag out of his mouth. "Now, from the top, tell me everything that happened the night Kyra got shot and then I want to know *exactly* where Marvin is."

After allowing Lo to speak for about fifteen minutes, I got up, pulled his head back and slit his throat open. I got all I could from him and hoped that it was everything I needed. After leaving out the back door, I hopped over the fence and that's when I noticed all of the blood on my pants. Wasn't half as much on my shirt. My phone vibrated and I didn't even look at it because I knew who it was. I made my way to my ride, jumped in and took off. After five minutes my cell vibrated again. It vibrated on and off for the next half hour. I knew it was Tasha before I finally decided to answer it.

"What's up?" I asked.

"What do you mean what's up? Where are you? You could have at least checked in. Your mother called looking for you, the boys called and I didn't know what to tell them." Tasha was amped. She had been blowing my phone up the last twenty-four hours, but I was on a mission. "Did you find out anything?"

"I'm on my way to the house. Let me call you when I get there."

"No. No, Trae. Come see me *now*." She had the nerve to have base in her voice. "I've been waiting for you, thinking something happened to you and now you think you can call me and brush me off? No. I don't think so."

I could see her stomping in place looking like our baby, Caliph. "What do you mean 'you don't think so'? I'm going home."

"Trae, I need to see you now. Are you in the city?"

"I'm about twenty minutes away."

"Then what are you doing that you can't come and see me? You know what?" She got quiet. I know she was thinking that I was doing some shit I ain't have no business doing. "Okay fine. Go home. I'll meet you over there."

"Girl, you see what time it is. You don't need to be riding across town this late. I'm on my way over to see you." I hung up before she could say anything.

TASHA

I didn't know what the fuck Trae was doing, but he was doing something. This nigga had been M.I.A. for damn near three days. Not answering calls from his moms or sons? He never does that. If he doesn't show up within the next twenty minutes I am going to go looking for him. I don't care what time it is.

I paced the floor from the kitchen to the living room to the front window and back again. After about fifteen minutes of doing this, I told Trina to get ready. We were going to find Trae. Just as we were about to leave he called my cell.

"Come downstairs," he told me. I could barely hear him. He sounded beat down.

"Who is that?" Trina's nosy behind asked me.

"I'm on my way down now," I told Trae. Then told Trina, "I don't need you. He's downstairs."

"You got me up out of my bed to get dressed, to go riding around town at two in the morning and now you don't need me?" She was twisting her neck and the whole nine.

I left her standing there and went downstairs to find Trae parked in front of the building. I went around to the driver's side and his window came down. Even though it was dark, I could see that he didn't look like a nigga who was out partying. He had hair on his face, he was dressed in dark clothes and he smelled.

"What is that smell?" I looked at his clothes. "Is that blood?" I already knew the answer. We looked at each other and no words were necessary. I've been doing this shit too long and I knew what time it was. This wasn't the first time that I knew of my husband killing someone and I'm sure it wouldn't be my last. I just didn't always know who the victims were.

"What's the matter with you, Tasha?" He shook his head, grabbed a bag off the seat and got out. "Stay right here." He went inside Trina's apartment building to where I was, the laundry room. About five minutes later he had changed clothes and was back outside.

"I just want you to tell me about Kyra, Trae. Where is she?" Not knowing was driving me insane.

"I'll be back over later today to fill you in. Go back in the house." The look he gave me said, *Do it now and don't make me say it again.*

I went upstairs and he pulled off.

TRAE

I wasn't ready to see Tasha. My mind was still at the scene of the murder. Taking another man's life gives me a high that hasn't been able to compete with anything else. Well, except when the twins were born. That shit there was the ultimate. However, seeing Tasha took me off my high and reminded me of what was going on in my world. My world was threatening to crumble around me.

After I did away with the bloody clothes and murder weapon I was on my way to our home but changed my mind. Tasha hadn't been there in a while and it was no longer the same. I can't even attempt to front about that shit. Neither of us was staying there. I made an illegal U-turn in the middle of the road and headed for my so called bachelor pad.

I turned onto my block and surveyed the area. I drove past my spot and a limo was parked in front. I started to keep going but thought, *fuck it.* I was tired. I hit the switch to open the garage door and placed my ratchet on my lap. I drove into the garage and hit the switch to close it. I got out my ride, and deactivated my alarm. I stepped inside the house and peeked out of the front window. *I'll be damned.* My blood pressure shot up as I watched Charli's ass get out of the limo. The bitch did not know when to quit.

CHARLI LI

I didn't know if he was going to return to the condo or not, but it was the last place I had seen him over a month ago. After sitting across the street from his house for about two hours, my excitement heightened as I watched the lights of an SUV come down the street and then pull into the driveway in front of the condo. I waited until he was out of the truck and for when I was sure that he was inside the house before I exited the limo. I began to knock on the front door. A few minutes later, he opened it.

"Charli, what the fuck? Do I have to buy one of them Rosetta Stone CD's and learn to speak Chinese? Because every time I tell you in English to leave me the fuck alone, you act like you don't understand me. What could you possibly want at 3:00 in the damn morning? Wait, let me guess. You've now become a stalker," Trae exploded.

"Mr. Macklin, don't flatter yourself. I didn't come here to argue with you."

"Then, what did you come here for?"

I looked up into the handsome face of the ebony god that stood in front of me and struggled to compose myself. I tried to read his eyes, but they were void of any emotion. "I came for three reasons. To tell, to give and to show. Now, if you would be so kind as to let me in, I could say and do what I came here to do and be on my way."

I watched him as he ran his hand across his face and rubbed his beard stubble. Exasperated, he said, "And for some reason, this couldn't wait until a reasonable hour? You just *had* to come here at three in the morning?"

"In China they say the early bird catches the worm."

"What the fuck you a philosopher now? They say that shit everywhere. Look, I'm tired Charli and I'm ready to blow. The only thing you can do for me is give me the money you owe me from the investment on that land project. I don't want to hear about fucking birds and worms."

"I have what you want. But I am not going to conduct business out here on your front steps. Now, may I please come in?"

"You got five minutes and five minutes only."

He opened the door and waved me inside. I closed it behind me. "I know I'm probably the last person that you want to see right now," I said as I followed him to the living room.

"No shit?"

I ignored his sarcasm . . . for now. "We definitely need to talk."

"You're now down to four minutes. Just give me what's mine."

I reached into my Louis Vuitton shoulder bag and withdrew an envelope. "I maneuvered some pieces around the board while I was gone and they proved to be quite profitable. You made it more than clear to me before I left that you wanted your money. So here. This is yours."

Grabbing the envelope, he pulled out the check and mumbled, "The whole eight million, huh?"

"Plus a little something extra as you can see. That's for any inconvenience I may have caused."

"That's an understatement. But I would have had a lot more respect for you if you would have kept this professional."

"As I was saying, Mr. Macklin, in the process of moving the pieces and procuring the capital necessary to pay you, I spoke with two associates of my father's and they've assured me that there wouldn't be any more trouble to the club." I paused to allow Trae to speak, but he remained silent. "In light of the way our last few conversations went, the least you could do is tell me 'thank you'."

"I'm not in a gracious mood right now, Charli. Plus, you owe me this. Why the fuck I gotta thank you for what's mine? You know what? It don't even matter no more. This check concludes our business. Now, I need you to stay away from me and my club." Trae replied over his shoulder as he pulled out one of those blunt things, lit it and sat on the couch. He inhaled twice and began to cough.

"Put that out Mr. Macklin," I said facetiously and walked a few steps towards him. "I'm pregnant and second-hand smoke is bad for my child. Our Child."

"This is *my* house. And I suggest that you stay your ass over there then. Why are you coming closer to the smoke? As a matter of fact, why are you still here? Because I ain't tryna hear that *our baby* shit right now."

"Hear it now or hear it later, Mr. Macklin." I pulled the tyvek envelope out of my bag and tossed it in his lap. "That's a sonogram that I had recently. I wanted you to see what you created inside of me."

"Charli, don't you think I already saw the first one you sent me?"

"I don't know. You don't return my calls, so it's obvious that you didn't. But if you want to continue to deny my child, our child, that's on you. The baby will be raised to have the best of everything. I will not force you to be a father. I have enough love inside of me for the both of us."

"Are you done? Because I'm starting to feel like I'm trapped in a Lifetime movie. I'm not in the mood for this, Charli, I just told you that." Trae inhaled that horrible blunt thing again. "You said you came here to tell, to give and to show. You told me about the baby, which I already knew. You told me about what you did for my club which I want you stay away from. You gave me the check and you showed me the sonogram . . . again."

"The sonogram was a part of what I came to give. I have something else that I want to show you." I moved so that I could stand directly in front of him.

"And what might that be?"

Stepping out of my Alexander McQueen's and lifting my skirt, I pulled my thong panties off.

"Charli—"

Leaning forward, I put my finger to his lips. "Don't talk. Since this is the last time that I might see you, just lie back and let me show you something that I learned in the Philippines." Lifting my skirt to my waist, I straddled Trae. Slow winding my body in his lap caused his dick to grow in his pants. I was soaking wet. I told him, "They call this the 'Couch Canoodle'." I reached under me until I felt his zipper. In seconds, I had his member free, big and thick in my hand. I rose up and rubbed the head of his dick all around my wetness. Quickly tiring of the foreplay, I lowered myself a few inches onto him. "Earlier you said I had five minutes. How many do I have left?"

Before he could say a word I leaned forward to kiss him. He turned away from me. I didn't care. I was getting what I came for. I used my pussy muscles to pull him all the way inside me. He didn't even budge. I bounced up and down on his dick until my pussy adjusted to his length and girth, then with my legs splayed apart, I bent my knees. I pressed my knees up against his chest, and then slowly leaned all the way back until my palms were flat on the floor. I was almost completely upside down. Without letting his dick escape from within me, I thrust my hips back and forth while opening and closing my legs simultaneously. And just when I thought that he might not take the bait he grabbed me by my hips and began to match every stroke. I was confident that by the time I starting working my pussy muscles like the Kama Sutra had taught me, that I would have Mr. Trae Macklin exactly where I wanted him. Checkmate.

TRAE

I could have stopped the whole thing from happening but fuck it. Why should Tasha have all the fun? She was out there fucking the next nigga raw, carrying his seed and acting like I'm some kind of soft ass nigga. Plus, when she mentioned couch canoodle I got curious. If I liked it, I would teach Tasha how to do it. And it didn't hurt that old girl was fucking the shit outta me, not to mention, y'all know a nigga loves that pregnant pussy. But for real, I may need this bitch later on so I'ma need her to act right so she can do what the fuck I tell her. Like they say, the game is chess, it damn sure ain't checkers. Every move I make is so that I can conquer and destroy. At one point I could have sworn that I heard her say she loved me. Fuck outta here with that bullshit! The bitch is definitely not playing with a full deck. It always amazed me how a bitch could allow herself to fall in love with the next bitch's dick then be shocked when you treat them like a ho. I let her get her shit off and then put that bitch to the bricks. I needed to rest up before I made my next moves.

KYRON

I had been blowing up Tasha's cell but she was adamant about not talking to me. She must have threatened Trina because she wasn't answering her phone either. I had Kendra call Tasha from her phone and she picked right up.

"What's happening Miss Tasha?" Kendra hit her speaker-phone button.

"Kendra, do you have me on speaker?"

"Yeah she do." I snatched up the phone, took it off speaker

and went where I could talk in private. "Tasha, why do I have to jump through hoops and shit just to talk to you? What's up? You told me you would be here by now." She was busted and I dared her to hang up on me.

"I need to sort this out first. I need a few more days."

"What's to sort out?"

"What do you mean what's to sort out?" She snapped. "I'm married, I'm pregnant and I don't know if the baby is my husband's or if it belongs to the nigga I was creepin' with. I have yet to figure the shit out, Kyron."

"Tasha, you know that the baby is mine."

"You don't know that, Kyron. And let's say that it is yours. What about me and Trae?"

No she did not just ask me that. I didn't want to hear that bullshit. "Tasha, don't get rid of my baby." I warned her. "Come back so we can sit down and talk about this face to face. You and that baby belong to me."

"Kyron, I told you before that you were just a revenge fuck. Our little game is over."

"Come and see me Tasha. I need to see you."

"Kyron, I won't just get up and come up there and see you on a whim. I need to have a sit down with Trae before I come back to New York. So, I'm going back home."

She then hung up on me.

TASHA

I can't believe this nigga. The way he said, "Come see me, Tasha. I need to see you." The power in his voice had my knees weak. I was damn near hypnotized. I had to hang up before I started packing my bags. But I couldn't lose focus. Not now. I had to try one more time with my husband. I could tell that Kyron was losing patience with me but I still hadn't figured out his motives. Deep down I had a feeling that I was carrying his seed, but I hadn't had the opportunity to sit down and go over the consequences of my actions, weigh my options and have the dreaded *discussion* with Trae.

I got off the phone with Kyron and I sat there for almost two hours trying to get my mind right. The conclusion I came to was to start piecing my life back together and the first step in doing that was to move back home. I packed up all of our belongings and loaded up my car. I didn't realize me and the kids had so much stuff and saw that I would have to make another trip. I took the first load to the house and unpacked. It felt so strange being there and I swear I wanted to grab all my shit and go back to Trina's. I was thankful that I had the house to myself because I needed uninterrupted time to think and be sure that this is where I wanted to be.

I knew that Trae wasn't spending any time in our home either but it looked like he had been there earlier and had the same thought as myself, to move back in. We were always so in tune. His stuff was already in the living room. He had gone to the drycleaners and had sorted and stacked our mail on the dining room table. I put his stuff away, as well as the kids' and saved my stuff for last. I cleaned up and decided that I would stop at the bank and do a little grocery shopping.

On my way out I decided to go through the stacks of mail. Trae had left some receipts and other documents in a folder. I went through everything with a magnifying glass, especially when I came across the documents of three brand new trust fund accounts for our sons at a half-million apiece. The muthafuckas were just set up yesterday and my name wasn't anywhere to be found. Then there was a large manila envelope addressed to Trae in today's stack of mail. It stood out like a sore thumb. I knew who it was from before I even opened it. She didn't want me to miss it. Inside the manila envelope was a white tyvek envelope that had the picture of an ultrasound belonging to his bitch Charli Li. *Sonofabitch.* I closed the folder. I had to really think about this shit but not on an emotional level, which was hard as hell. I felt like my emotions were in the Matrix. They were twisting, turning, going upside down, inside out and I had broken into a cold sweat. I must have sat there for almost an hour before I regained my control. I took the envelope and put it away.

I then turned my focus to the three trust funds. It took me a while to formulate my strategy but I just about had it all figured out.

Then there was the matter of the receipt of the big ass, seven figure bank deposit. This Chinese bitch was undoubtedly somewhere close. Here I was ready to try and piece back our family and this nigga was still fucking with her.

I called Trae and got his voicemail. "Trae, come home *now.* We need to talk. *Now* Trae."

SIX

TRAE

Tasha left me a message that she needed to see me *now*. I could tell by the tone of her voice that she was ready for war but, I couldn't put my finger on why. She said she was at home. Why was she even at the house? I thought that it was ironic that she was trying to have an attitude after she goes and fucks another nigga. Then it hits me like a ton of bricks. She was back at the house and was going through my shit. *Damn* . . . I left all of the mail and the entire bank folder on the dining room table. *Fuck!*

TASHA

The sunlight peering through a slit in the drapes woke me up. I buried my face deep into my pillow and tried to go back to sleep. I was drained. I had waited up until after three for Trae. He never answered my calls nor did he bother to call me.

On another note I was relieved that I was not suffering

through morning sickness, but at the same time it had me skeptical. Carrying each and every one of Trae's seeds had me sick as a dog for months. Could this really be Kyron's baby that I was carrying in my stomach?

I looked at the clock, it was only 7:22. I couldn't go back to sleep, so around eight o'clock I finally got my ass up and out of the bed. I was dressed and ready to handle something when I dialed my cousin Stephon's cell.

He picked up immediately. "What's up, cousin? Where the hell have y'all been?"

"I need you to do something for me." I didn't have time for the small talk. The nigga had me and Trina's number so if he really wanted to get in touch, nothing was stopping him.

"Is everything alright? I haven't heard from anybody."

"I need to see that bitch, Charli. Get her to the office today. Just let me know what time."

"Oh, nonononono. I love you and everything but you are not going to get me mixed up in this bullshit."

"Nigga, you already are mixed up in it. For one—"

"Tasha come on now."

"For one you introduced her to us. Two, you owe me and three, I know you don't want me to tell Trae that you knew about Marvin dealing out of the club. You know he will make sure you will never run another club in this life or your next one."

That shut his ass up. He thought I didn't know about him knowing. This nigga has gotten so Hollywood that he thinks he can't live without running a club.

"I'll see what I can do," he mumbled.

"Today, Stephon! I need you to make that shit happen today!" I was sure that I had got my point across so I hung up.

TRAE

My wife had been blowing my phone up all night. After I found out from my man Lo where Marvin was resting at, I turned the shit off.

It wasn't even five in the morning and here I was landing in fuckin' West Bubblefuck, Kentucky. Since I was on a mission I rented an inconspicuous ride to get around in. As I walked up the driveway I hoped that this was the right house. A little girl's bike was laying on the lawn as well as some pink roller blades. Looks like something Aisha would have. I stepped on a squeezie toy, announcing to the whole block that I was here. Dogs started barking and the curtain of what I hoped was Marvin's window moved.

I made my way up the steps and rang the doorbell. After several minutes, a little Mexican shorty came and opened the door. Well, I don't know if she was Mexican, but she was mixed with something.

"Can I help you?" she asked in a thick Spanish accent.

"Is Marvin in?"

She smiled, "No, he isn't. Mr. Marvin is out of town."

"What about my niece, Aisha?"

"Aisha is your niece?" Her left eyebrow rose up. "What's your name?"

"Trae. He didn't tell you that I was coming?"

"Uncle Trae!" she squealed with excitement surprising the shit out of me and opened the door. "Oh my heavens. Come in! Miss Aisha talk about you all the time. Come in! I feel like I know you. Your wife is Auntie Tasha. There's also Auntie Angel and Jaz. The twins and Callie." Oh, I can't wait to go to California. Mr. Marvis promise me he take me soon."

"Caliph." I corrected her as I stepped inside.

"Mr. Marvin didn't tell me you were coming. He won't be

back for a couple of days. Can I fix you something to eat? You came all the way from California and he didn't tell me? He must have forgotten."

I couldn't get a word in. She was talking non-stop. I wasn't listening, just disappointed that I came all the way down here and the nigga wasn't even home. Now I had to decide if I wanted to camp out for a few days or take my ass back home and check him out next week. But then there was always the chance that the nigga would get ghost once he learned that I knew where he rested. The good thing was, this chick wouldn't stop talking. Whatever information she had, I would have no problem getting. She guided me into the kitchen and sat me at the kitchen table. She started going through the cabinets and refrigerator, preparing to cook something up. I sat back and allowed her to ramble on.

STEPHON

I didn't want to believe that my own blood threatened me like that. Shit, she was fucking with my livelihood and she knew it. Yeah, I knew that Marvin was running a little get high from the club but, Who doesn't? And if I would have ratted him out what would he have done to me? I didn't know Tasha knew what was going on but if she rats me out to Trae that could be a problem. By the skin of our teeth we were able to get the club re-opened. It's not back to how we had it, not yet, but at least we are open and it's running.

I was caught between a rock and a hard place. Adding Charli Li to the equation, what was a nigga supposed to do? I called her and she answered on the second ring.

"Well, well, well. What a pleasant surprise. I was just beginning to feel insulted."

"My favorite lady friend," I teased. "How are you and where the hell have you been?"

"If you would have been keeping in touch the way you were supposed to you would know, Stephon."

"Don't put all the blame on me. You haven't called me, texted me, anything."

"I told you that I had business in Seoul, remember?"

"Vaguely. Stop by the club. I have some things to run by you."

"Is everything alright?" I could hear the genuine concern in her voice.

"I need to talk to you. How soon can you get here?"

"You don't mean today do you?"

"Yes, today."

"Did Trae put you up to this?"

"No. Well . . . I need to run a few things by you."

"Stephon, is everything alright?"

"Yeah, girl. I need to talk to you, that's all I want to run Vegas by you." I could hear her fumbling around in the background.

"Vegas?"

"Yes, Vegas. This could be big, Charli, I'm telling you."

She laughed, "Fine. I can get there anywhere between noon and one."

"Bet. Thanks Charli. I'll see you then."

CHARLI LI

Stephon and I have been friends for about five years. He walked into Hammerstein and Li one day and I was temporarily smitten.

The tall, dark and handsome, bald-headed stranger reminded me of Boris Kodjoe and as quiet as it's kept, I'm so intrigued with Boris Kodjoe. The fact that he was charming and intelligent was an added bonus, so I decided to wrap my lucious lips around his member that very same afternoon. But after spending a few days and nights with him, I learned that his swagger was contrived, it was completely made up. Stephon turned out to be a watered down thug, business man who had emulated his identity from Sean "P. Diddy" Combs. And if that wasn't bad enough, the dick turned out to be garbage, a total waste of my time. So I dropped him faster than Charlie Sheen would check out of rehab. Despite all of that, we remained business partners and friends. I admired his hungriness and in business he was always up front and honest with me. Over the years, he became like the sibling I never had.

Dropping my cell phone back into my Chanel clutch, I thought about his call. I had planned on calling him in a few days anyway. For some reason, something inside me initially told me to decline his invite to the club, but then my body screamed, "Go. Mr. Trae Macklin might be there." What other reason would Stephon have to tell me to come to the club? And on such short notice. If it was really important, he could've come here to my office. The more I thought about it, the more I convinced myself that Trae was behind the call. The 'Couch Canoodle' move that I put on him probably had him yearning for me. So after I freshened up, I left the office.

In the lobby I saw my long time driver and bodyguard.

"Luther, leave the limo, get the Murciélago out. I need to be across town in the next 30 minutes."

To myself I thought, *I'm coming, Mr. Macklin. I'm coming.*

TASHA

By the time I pulled into the parking lot of our club, it was 12:35. Stephon had called me and told me she would be here between noon and one. His scary ass had the nerve to tell me to act like I had just happened to drop in. *Whatever.* Anyhow, I didn't want to be too early and I definitely didn't want to be too late. I had vowed to myself never to step foot in Club New York again—since it, like my home—basically belonged to that Chinese bitch. But being a street bitch at heart, a sista gotta do what a sista gotta do.

The lot was empty except for Stephon's big ass metallic silver Hummer H1 parked in the spot reserved for the owner. Next to it was a black drop top Lamborghini Murciélago. Standing next to it was a Chinese man of average height dressed in a black suit. His presence told me what I needed to know. Ms. China Ho was inside the club and for the moment, that's all I cared about.

STEPHON

I'm sitting here chattin' it up with the woman who put me on in this city and now I'm in panic mode. This chick just sat here and told me *everything*. I did not know that she was pregnant by my cousin's husband. Right then and there I knew I had to get her the fuck outta here before Tasha showed up. My slick ass cousin set me up . . . big time, and now it may be too late. I then knew I was fucked when I got a text message from Tasha telling me that she was in the parking lot and on her way up.

"Stephon are you listening to me?" Charli asked me. I was hoping that she didn't notice the sweat beads popping up across my forehead.

"Sorry, babe. Something came up. I got to get up out of here."

"Something came up? I just arrived. You invited me and you still haven't said a word about Las Vegas. I'm all ears but I still have to tell you, Vegas is the big league. Do you really think that you are ready for Vegas?" She had the nerve to look like she was getting comfortable in her seat.

"Babe, I apologize, but this is even more urgent."

"Same ole Stephon. Then let's play catch up and do brunch on Sunday. How does that sound?"

Shit. Will you be around to see Sunday? I stood up. "That sounds like a plan. What spot do you have in mind?"

"Let me surprise you." Charli smiled at me.

By the time I locked up my office and turned around, Tasha was coming up the stairs looking as if she was on a mission and looking like a runway model. Where was *Hip Hop Weekly* to get this picture? She was dressed to the nines in a pair of Antik Denims that hugged her just right. She had a low cut yellow blouse and was carrying what looked like a brand new croc print Gucci bag. My cousin takes no prisoners when she steps out.

This was the first time I saw someone smiling with slits in their eyes. She was looking like the devil. I looked at Charli to see if I could read her body language. She appeared to be cool. It was as if she welcomed the challenge.

"So, Steph. Is this why you invited me here? You naughty boy." Ice dripped from her tone. I knew I was fucked.

"Is my husband here?" Tasha asked as she came up the steps. She was acting as if she didn't see Charli.

"Nah. I haven't heard from Trae in a while."

"Then why is this bitch here?" Tasha snapped.

Even though I was looking right at Tasha, I didn't see what happened. She was that slick with it. I don't know if she pushed her, nudged her, tripped or clipped her but Charli went tumbling down about twenty steps. *Shit.*

TASHA

Yeah, I did it.

My punk ass cousin was now at the top of the stairs pacing back and forth, rubbing his hands across his head yelling, "Oh shit. Oh, shit."

"Shut the fuck up, nigga. The bitch ain't have no business being here. The last time I checked, her restraining order was still in effect."

"Tasha, what the fuck is wrong with you? The woman is pregnant." Stephon's ass was turning pale.

"So, the fuck what! She shouldn't have fucked *my* husband."

I looked down at the bitch. She was at the bottom of the steps out cold, not moving. I believed my work here was done. I started my descent down the steps.

"Where the fuck do you think you're going? You can't just leave her there." Stephon was panicking.

"She's your guest Stephon, not mine." I kept on going but stopped when I reached the bottom of the stairs. I swear I was tempted to stomp that fuckin' baby out of her stomach. My cousin must have sensed it because he came flying down the steps and pushed me away from her. "Get your hands off of me, Stephon. Why the fuck do you care about this bitch, anyway? You fuckin' her too?"

"Tasha, get the fuck out of here. I need to call an ambulance. What if she's dead? How are we gonna explain this shit to Trae? Shit, how can I explain this to her people? You don't even have a clue as to what you just did, do you? Don't answer that. Just leave! Now! Get the fuck out of here! Tasha, go!"

"Fuckin' weak ass bitch." I stepped closer to Charli, when I was directly over her I hawked and spat in her face. Then I left, totally feeling myself. What I just did felt good at the moment and I didn't give a fuck about anything else.

TRAE

Since I was already in Kentucky, I decided to stay a few days to see if Marvin would show up. Frangela, the housekeeper and nanny, only knew what Marvin wanted her to know and that wasn't much. After all that talking she did I found out that, not only did she not know where Marvin was but she had no clue as to when he'd return. What I did know was that wherever he went, he took Aisha with him.

After paying her a few dollars to keep my surprise visit still a surprise, I left and checked into the Hilton. I was enjoying the solitude until my phone started blowing up nonstop. I was getting back-to-back calls from Stephon and then Tasha. I didn't answer any of them. I wanted to stay focused for the unpleasant job at hand. Then I got a call from Benny, my lawyer. If Benny was hittin' on my cell phone, then something was wrong. His second time calling, I picked up. What he told me gave me an instant headache.

"Shit!" I gritted as I ended the call. That's why Steph and Tasha were blowing up my phone. They needed me to do damage control. Tasha's vindictive ass had pushed Charli down a flight of stairs. No one knew her health status and now Stephon was scared shitless. I went back to Marvin's house, reminded Frangela

to keep our secret, and said my goodbyes. Then I was on my way
back to California.

TASHA

Last night I heard Trae come in and then immediately leave
which only left me to believe that he went to check on his Chinese ho. That very thought felt like a stab in the chest. But what's
done is done. I knew what I had to do. So the first thing I did
before I got out of bed the next morning was call my sister. "See
how soon you can get me a flight out to New York."

"Why? What's going on? You don't mean today do you?"

"Yes. Today, Trina." She had no clue as to all that had gone
down the day before. I told her, "Get me as far the fuck away
from this nigga as possible. I'ma get my kids and ride off into
the sunset somewhere."

"Yyesss! I'm coming with you."

Here I was ready for war and this bitch was all excited about
going to New York. "Trina, just make the reservation and come
pick me up."

I hung up and then continued to map out my strategy. My
first instinct was to chop off his dick. The more I thought about
it, the more I saw that I probably could pull it off and get away
with it.

KYRON

I was with Kendrick when he got the call from Trina that she
and Tasha would be catching a red-eye up this way. I immediately called Tasha to question her as to why I had to hear the

shit from someone else. Of course she wouldn't answer my call. But that ain't stop shit. I snatched up a total stranger and borrowed his phone.

"How come I'm the last to know that you are on your way up? What? You're not planning on seeing me? And why are y'all taking a commercial flight? You have access to a private jet."

"Kyron, I know you gonna let me do me!" She snapped.

She sounded vexed. I had asked Trina if she and Trae had a fight and Trina's response was she 'didn't think so.' I figured that she wanted to be around her girl Angel so I asked, "You staying at my brother's?"

"No, I'm not. I don't need them to be judging me and I don't need them all up in my business."

"Then where are you staying?"

"At a hotel, Kyron."

"A hotel?" She was really starting to piss me off. "Tasha come on now. You have keys to my crib."

"No, Kyron. I don't have your keys anymore. And no, I'm not staying with you; we are no longer fucking around like that. Remember?"

"Who said anything about fuckin' around? We are supposed to be talking about me, you and the baby *remember*? You know what? Fuck it. I'll see you at the airport."

"No!" she snapped. "I'm serious Kyron. Don't waste your time. I'll let you know when I'm ready to talk to you."

"Talk to me?" I laughed it off. "The only thing I want to hear is you calling my name as I'm beatin' that pussy. So bring it to me."

I hung up on her this time.

CHARLI LI

When I awoke, I looked around and realized that I was in a room at my father's palatial estate Rancor Los Arboles, in Rancho Santa Fe, California. The room had a panoramic view of the clear blue sky. The walls were made of glass and there was a 60 inch plasma screen T.V. made into the wall over top of the fire place. The floor was bare except for one white Asian throw rug that matched the king-sized white bed that I laid in. In the corner of the room stood my chauffer and bodyguard Luther. As soon as he saw me eyeing him, he left the room immediately.

My whole body ached and I noticed that I was attached to a single I.V. drip. I heard the door to my room open and in walked my father, with two of his men. My father came straight to my side, bent down and kissed my forehead.

"My child, you had me worried. The doctor just left and he assured me that your concussion was minor. He examined you and found no broken bones. You have a few bruises and a knot on your head from your fall. The paramedics inside the ambulance discovered that you were bleeding below the waist. At the hospital before I had you moved, I was told that you were with child—but you miscarried. I'm disappointed, Charli! You never told me that you were pregnant."

I looked into my father's eyes. They held so much wisdom and history and pain. Once being a part of the Triads in China, he migrated to the U.S. to find another way to live. In the states, old habits were hard to break and three years after landing on American soil, Charlie Li was the overlord of a large Chinese underworld that specialized in selling knock-off clothes, narcotics and counterfeit money to the highest bidders.

Him ruling the underworld was 30 years ago, three years

before I was born, and now my father looked old. Years of war, love, betrayal, killing and prison had taken its toll. Where his once silky black hair used to be, was now covered in grey. The only thing that remained the same was his smile and his eyes.

"I had just found out myself." That was all I could say before I started to cry.

"Tell me, my child, who did this to you? You sustained a fall at Club New York. Was Mr. Trae Macklin the person who hurt you?"

"No." I must have responded a little too quickly. My father's eyebrow rose. I continued, "Mr. Macklin had nothing to do with it."

"Then what happened to you? Did you fall down? "

"Mr. Macklin's wife seems to believe that I wanted to take her husband away from her. Her name is—"

"Tasha. Rosalyn Tasha McNeil is her maiden name. It became Macklin after she married."

"But how do you know—"

"My child, it is my business to know everything. The minute you told me about your business venture with Trae Macklin, I had him checked out. He was born and raised in New York. He and his partner, a mister Kaylin Santos, attracted the attention of both the Columbian and Italian mob bosses there. They were used by the dons to amass a lot of wealth. But in the meantime, Mr. Macklin and Mr. Santos invested wisely and left the family business or at least they tried to leave. But the dons will not let them leave. In this business, it's blood in, blood out. You come in walking and you leave in a box. Mr. Santos established himself in New York with a soon-to-be music empire, while Mr. Macklin elected to come here and start a new life. I know everything there is to know about Trae Macklin, his wife, his children, his entire family. Are you telling me that Rosalyn Macklin attacked you?"

I nodded my head.

"Since you got yourself into this mess, I should let you handle it yourself. After all, getting pregnant by a married man is not a noble thing."

"Father, I will handle this myself."

"No. The girl will be dead by tomorrow—"

"No, Father I have other plans for Tasha Macklin. I want to deal with her personally."

"I will kill her husband—"

"No! Father, please let me handle both Trae Macklin and his wife. But there is one person that you can kill for me. Before this day, I loved him like a brother, but he has betrayed me."

"And who might this be, my child?"

"Stephon McNeil."

"Ah, yes. Mr. Stephon McNeil. Rosalyn McNeil Macklin's cousin."

I nodded. "He's the one that arranged the meeting between myself and Mr. Macklin. He knew what was planned for me. His actions are inexcusable." I was disappointed in Stephon.

My father was dressed in his ever-present black custom made shirt, black slacks and Chinese-made suede loafers. He paced the floor in front of my bed. It was what he always did when he made decisions. "It will be taken care of." My father spoke in rapid Mandarin to one of his men, Samu who left the room quickly. Moments later, he returned with a wooden box. He gave the box to my father, who brought it over to me. He placed the box on my bed and opened it.

"Our people have made knives and swords for centuries,

but the greatest knife makers who ever lived weren't in the renaissance or some other period; they're living and working right now." He reached in the box and pulled out a knife of some kind. "No one from any era in the past can touch what the best craftsmen are doing now. This knife is the Rembrandt of knives. It was made—hand-carved by a man named John Jensen. This replica cost me 100 thousand dollars. Isn't it beautiful?"

I looked at the hand-carved knife that had swirling designs carved into the blade. The handle was bejeweled. It was indeed beautiful. "Yes, Father." Like a child on Christmas my father's eyes lit up. Then in an instant, the light was gone, replaced by darkness that seemed cold and distant. My father walked over to my bodyguard Luther.

"Where were you when this woman was assaulting my daughter?" he asked Luther.

"Outside by the car. I—"

"Silence! Your job was to protect my daughter, but she still ended up hurt. You failed her. You failed me and you failed your family." My father turned and plunged the knife into Luther's chest. "Failure is unacceptable."

Luther fell to his knees; he grabbed the knife and pushed it further into his chest, "I don't deserve forgiveness. I will regain my honor in my next life." He knew that he had failed my family.

TRAE

When I pulled up in front of the house, Tasha was sitting on the porch but got up and went inside before I could even shut the car off. When I stepped into the house she was seated at the dining room table thumbing through that damn folder. I got caught slippin'.

So I immediately told her, "Tasha, don't start trippin'. It ain't what you think it is."

"Oh, I ain't trippin'. Not yet."

"What is that supposed to mean?"

She didn't answer my question but stood up and grabbed the folder. "Let's go to the bank. These trust funds need to be amended to include my signature. I need to be able to have access before the kids turn of age. With you being so fuckin' reckless, anything could happen to you. I'll be in the car." She walked out of the dining room, leaving me alone.

I stood there thinking about what she said. Shit, I figured she was right, especially since I had just began my killing spree. That shit could go either way, since I had yet to catch up with Marv. I turned the dining room light out, got outside and locked the front door. I kept going over what she had just said. Tasha was too calm for me and I knew she was up to something.

"What happened between you and Charli?"

"Don't you dare question me about your jump off. You probably was with her last night, so I'm sure she told you what happened."

"I was not with her. I wish you would stop insinuating that I still fuck with her. That shit is gettin' old Tasha."

"Whatever, nigga." She turned her back towards me.

I wanted to reach inside the truck, yank her ass out and put my foot in her ass. Instead, I took a deep breath, walked around to the other side and got in the truck. I drove to the bank in silence.

We arrived about a half hour later and got out. I followed

Tasha inside of the crowded bank and went to take a piss. When I came out Tasha had her arms folded across her chest and I knew that she was ready to argue. So I sat across from her and picked up a brochure off of the waiting room table.

As we sat and waited for our banker to see us, she looked over at me and asked, "Why are you still fuckin' with that bitch, Trae?"

I sighed. I was tired of this game. I played, I lost and now I needed to figure out how to get back right. "Tasha, I told you. I—"

"You ain't tell me shit." She snapped, not bothering to lower her voice.

"Well, I'm telling you now." I spoke low, through gritted teeth. "I ain't fuckin' her. She owed me money. That's it. That's all."

"Nigga, please. The last time she owed you money your dick did all of the negotiating. What were you planning on using this time?"

I shook my head after an older white woman frowned and covered her child's ears. I didn't respond because she was starting to get loud and I knew this was an argument I wasn't trying to win, especially not in no damn bank lobby. I'll handle the shit when we get home.

She obviously didn't like the fact that I wasn't responding, because she said, "Well, you can have her . . . or what's going to be left of her once I finish doing what I gotta do."

"What?" I stared at my wife who had a crazed look in her eyes as she stared back at me. Then our banker Mike came and greeted us. We stood up and followed him to his office. I let Tasha do all of the talking as I kept thinking about her last threat. She kind of had my ass buggin' at that shit. I hadn't spoken to Charli and didn't intend to. But I did meet up with Stephon and Benny last night and Stephon was scared shitless.

My train of thought was interrupted when she said, "Last but not least, we are going to add another million dollar trust fund to our portfolio for the baby I'm carrying."

"Come again?" I turned to face her. I needed to make sure that I was hearing her right.

"Yes, you know that you are hoping that this baby is yours and if something happens to you, this baby needs to be taken care of as well."

Mike's face turned beet red. He was hearing some Maury shit, up close and personal. Without even consulting with me he got up to follow Tasha's instructions. My wife was really fuckin' with my head. I began to entertain the thought of the baby actually being mine. And before I knew it, Mike was back at his desk with the papers.

Tasha wasted no time. She pointed to the documents. "Sign here. And here. And here."

I had to look at my wife to make sure she was serious. Maybe I was being *Punk'd*. I looked at Mike and he looked serious, Tasha looked like a mad woman. I looked around at my surroundings and nothing seemed out of the ordinary.

"You must be out of your got-damned mind. I'll put you on my kid's paperwork, but you let that nigga pay for his own seed, that's if the muthafucka make it.

"Aiight." Tasha said, real cool. "Okay. This is how you wanna play?"

"What the fuck you mean is this how I wanna play? That ain't my fuckin' seed! What the fuck do I look like to you, Tasha?"

"Nigga, are you sure the ones you are signing for belong to you?"

I lunged at this bitch's throat and I swore that I was going to kill her at that very moment.

Mike's ass was hysterical as he called for security to come and save Tasha from me.

"Mr. Macklin, please. Please let her go."

As Tasha fought to catch her breath, I ripped up all of them muthafuckin' documents. "Bitch, you must have bumped your head." I stormed out of the bank and headed for my ride.

It wasn't the money. Shit it was only a million dollars. If it was going to get me back tight with my wife, a mil was more than worth it. But she asked me to put up for some other niggas baby? Then she had the nerve to insinuate that our kids wasn't from my loins? She had to be trying me. No, I think the bitch was trying to run me crazy.

I was driving us back to the house, looking straight ahead, when Tasha hauled back and punched me dead in the face. The truck swerved, horns started honking as I yelled, "What the fuck is wrong with you?"

She started spazzing on me. "I actually came back to our home thinking that we could work our shit out. And you still fuckin' with that ho?" She punched me again. This time I pulled over, threw the car in park and was getting ready to fuck her ass up, but she jumped out of the truck and started walking down the street. The sun was glaring down on her and it looked like she didn't have on any panties on under that sundress.

I got out, caught up to her, snatched her by her hair and dragged her ass back to the truck. "What? You done lost your fuckin' mind? Right now you don't want to try me, Tasha. Now, get out again."

I dared her. She must have seen that I was not fucking with her because she got in, sat back and put her seatbelt on.

TASHA

I may have gone too far. I should have quit while I was ahead. Realizing that I should have just chilled out because I fucked up the trust funds. But the more I thought about him and that Chinese bitch, the madder I got. The next thing I knew, I swung on him. But now this nigga was standing by the truck looking at me as if he wanted to kill me. I was looking out of the window and praying that he got his ass back in the truck and drove me home. I was holding my breath as he stood there. I could tell that he was debating on whether he should whip my ass or not. Finally, he made his move, came around and got in.

"I know I fucked up," he mumbled as if it hurt him to acknowledge that yes indeed he did fuck up!

I looked at him. The wise Tasha was saying, *"Don't say a word. Just get home, get your shit and leave."* I fought like hell to keep the scorned Tasha at bay until we pulled in front of our house. But the scorned Tasha . . . now that bitch was causing me turmoil. I lost control of her. And the minute we pulled up, she let loose. I jumped out of the car and so did Trae.

"You know what nigga? Yes, you did fuck up. You started all of this shit and you best believe I'ma finish it."

"You finished it already! Have you forgotten that you fucked a nigga? Whose baby are you carrying Tasha?"

Even though I started laughing, his words cut through me like a knife. And the look in his eyes was more hate than love. I started to just walk away, but fuck the bullshit, I had to respond since the muthafucka asked.

"Did you forget that not only did you fuck the bitch, but then you had me, your wife, sitting in the fucking doctor's office getting medication for a gotdamn STD? Do you know how embarrassing that shit is? So don't get in my face about me fucking another nigga. At this point I don't give a fuck whose baby it is! You want to rumble muthafucka, let's rumble." I stood there glaring at him. He stood glaring at me. I finally took my ass in the house and was going to get my shit and leave for good, but with each step I took it was harder and harder. The Tasha who he had swept off her feet was hurting real bad and she didn't want what she had with the fuck up outside to be over.

TRAE

I followed her in the house, thinking about Sabeerah, the bitch who drugged me a while ago and took the dick. But I knew not to reveal that. Simply because if Tasha knew it was two bitches that I fucked instead of one it would definitely be over. When I came out of that daze Tasha was walking down the hall heading towards our bedroom. So I went after her. When I entered the room she was sitting on the bed staring at the floor with tears running down her face.

"Oh, God. How did we get here, Trae? What happened to us?"

There was no doubt that I had disappointed my wife. I let her down. I had sworn to her that I would never do what those other niggas did to her . . . but I did. Not because I wanted to but shit happened and I couldn't take it back. No matter how bad I wanted to.

"I fucked up baby. And I take full responsibility for my actions. You fucked up trying to get back at me. So it is what it is." I said as I lowered myself to her feet.

"I wish we would have never moved out here. Kyra is dead, our marriage is dead. Everything we built together is crumbling." She was crying for real and it was tearing me up.

"I'ma make it right. I promise."

My wife looked at me with disbelief in her eyes and shook her head. "Promise? I used to be able to put my life on your promises. But not anymore. It's over for us, Trae. We need to start accepting that."

"Baby, look me in the eyes and tell me that you really believe it's over between us."

"It's over, Trae."

"Baby, your mouth is saying that, but you looked away. You know you don't believe that."

"What am I supposed to believe then?" she cried louder.

"Believe that we can work through this. Believe that we are *supposed* to work through this. Just because we are thrown a curve ball, it don't mean that we're out." She looked at me and was looking at me hard. I could tell that she was wanting to believe me and was wondering if what I had just told her was humanly possible. "I'll never stop loving you, Tasha. You are my world. Now tell me that you don't know that."

"I used to know that, Trae. There used to be no doubt in my mind. Now, I honestly don't know shit anymore. I don't know what to think." She reached over to the nightstand and grabbed some tissue.

"Think about us, baby." I was damn near begging.

"But . . . this . . . baby." She said it. It was forced but she said it. I could tell that the baby situation was tearing her up. Hell, it was tearing me up. "What do we do about the baby?"

"Let's find out whose it is first."

"Then what?"

And just as the words left her mouth I leaned in and kissed her lips and it was the sweetest kiss we had ever shared and it was the first one in a long while. Then she stopped me.

"No, Trae. I don't think we need to let this happen." She was dead serious. "It's only going to confuse things."

Confuse things? "It's already happening." I said as I laid her back. "You belong to me, Tasha Macklin." I kissed her again. She tried to resist. "I love you more than any other nigga ever will. You can put your life on that."

"Then why Trae? Why did you—"

I covered her lips with mine and I thought no kiss could be sweeter than the last one, but it was happening again. I slipped my hand up her dress and as always got hard instantly, thanks to her not having any panties. I stopped kissing my wife and looked down at her beautiful face. "So what's up?" I eased off of her, stood up and unzipped my jeans. "You was planning on giving me some pussy?"

"I was last night but since you didn't come home, you blew that."

I was stripping as fast as I could. "I had to meet up with Stephon and Benny to see what the fuck you had done. I knew I couldn't count on you to tell me everything."

TASHA

You damn right you couldn't. And if that trip down the stairs didn't flush that muthafuckin' bastard out of her womb, I was going to plan B.

My husband stood there bucknaked, massaging his dick. I tried to resist but the more I watched him, the hotter and wetter my pussy became. I finally stood up and tossed my dress onto the floor, climbed onto the bed and crawled to the edge. I was convinced that my husband had the prettiest and biggest, black dick in the universe and I couldn't remember the last time I had sucked it. It was sticking straight out at me and I could have sworn that he whispered my name, so I answered him.

I used my lips and tongue to play with the head. This always drove him insane. He was anxious for me to deep throat his shit but he had been a very bad boy and didn't deserve it. He grabbed my hair.

"Baby, what's good?" he asked me in desperation as I continued to tease him without mercy. "Swallow my shit," he begged.

I stopped giving him head altogether and leaned upward remaining on my knees.

"Oh, it's like that?" He had the nerve to sound as if he had a slight attitude.

"Yeah, nigga it's like that. But I'm not stopping you from doing you."

Still on my knees, Trae leaned me backward. He spread my thighs and pulled me to the edge of the bed. Holding all of his weight up, he climbed on top of me and made penetration. Now it was his turn to tease me and drive me insane. Since my legs were folded back, I couldn't move. He had total control. I could only tightly clench my sheets. He fucked me the way he wanted to. Going all the way in, coming out, hitting my spot and then acting as if he couldn't find it. He wanted me to beg. Beg him to fuck me harder. Beg him to punish my spot until I came. Beg him to stop pulling all the way out and then plunging in deep and stopping. But I wouldn't beg. I refused. Then his mouth covered mine. We kissed as he stroked real slow. The tears fell from the corners of my eyes. He was on my spot again. And then I did what I said I would never do again, I begged. "Babeeeee, pleasssse." He had a smirk on his face that said he won. I submitted to him. And for that I was rewarded with a dick that murdered my g-spot and an orgasm filled with fireworks.

TRAE

Lil' Wayne said it best, "Oooh shit, muthafucka, got damn!" You talking about pussy being good. I know she thought that I was trying to be funny and get her back for not swallowing my dick, but that was not the case. Her pussy was so good, that if I didn't keep changing up my strokes I would have become a one minute man. The thought of her possibly being pregnant by some other nigga made me angry. That's when I was finally able to grab this horse by the reigns and bring it home. I was no longer reveling in how good the pussy felt. I started hittin' my baby's spot and when she started speaking in tongues, I knew she was gone.

"This is what you wanted right? That's why you ain't have on no panties. You wanted me to fuck you just like this. Didn't you?" I was talking shit as she was cumming. I held mine back because I wanted to come in her mouth. I pulled out and dived straight into the pussy. I needed to taste that sweet nectar that was just released. She tried to stop me but I kept feasting while bringing her to another body wrenching orgasm.

"Oh shit." She kept mumbling. "Shit."

I got up off the bed, and stood there, patiently waiting, and watching her recover as I stroked myself, my dick on swole. My wife was so fuckin' beautiful. Her hair was sprawled across the sheets; her breasts and stomach were glistening with sweat. Hands down, she was just a fuckin' dime. She opened her eyes and saw me standing there. She smiled, stretched out her legs and watched me continue to do me.

"Come over here and talk to him. Tell him how much you miss him." I said as I continued to stroke my handle.

Tasha lay there from back-to-back monster orgasms. If she didn't hurry and get up, I was going to have to slide up in that pussy again, even though I wanted to feel her lips wrapped around my dick. I was beyond ready. She must have read my mind because she slowly and seductively got up off the bed and came over to where I was. She placed one hand around the back of my neck and started tonguing me down and grabbed my dick with her other hand. I closed my eyes as she began to plant kisses on my neck, chest, and getting down on her knees, she licked and sucked my abs.

Finally . . . her lips were wrapped around the head and she was sucking it as if her life depended on it. When I felt my joint going down her throat, I said it out loud this time. "Shit, muthafucka, got damn." I was through at that point. I busted all in her mouth and as my knees buckled, I watched as she slurped and swallowed until her heart was content.

She finally stood up and we went wild tasting each other's juices as we always do. Her cell was constantly ringing and then she stopped kissing me and mumbled, "Shit, I forgot about Trina."

I said, "What? Shit, I was getting ready for round three." She rushed to the nightstand to answer her phone. I went and stood behind her, planting hickies on her neck. I could hear Trina's big ass mouth loud and clear.

"Tasha, what the fuck are you doing? Why aren't you answering the phone? I'm on my way to pick you up. We can't miss the flight. I already told Kendrick what time we would get in."

"Let me call you right back."

"Call me right back for what? I'm packed, in the cab and on my way over."

"Trina, let me call you right back." She hung up the phone.

I stopped kissing on my wife and stepped back. I wanted to see if Tasha was going to lie to me. "What was that all about?"

"I told Trina to make reservations for us to go to New York."

"What the fuck for?"

She hesitated and then said, "I was planning on leaving you and getting my kids."

"Your kids? Those are *our* kids. And leaving me? For what? So you could be with your little boy toy? Leaving me? Why?"

"Trae, what do you mean why? We haven't been on the best of terms lately, have you noticed? I was mad and hating you, you were mad and hating me, so what do you mean for what and why?"

"You want to leave?" I yelled as I snatched up my boxers and jeans and put them on. "Your ass is here fucking me all the while making plans to go see your fuckin . . ." I was so heated I couldn't get the words out of my mouth.

"I told you I was mad, Trae. I was leaving you. It wasn't like I was fucking you and planning to leave at the same time." She was now yelling and putting on her clothes.

"So what's it going to be *Tasha*?"

"At this point. I don't know. You tell me *Trae*."

"Oh, you don't know? Well I'ma tell you what you're gonna do. I grabbed her by her throat. "You're gonna call this nigga and tell him you ain't coming up there because y'alls little game is over and if the baby is his, you are getting rid of it. And then pass me the muthafuckin' phone." I pushed her onto the bed, snatched up her cell phone and threw it at her. "Call him Tasha. 'Cause you really got me fucked up."

"Nigga, please, don't act like your ass is such a fucking angel," she screamed and threw the phone back at me. I caught it before it hit me in the face.

"I fucked up. I know it. How many times do you want me to say the shit?"

"That depends on how many times you kept fucking up, nigga!"

"You know what? Get the fuck out. Go be with your little boyfriend. And make sure that when you kiss him, and when he eats your pussy you let him know that he's sucking my dick."

"I will. And make sure you let your little Chinese bitch know that she's sucking my pussy."

"See. That's your muthafuckin' problem. You still think I'm fuckin' with her. You just refuse to let the shit go. I'm trying to make shit right, but it's obvious that you don't want to, so fuck it. I'ma do me and go ahead and fuck the bitch since that's what you want to hear."

Just that quick, our home turned into a war zone. My wife hauled back and slapped the shit out of me. Without thinking, this time I grabbed her neck with both of my hands and was trying to strangle her to death. Her eyes started bulging and the color was draining from her face. She was frantically flailing her arms. That's when I caught myself. *Shit.* I had temporarily lost it. I let her go. And she was coughing and gagging. I stood there rubbing my hands across my face and heard, not believing that I was that close to taking my wife out.

"You . . . tried . . . to . . . kill me." She burst out crying. "You actually tried to kill me. This was the second time today," she said as if she didn't believe what just happened. She now looked scared.

"Tasha I—"

"Get the fuck away from me!" She was moving to the other side of our bedroom like a frightened child.

"Tasha you know—"

"Get away from me, Trae. I'm out of here."

TASHA

I couldn't believe *my* Trae had just tried to kill me. And on top of that, he had the balls to say that he was going to fuck that Chinese bitch. That made me madder than him trying to kill me. "Fuck you and that Chinese, Korean, Jamaican, mutt. I hope y'all make another baby because I damn sure knocked that one out of her."

He pushed me backwards and I fell onto the bed.

"We've been reduced to you putting your hands on me now? I hate you. And I'm out of here. If we weren't finished before, we damn sure are finished now." I screamed at him as he hovered over me. I could tell that he was not himself and I needed to get the fuck out of there before it was too late.

"You're not going anywhere." That's when I kicked him in the balls. That shit took his ass down to one knee. I jumped up. "It's over. I'm moving out for good and I'm taking the kids with me. I hope you find what you're looking for in that little Chinese bitch." I ran outside praying that my sister would be out there waiting.

TRAE

This shit was unreal. I didn't know who this lady was. She was not my wife. Hell, I didn't know who I was. I would never put my hands on Tasha like that. And she would never have kicked me in the nuts, fuck another nigga, threaten to leave me *and* take our kids. I tried to stand up. I couldn't let her leave me. But shit, that kick in the nuts knocked all of the wind out of me. By the time I was able to make it downstairs, she was walking down the block. I ran after her.

"Baby, listen. Please."

"Listen? What could you possibly say?" I tried to reach for her and she started spazzing out. "Don't you fuckin' put your hands on me! You forgot that you just tried to kill me? You already said we are finished! So we are finished." She turned around and started walking faster.

"We are not finished and you ain't bouncin' on me like that." I quickened my steps to keep up with her.

"Watch me. It's over, Trae. Accept it. I can't believe you still fucking her."

She refused to let that shit go. "I'm not fucking her. She came by to drop off some of the money that she owed me."

"She came by?" She stopped dead in her tracks. "She came by? *Some* of the money? She could have mailed that shit, Trae. She knows Benny. And *some* of the money? That means she has to come by again. You know what, go ahead and do you."

A cab pulled up and the back door flew open. "Tasha, are you—"

"Don't get out of the car Trina." Tasha had the nerve to yell at her sister.

"You got your stuff?" Trina was standing there looking at the both of us, trying to figure out what had just happened.

"I don't need shit. I'm out." She pushed Trina over in the back seat and got in.

And just like that, she was gone . . . again.

SEVEN

FAHEEM

Oni was dropping Faheem off at seven this morning. I couldn't sleep so I got up and headed for my backyard. The early morning was my favorite time of day. I had to admit, my garden was the shit, the best on the entire block. I turned on the sprinklers and admired my landscaping. I had a man-made pond that had four different tropical fish and three exotic turtles. It had a five-foot waterfall that constantly ran and gave off those soothing, running water sounds. I sat on my stool for the next half hour and got my meditation in. I then did a few hundred push-ups, turned off the sprinklers and hit the shower.

I was surprised when I got the call last night from Oni, asking if she could bring my son over the following morning. This would be the first day that me and my son would spend time together. My plan was to stay around the house and get to know him. Jaz was taking Kaeerah to her soccer game, leaving me and little man to get acquainted. She was excited for me.

"Daddy, I want to meet my little brother," my baby girl announced as she followed me downstairs into the kitchen. "Can I? Can I, pretty pleeeese?"

"Of course you can. Right after you wash your face, brush your teeth and go to soccer practice."

"I don't wanna go to soccer practice. I can stay home right, daddy?"

"What was our agreement? No more missed practices, right?"

"Awwww dad."

"Don't aww dad me. You know what our agreement was." I watched as my smart little angel made an about face and marched upstairs.

ONI

I hadn't seen or spoken to Faheem since the night he left my house in a tizzy. Lil' Faheem's babysitter went to Florida for a week, so I didn't have a sitter. I didn't trust just anybody with my son but I did trust Faheem. So I took a deep breath and called him. I usually worked from Friday night to Sunday afternoon straight. The weekends are the most busy times at the hotel. Me and my brothers own and operate three Suite Tree Hotels here in Atlanta. Each one of us is responsible for one hotel, but we run all three together. We cater to families on vacation and to the business traveler.

I hated that Faheem was now living in the same state and now I was forced to deal with him. I wasn't trying to kid myself, I still was not over him and I knew that having to interact with him was not going to be easy. So here I was, standing on his porch at 7:30 in the morning, ringing his doorbell. My . . . our son was excited. After days of questioning me, he was finally at his father's house. But actually I think he was more excited about meeting his sister than getting with his dad. I smoothed over his clothes and checked his backpack for the hundredth time to make sure I didn't forget anything. Then I stood there fidgeting with my hair and clothes.

Faheem answered the door and stepped out onto the porch. He didn't acknowledge me but smiled at our son. Before he could say anything, Lil' Faheem asked, "Daddy, is my baby sister home?"

Faheem was still smiling. "Yes she is, but she's not a baby. The both of you are the same age."

Lil' Faheem then turned to me and said, "Mommy, you said she was the baby."

Faheem didn't give me a chance to respond to him. "Well, I'll tell you what. Say goodbye to your mom and we'll go inside. And when you see her, you tell me if she's a baby or a big girl. Do we have a deal?"

Lil' Faheem nodded in agreement, looked at me and waved goodbye. They both disappeared into the house. I was left standing on the porch wondering how long Faheem planned on giving me the silent treatment.

Phoenix, Arizona

Nurse Wright yawned, looked at her watch and stood up. It was 4:44 a.m. They were short staffed as usual, so that meant that she had to sponge bathe her three patients and probably two more. Since Brown Doe was the smallest, she decided to start with her first. She stepped inside of room 703 and turned on the light. In all of her sixteen years she had never seen anyone in a coma who was so strong willed. Brown Doe was hanging in there. She had been transferred around as if she was a foster child. The coma patients she had previously cared for, most them either gave up or their families gave up and pulled the plug. Well, if Brown Doe had a family they probably would have lost patience and given up too. It had been months and Miss Brown Doe needed to wake up soon because her charity was running out.

Nurse Wright began humming her song for the day, "Amazing Grace," as she prepared to give Brown Doe a sponge bath. Calling someone Jane Doe was so impersonal to her and she didn't get down like that. Plus the young lady had such a rich brown complexion. If it wasn't for the stretch marks on the girl's stomach, she would pass for a teenager. That's what everyone else thought but Nurse Wright knew better. This was a grown woman and judging by the old scars on her arm, she knew that this young lady came with some history.

Nurse Wright wiggled Brown Doe out of her hospital robe and sponged her down. She then lotioned up her body with the Avon lotion she brought from home. It kept Brown Doe's skin nice and soft. She then eased her small frame into a clean gown. As Nurse Wright stood there looking over her patient, she decided that she would swab Brown Doe's mouth, since it was so hard to use a toothbrush and then the last thing she would do was twist her hair. She smiled at that thought. Since Nurse Wright had long, dark, red locks up in a bun, she kept Brown Doe's locks up in a ponytail. They weren't long enough yet to twist up into a bun.

As she busied herself with dumping the pail that was used for the sponge bath and filling up the small toothbrush bowl, she recalled the big ugly scar that was on the right side of her head. Now, with her new growth of hair, it was 90% covered. Wetting the swab first, she smeared a smidgen of tooth gel on it. She held Brown Doe's mouth open while brushing her teeth and gums at the same time. To Nurse Wright's surprise Brown Doe started gagging. She stopped swabbing and stood back. Brown Doe kept gagging and then she started choking. Her eyes popped open and then she sat straight up, choking and gagging.

The heart monitor began beeping fast and steady.

In a room down the hall, Brown Doe's doctor and a nurse watched the heart monitor screen light up. "Is that room 703?" Nurse Nevins asked Dr. Shalala.

"My sweet Jesus!" They heard Nurse Wright shriek from way down the hall. "Oh my God!" The young lady who she had been taking care of for almost five months was throwing up. Nurse Wright hit the call button. "Brown Doe is awake! Brown Doe is awake!" she yelled. "Get Dr. Kerr or Dr. Shalala in here *stat!*"

Dr. Shalala and Nurse Nevins were already sprinting down the hall.

FAHEEM

After leaving Chuck-E-Cheese, me and Kaeerah dropped off Lil' Faheem at his mom's. When we pulled up into the driveway, she came out the house and met us.

"Would you like to come in?" she had the nerve to ask me. I waited until my son grabbed his toys and got out before responding.

When he was up on the front porch I said, "I want you to

remember that I ain't ya fuckin' friend. Seven fuckin' years, Oni?"
I wasn't trying to hide my disappointment and disgust. She hung
her head and I put the car in reverse and left.

The more time I spent with my son the more venom I had
towards her. The little guy was brilliant. I was like a superstar
to him, well, that was until Aisha came home. I got a kick out
of watching them interact. Once she got there and they started
playing, he conveniently pushed me to the side. I guess it's true
what they say about a brother and a sister's love.

ONI

I stormed inside of my house, my mood for eating the big dinner I just cooked up . . . gone. *I ain't ya fuckin' friend.* He wasn't
saying that bullshit when he was all up inside me. His remark
caught me off guard and Lil' Faheem rambling on and on about
how much fun he had with his dad and his baby sister wasn't
helping matters at all. Well, even though she wasn't a baby, he
felt that he was the oldest, especially since he was a little taller.
As he excitedly rambled on about Chuck-E-Cheese, I couldn't
shake Faheem's blunt remark. That shit got under my skin and
I couldn't shake it. Again, I wasn't trying to fool myself. Hell, I
fantasized so many times about Faheem being with his father
that it sometimes would make me sick. But now, I didn't know if
I was more mad at him for refusing me or more mad at myself
for inviting his obnoxious ass in. But shit, I'd be damned if I was
going to put up with his disrespect. He's in his son's life because
I'm *allowing* him to be.

The more I thought about the situation the angrier I became.
So, after I put Faheem to bed I decided to call him.

JAZ

Me and Faheem was curled up on the couch watching television and talking when the house phone rang. Faheem picked it up.

"Hello."

His body stiffened right up.

"What do you mean I could at least respect you as the mother of our son? I would have never known I had a son if I didn't run into him at some fucking ghetto-ass mall!"

Faheem had moved me off of his chest and was sitting straight up.

"What the fuck do we have to talk about, Oni? Tell me."

Just when I had started to run into the kitchen to pick up the other phone so that I could listen in, he hung up on her. I will be paying this bitch a visit tomorrow to check her about getting my hubby all riled up.

ONI

I had called and left Faheem a message to come by after seven. I knew that I had gotten him amped up on the phone last night but hey, I had to get the lines of communication up and running somehow. Even if we were having angry dialogue, it was nevertheless dialogue.

I sent Lil' Faheem to his uncle Damon's house. And by 7:00 I was sitting on my front porch looking pretty, awaiting the arrival of my baby daddy. At 7:10 Jaz pulls up into my driveway. This bitch had the nerve to be alone.

EIGHT

TRINA

I don't know what happened back there when I pulled up to get Tasha, but she has been fuming ever since. It looked like they had been physically fighting but when I asked her, she didn't respond. Physical fight or verbal, whichever one it was, had my sister bent the fuck up.

We were riding stand-by since everything was spur of the moment and because of that we had to hang out at the airport before catching the red-eye to LaGuardia. I had to sneak off to call Kendrick and let him know what time we were coming in, since he was the one picking us up. He told me that Kyron had gone out of town to take care of some business but he had brought Tasha a car to use to get around the city. I was like *damn, the power of the pussy.* I didn't tell my sister about the car, I would let Kyron do that becuse I know she probably would start trippin'. But shit, what were we going to drive around in once we got into the city? I hated cabs and I damn sure wasn't riding the bus or train. When I was ready to move, I was ready to move, so I had no problems with Kyron trickin' off some wheels for my sister.

Suprisingly, when Kyron did catch up with her, she didn't trip. And since he was out of town, Tasha decided to crash at his apartment while I camped out with Kendrick. It was all good but the minute she heard that Kyron was on his way back she packed up her little bags and went to a hotel. She tried to talk me into going with her, but unh, uh. I was laying up under the dick.

TASHA

I finally went to the doctor's office this morning and yes, I am pregnant. When she told me the results she said that I looked at her as if to say, *No, it can't be. Take it back.* I told her she didn't know the half of it. She told me to try her because in fourteen years of practice she had seen and heard it all. I got up and left. I needed to see my children.

Yeah, Kyron brought me a 2010 Jaguar. It was white on white. That bitch was almost prettier than me. The nigga put it in *my* name. He joked that he couldn't have his baby momma running around the city flagging down taxis. He knew that I had a garage full of wheels at my home out West, but him trickin' his dough on my new ride simply reminded me that I still had *it*. He had left it parked in the garage under his building and he left the keys and all of the paperwork on the kitchen counter. I called him to thank him for the ride but mainly to find out when he was coming back. That's how I knew to leave when I did. He didn't come out and say it, but I nosed around and got an idea. I couldn't see myself driving the car . . . not yet. You know when a nigga buys you anything big, especially a car, *and* puts it in your name, you better believe he thinks that the pussy belongs to him. I gave the keys to Trina and told her that she could chauffeur me around. She was grinning from ear-to-ear. All this bitch needed was a chauffeur's hat.

After my doctor's appointment, I went shopping for the kids and we headed over to their grandparents house. I told Trina to pull up into the driveway and park. Pop Pop, Trae's father, was standing in the front door. He was surprised to see me and he came out onto the porch.

"Is that my precious daughter-in-law?" He made his way down the steps.

"Yes, Pop Pop, it is I," I teased and gave him a hug. "You met my sister Trina before."

"Oh yeah, how could I forget? She looks just like you."

"Hello, Mr. Macklin." Trina came around the car and gave him a hug.

"Call me Pop Pop like the rest of the family. I've gotten used to it by now," he told her.

"I brought the boys some things and I want to take them for the night." I gave him a couple of the bags to carry inside while I carried the rest. "What have they been up to? I miss them."

"Nana called last night. They are having a good time."

"Last night? Where are they?" I was hoping that I was hearing him wrong. Was he saying that my sons were not here?

"They're in Florida. You didn't know? No one called you? They've been gone for three days now."

"Florida?" My voice squeaked. It felt as is a ton of bricks had just been dumped on me.

"They went to hang out with Mickey Mouse. Come on in. Let's get this stuff inside. It's not like they need it," he mumbled that last part but I still heard him.

I was speechless. This muthafucka! Trae is going to make me kill him. I know he did this shit on purpose. I had to take a deep breath to try and calm myself down. I couldn't go off on Pop Pop, because it wasn't his fault. But still, no one had the courtesy to let me know that my kids were across the country. I had our next two days planned out. We took everything inside and then I called Nana and spoke to the boys. They were having a ball. Pop Pop fed us some of his chili, which I didn't like and then we left.

We were getting ready to back up when a Navigator pulled up behind us and blocked us in. "What the fuck?" Me and my sister said at the same time.

Then she gritted. "No this muthafucka did not just hit *my* cocaine Jag."

TRINA

I was starting to like this new jag and was thinking about asking Kendrick to get me one. No nigga ever brought me a new car and put it in my name. "Where to sis?" I put the jag in reverse and started to back up when this big ass truck rammed into us. He didn't hit us hard but he hit us. But that wasn't the kicker. When I saw a nigga jump out and come towards the driver's side and that nigga was Trae, I was too through. I hit the locks real quick and said, "Oh shit."

He didn't realize it was me and barked, "Whose car is this, Tasha?" When he saw that I was in the driver's seat he went around the front of the car and he headed for Tasha. I looked at her and she was in shock. My sister actually looked scared and the shit was spilling over on me.

"Just tell him it's mine," I whispered. I could see that this nigga was certifiably crazy. And if we had planned to get out of this situation in one piece I had better play my role.

"Whose car is this, Tasha?" He had mad bass in his voice and I could tell that he sensed that this car was brought by some nigga.

"Why didn't you tell me the boys were going to Florida, Trae?"

"Whose car is this Tasha?" He was seething and was only concerned with whose car this was.

"It's Trina's," my sister lied.

"This ain't her car," he had the nerve to say it as if I wasn't good enough to be driving a Jag.

"It is hers. Now can you move your truck? We are trying to leave."

"Let me see the registration and insurance card."

"Can you move your truck please?"

Trae tried to open the door but I had already locked it. "Open the door, Tasha."

"No, I am not opening the door. What for? So you can strangle me to death?"

"Oh, you'll get out." He walked away and disappeared behind the Navigator.

"What the fuck is he doing?" I asked my sister.

She frantically reached into the glove compartment and threw me the documents. "Put them in your purse." Right after I said it, I saw Trae coming back and carrying a lug wrench.

The next thing you know he had raised it up in the air,

brought it down and smashed the passenger side view mirror. "Get out . . . the. Fucking. Car. Tasha."

Oh shit. I knew it was about to get ugly. My sister was speechless and the bitch was shaking.

He raised it again and it came smashing down on the front window.

"Stop it Trae!" my sister screamed.

"Get out the fuckin' car, Tasha, and bring the papers with you," Trae yelled as he moved to the back and brought the lug wrench down on the back window.

"My fuckin' car. He's ruining my fuckin' car." Tasha jumped out of the car and went after him. "Trae, what the fuck is the matter with you?"

"Whose car is this?" He came at her like a pitbull.

"I told you, it's Trina's," she said as she was backing up. " I'm not sure if she rented it or not. You know you are going to have to pay for all of this shit."

"Why are you worrying about it, if it ain't your car?"

This nigga was now opening the door and rummaging through the glove compartment.

"This *is* my car. You know I'm filing a police report if you don't pay for it?" I said.

Frustrated that he couldn't find the registration papers he got out, not even bothering to close the door. "Fuck a police report. Show me the insurance and registration or rental papers and I'll pay for the shit right now."

I couldn't say or do anything but look stupid.

"That's what the fuck I thought," his smart ass had the nerve to say with a smirk plastered on his face. He then grabbed Tasha by the arm. "Come on. We are going to the doctors."

Tasha yanked away from him. "For what?"

"To take a DNA test. I need to know if you are carrying my seed."

"No, Trae. I am not taking a DNA test."

"Why not?"

"Because it is too early and they will have to stick that needle up in my uterus."

"I don't give a fuck."

"Trae, that is dangerous. The baby isn't even developed and it is very risky. So, no. I am not going to the doctor's with you."

He now had Tasha pinned up against the car and she was trying to push him away. He was saying something but I couldn't hear him. I'm sure it was nothing pleasant. The next thing I knew Pop Pop was jumping off of the porch. He had grabbed Trae and yanked him off of Tasha and threw him over the hood of the car.

"Boy, what is the matter with you? Don't be carrying on like this in front of my house. Have you lost your damned mind? You take shit inside of the house. You ain't ever saw me and your mother carry on like this outside." He had grabbed Trae and was pushing him. "What is the matter with you?"

TASHA

Thank God for Pop Pop. Trae was just threatening to kill me. I yanked open the car door and grabbed my purse. "Let's go, Trina. Fuck this car." She grabbed her bag and came around to where I was. We rushed off of my in-law's property and went looking for a taxi. They now lived in Rockland County, a rural area called Nanuet. It was close to Lake Nanuet Park. I was praying that we didn't have to walk damn near two miles to get to a main street.

"Call a cab," my sister yelled. "My feet are hurting."

"I don't know no fuckin' cab number. You call one." We were walking so damn fast my feet were starting to burn. It felt as if we had already put in a good mile. Then we heard tires screech around the corner and we both looked back and Trae was turning the corner on two wheels. We took off, haul assing down the street when the heel of my stiletto got caught in the crack of the sidewalk. I twisted my ankle and went down. I fell flat on my chest. My sister came down with me and it was a good thing that she did because Trae slowed down as if he could smell us. Trina had her hand over my mouth because my ankle was on fire and I was screaming.

"Shhh . . . Shut up bitch."

We were hiding behind somebody's Cadillac. We waited until it got quiet and Trina got on her knees and peeked over the hood of the ride. "He's gone." She let out a sigh of relief. "Can you walk?" Trina asked me.

"I don't know. Ahhhhh fuck." I gritted as I tried to stand up. I swear I wanted to cry. The heel to my $900 stiletto was ruined and my ankle felt as if pins were sticking in it. Trina saw that I was in pain so she helped me up. But as soon as we stood up, Trae had circled around the block and was flying back down the street.

"Here he comes again!" Trina yanked me down, damn near breaking my shoulder. "This muthafucka is crazy." She mumbled as we huddled together like two frightened school girls. An old white lady walking her dog passed by us. She stopped and looked at us but kept on going.

NINE

BROWN DOE

"Dear Lord, thank you for answering my prayers and keeping Brown Doe on this good ole earth just a little while longer. I've grown very fond of her and she is one of your children out here in the wilderness. So Lord, please look after her. Guide her and stay with her. Bless her to get back whole again. Amen."

Nurse Wright was on her knees inside of the rehabilitation center's chapel. I was kneeling down beside her. She said my name was Brown Doe. She nudged me and told me to ask the Lord for whatever I wanted. I bowed my head and closed my eyes and said, "Lord, help me. Why am I here? I don't know this lady. She said that I've been out of my coma for almost two months now and made excellent progress. They are telling me that tomorrow I have to go home. Where is my home? Will you help me find my way? If I do have a home, who's there waiting for me? Lord, this is so frustrating. Nurse Wright said from the stretch marks on my body that I had to have given birth before. If so, then where is my baby?" And before I knew it my eyes got wet. I welcomed the emotion and it felt so good to cry. I felt so alive.

JAZ

Umm hmmm. When I pulled up in this bitch's driveway, I could tell that she almost shit on herself. This ho sittin' up here, weave blowing in the wind, nails all polished up, jewelry around her neck, legs crossed and stilettos on her feet. I got out of my car and went marching up her front steps. "I can see that you thought I was Faheem." She rolled her eyes at me and looked in the opposite direction. "I don't appreciate you calling my husband starting unnecessary bullshit. We know that Faheem is his son. We all agree that Faheem is going to be a big part of his life, but that is as far as it goes. You need to get that 'me and my son come as a package' bullshit out of your head. Forget about rekindling your 'in the past relationship' because it ain't going down like that. Unh unh. Not as long as I'm in the picture. You need to believe and understand what I'm telling you."

"Are you finished?" This bitch had the nerve to ask me.

"Yes I am."

"Good, because you need to *believe* and *understand* that we do come as a package. I'm his mother. And if he wants to be a major part of his son's life, he has to come through me. Why? Because we have to have some level of a relationship if we expect to raise *our* son right, whether you like it or not. I figure it might as well be a cordial one instead of one filled with hate."

I chuckled. "Bitch, try me if you want to but don't say that I didn't warn you. Because you really don't want to fuck with me. Act like you know and we can handle this in a civilized manner but if we can't, shit is going to get real ugly, real fast." I turned around marched back down the steps, got back in my car and left.

ONI

No she didn't just come on my property and lay down some got damned ground rules as if I was a child. She obviously don't know about me. The bitch was actually calling me out. Talking about, 'not as long as she's in the picture.' Don't she know that I can get her out of the picture? Shit, I know people in high places.

MARVIN

I heard a television going as I knocked on Isis' door with my free hand. Nobody was answering but I knew she was home. Dope fiends didn't have a lot of places to go when they were high. Finally, I heard footsteps.

"Who is it?"

"Open the door, Isis, damn." She cracked the door and peeped out, "Blue? Is that you?"

"It's me. Hurry up, I got my daughter in my arms and she heavy as shit."

The door shut and she took the chain off. "Blue, what are you doing here? And with this baby?" Isis grabbed Aisha and laid her on the couch. It was one in the morning and she was out cold.

"I came to pick up something from Lo. He moved and ain't tell me. Where is he, Isis?"

Her face twisted all up. "Blue, Lo is dead. Somebody killed his girlfriend Brenda in her bed, and then tortured Lo. They found him tied up, stabbed and Tank said that his throat was cut."

I was mute in disbelief. Lo being dead was a blow to the gut.

"And he ended up dead right after your brother-in-law came by looking for him. I told you to leave me a way to call you. He—"

"Trae?"

"—asked about you and Kyra. Yeah—that's his name. He told me he was Kyra's brother. I remembered him from being at one of the cookouts you had."

I knew he was coming, but why come to Isis? "What did you tell him?"

"What could I tell him, Blue? I don't know shit about Kyra. And I damn sure don't know where you rest at. I only knew where he could find Lo. At the time, I didn't know that Lo could get his throat cut."

"You told him where Lo lived?" I asked in disbelief.

Isis dropped into a La-Z-Boy chair and threw her head back. "Yeah. I told him that Lo was at Brenda's, but I didn't know the address. He said that it was important that he caught up with him."

"Isis, you talk too much, you shouldn't have said shit. You should've checked with me."

"Nigga, how could I? You just up and disappeared. Everybody looking for you. I don't even have a number for you. Lo would never give it to me. So how the fuck I'ma check with you?" Her neck rolled as she spoke.

Isis started rambling on about some other shit but I wasn't listening. I could only think about Lo and my money. I still couldn't digest the fact that my cousin Lo was gone. He had saved my ass on several occasions and when he needed me most, I wasn't there. I am 98% sure that Trae killed Lo. But why? What info did he get out of Lo? I stood there and thought about the possibilities. Shit! I had a stash at Lo's house and I needed my loot. That was the reason I made the trip in the first place. "So who is at Lo and Brenda's now?"

"Fool, ain't you heard a word I just said? I just told you what happened in there. That place was a crime scene with yellow tape everywhere. They had dogs and everything up in there. Whatever you had in there is gone. You should've left something here with me."

Without another word, I stood up, grabbed my daughter and bounced.

ONI

All week I had been trying to set up a meeting with Faheem, but Jaz was on me like white on rice, blocking every damn time. Even when I tried to get him over for my birthday she blocked. It was obvious the bitch wanted war. So you know what? I'll give it to her. Afterall, I did warn her. She didn't know me and she damn sure didn't have a clue as to what I was capable of.

"Oni!" My twenty-four-year-old nephew Ronnie yelled out as he banged on the screen door, before barging into my house. He was so tall he had to bend his neck to come into the living room. He was one of ATL's finest detectives. We all swore that we wouldn't taint him but desperate times often called for desperate measures. And I was desperate.

"Ronnie." I got up and gave him a hug.

"What's up auntie?"

"You want to help your auntie out while at the same time make a nice piece of cash?"

"All depends, auntie. You know that."

"Well, I really need this favor. And if you can't do it, hook me up with someone who will."

"Chill out, auntie. Let me hear what you got to say first."

STEPHON

"Yeah, baby . . . yeah. Right there . . . Keep your head right there. It's so snug, baby right there. You got this big dick in your throat and it feels so good. Okay, baby . . . go head. That's right . . . stroke that dick . . . while you eat it. Uh . . . Uh . . . um . . . . mmmh. You a beast, baby! Good gracious! That's right . . . eat that dick up . . . eat it! I'ma . . . I'ma . . . 'bout to cum, baby! Aw-w-shit . . . gotdamn . . . here it comes . . . a-a-r-r-g-g-h-h-h!"

I looked down in my lap at the head that was bobbing and stroking me at the same time. She was deep throating my dick and swallowing my seeds. And the crazy part was I didn't even know her name. Finally, the face of the beautiful mixed brown skinned honey with the long, jet black hair and a sexy body lifted up and let my now flaccid dick plop from her mouth.

"You a beast, baby. What's your name again?"

"Mishawnna." The beautiful lady said and licked her lips and fingers.

"Mishawnna, huh? Well you are hired, Mishawnna. Can you tend the bar?"

"That's what I do best, besides give good head," she giggled.

"You ain't never lied. Go back downstairs and tell Mick, the guy cleaning the bar, that you're his new bartender." I put my dick up and zipped my pants. As Mishawnna stood up and turned around I smacked her ass. "And tell Mick to send me up one of his special Guava Lehuou Twists."

"Anything for you, bossman."

"That girl's got a hell of a head on her shoulders. A lot on her mind." I said to myself and flipped up my laptop. Checking my e-mails, I looked to see if any info had been sent to me about Charli. I found nothing. Where is she? How is she doing? No news is always good news . . . I guess. So I made a few phone calls and prepared for the club's new grand re-opening.

With everything done that I needed to do, I checked my watch. It was a little after 8:00 p.m. I thought about my date with Amber Rachen. Amber Rachen was the new Kim Kardashian in L.A. and I just happened to be her new business partner slash sex partner. I locked the club up and walked around the corner to my brand new Rolls Royce Phantom Drophead coupe.

I was leasing it for now. That's how confident I was in the reopening of the club. I heard the sounds of a motorcycle drawing near before I actually saw it coming in my direction. I stood frozen in my tracks as the motorcycle stopped a few feet in front of me. A person jumped off the back of the bike and approached me with a helmet on. *Who the hell?*

The person reached behind him and pulled a gun. Before I could utter a sound, the killer squeezed the trigger.

TEN

TASHA

We parked our asses on someone's front steps. My ankle was killing me and was starting to swell. A cab was coming our way and Trina got up and began to frantically wave him down. It was for nothing because it kept going.

"Fuck you, faggot!" She screamed after the cab. "You see that shit Tasha? The nigga ain't even have no one in there. I hate that shit," she bitched.

"Girl, stop whining and flag this next one down," I told her. She did and he stopped. I stood up, forgetting that my ankle was messed up and put all of my body weight on it. I fell back onto the porch. "Ohmygod." I bit down on my bottom lip, damn near drawing blood. "Trina. I can't get up."

My sister opened the cab door, said something slick to the driver and came over to where I was. "Can you stand up? No. Wait. I got you." She took my arm and placed it around her neck.

"I know you don't think I'ma let you carry me."

"Then stand your ass up and get your own damned self in the car," her smart behind had the nerve to say.

"Girl, just help me to the damn car." My ankle felt as if it was on fire.

TRINA

My sister was trying to play strong but I could tell that she wanted to cry. Trae was acting like a damn fool, having us on the run as if we were a couple of crackheads that stole something. I managed to get her into the car but not before she put pressure on it causing her to yell out. As she leaned her head on the window and closed her eyes, I dialed Kendrick. I looked over at my sister and tears were streaming down her cheeks.

"Whad up?" he answered. I had him on speaker.

"There's been a change in plans. Don't look like I can come over tonight." He wouldn't respond. "Did you hear me?"

"Yeah. I heard you. Why? What happened?"

"No. Don't cancel your plans. I'll be fine," Tasha said to me.

I ignored her. "We ran into Trae. He smashed up her car, chased us down the street and she twisted her ankle. So right now I need to be here for her."

"Damn. Did she call my cousin?"

"Now you already know the answer to that."

"Where y'all at now?"

"In a cab."

"I'll call you right back," he told me and hung up. I know that he was getting ready to call his partner in crime.

I glanced over at Tasha and the look on her face made me think, damn, was I really responsible for all of this drama in

her life? I thought aboout it for a few minutes and then said
to myself, "No I wasn't. Trae started the shit by cheating with
them hos. I heard Tasha's phone ring but knew she wasn't
going to answer it. I knew it was Kyron so I braced myself
for what I knew was coming next. As soon as my cell rang
I answered it.

"Yo, Trina, pass Shorty your phone."

"Kyron, she's not in the frame of mind to speak to you right
now." My phone beeped and I saw that it was Kendrick calling
me back.

"Trina, put her on the phone."

"She won't take it Kyron, damn. What you want me to do?
Hold her down, tie her up and make her talk to you?"

"Did Trae put his hands on her?"

"Yeah, and he fucked up her ride."

"Fuck the car. What did he do to her? Is she alright?"

"Choked her up, threatened her and then chased her down the
street in his truck. She fell and twisted her ankle."

You could hear a pin drop on the other end. I had started to
ask was he still there when he asked, "Where are y'all?"

"We're in a cab. I'm taking her to her hotel." What did I say
that for? This nigga started spazzing the fuck out.

"What the fuck you mean a hotel? Tell the driver to bring
y'all over here." He was yelling at me as if he was my pimp and
I was his ho.

Tasha apparently heard his big ass mouth because she calmly said
without even opening her eyes, "Tell him, I'm going to my hotel."

"She said she's going to her hotel," I told Kyron.

"Trina, I don't give a fuck what she said. Tell the fuckin' driver
to bring y'all over here. Do this for me and I'll make it well

worth your while. I need to see her and you know I got her. Plus, Kendrick is waiting on you."

I thought over what he said. He obviously knew what buttons to push. Make it well worth my while. Kendrick is waiting on me. I knew she didn't need to be by herself and he would look out for her. Even though we were a couple of blocks from the hotel, I blurted out Kyron's address to the cabbie.

"Trina, what are you doing? No cabbie, take me to the hotel."

"Ladies, where do you want me to go?" He was looking at us through the rearview mirror, obviously confused.

"Sir, I'm the one paying, so turn the fuck around. I'll have a big tip for you," I told the cabbie, not caring that Tasha was going to be pissed at me. The cabbie then made a sharp left turn and we damn near was laying down in the back seat.

I was sitting there conflicted. Tasha was yelling, he was yelling. I was about to cuss Kyron's ass out and he must have felt it because he reiterated, "Trina, I'ma make it well worth your while. Get her here. I'll take care of her. I'll be out front when y'all pull up." He hung up.

"Trina, I can't believe you did that shit. If my ankle wasn't tore up, I'd leave you sitting in this cab to go over his house your damn self."

"Tasha, sue me, alright. Your ankle is fucked up. You don't need to be in no damned hotel all by yourself. What the fuck are you going to do? Hop around all night? You told me you didn't want me to cancel my plans with Kendrick. What, so you changed your mind? The nigga is genuinely concerned and wants to take care of you so again sue me."

"So what's in it for you, Trina?" she snapped.

Kendrick called me right on cue. I welcomed his call and

kindly ignored my spoiled-ass sister. Did she even have a clue as to how many bitches wish they had a nigga who wanted to look after them?

TASHA

This bitch! I can't believe that she had the nerve to stiff me off like that. I don't know what Kyron offered her but it had to be big. I would have been hopping around all night but I think I could have managed alright by myself. I needed to be alone. And Trae? That nigga is starting to make me believe that he has seriously lost his damn mind. And now he had the nerve to be blowing up my phone. Thinking about him caused my stomach to knot up and made me visit a place where I did not want to go. I was mad because I was still in love with him and I knew that I would always be. Before I knew it, we were pulling up in front of Kyron's building and he was yanking on the door.

"What happened, Tasha? He put his hands on you, didn't he? Don't try to cover for the nigga."

"He just pushed me up against the car, that's all. I twisted my ankle running down the block." Just then Kendrick pulled up next to the cab and jumped out. He rushed over to get a good look at me. He pulled Kyron to the side, saying some things that I couldn't catch.

Then Kyron said, "No, no man. I got this. Let me handle it. Take care of the driver for me so I can get Shorty upstairs." He then turned his attention on me. "C'mon Shorty. There's a doctor in the building. I'ma have him look at your ankle." He bent down to take me out of the cab.

"Be careful. I don't want to hit it." I then wrapped one arm around his neck, grabbed my bag and the broken shoe as he lifted me out of the taxi. I wrapped both arms around his neck, buried my face against his shoulder and tried not to cry. This shit was unreal. How the fuck did I end up in another man's arms?

KYRON

My heart was happy. I told Kendrick to take care of Trina for me and sent them on their way. I had my Shorty and she should be hoping that I don't hold her hostage. There was a cool ass young doctor that lived right upstairs and I was lucky that he was home. He was waiting on Tasha to come so that he could look at her ankle. As I stepped onto the elevator I had to chuckle.

"What's so funny?"

Shorty looked up at me, with tears streaming down her cheeks. I kissed her on the lips. "Déjà vu. You remember the night we went to Atlantic City and you was too high to get out of the car? I had to carry you just like this up to the room. You were telling the ladies on the elevator, two total strangers, how fine I was and that you weren't going to fuck me."

She smiled through the tears. And I was happy to see that. "And just like we didn't fuck that night, we are not fucking this night either," she said.

"You joking right?"

"No, Kyron, I'm not."

"We'll see about that," I told her as she tightened her grip around my neck and I slipped the key in my door. We made it inside and I sat her down gently onto the sofa. I made a call to the doc and told him she was here.

"Who was that?" Tasha asked me.

"I got somebody to take a look at your ankle. You're pregnant Tasha. Why are you walking around in ten inch heels? You're not supposed to be wearing those."

"Says who? And they are not ten inches."

"Says me. Ten inches, twelve. They are too damn high." She rolled her eyes at me.

"Who is this doctor? Is he a real doctor?"

"Of course he is. He lives right upstairs." The bell rang. "That should be him at the door now." I went to let Jeff in.

TASHA

I waited as Kyron left to go open the door for the doctor. After several minutes he returned with this skinny, young white kid carrying the typical black doctor's bag. He introduced him as Dr. Jeff Raskin.

"Mrs. Santos, how is the ankle?" He asked as he sat down in front of me, opened his bag, took out a cap with a light on it and placed it on his head. I tried not to laugh as I wondered why he needed a light. He wasn't about to perform a major surgery. With the black rimmed glasses on and the hat with the lamp he looked more like a coal miner than a doctor.

"It hurts." He rolled my jean leg up and started prodding at my ankle. "Owww! Shit. That hurt."

"Where? Right here?"

"No."

"Right—"

"Owww! Yes! Right there. Oh my God. Please don't squeeze it right there." I was ready to pull my hair out.

"Good. At least it's not broken. But you definitely sprained it. I'm going to leave you with a solution to soak it in two times a day for thirty minutes at a time. I'll show Kyron here how to wrap it up and as long as you don't put pressure on it for about four days it should be fine."

"What about the pain? I need something for the pain."

"Uh, Doc she's pregnant. She can't have nothing."

"She can have some Ibuprofen, as long as she doesn't overdo it."

"Thank you, Jeff." I rolled my eyes at Kyron, who didn't care because he was standing over Jeff waiting to see what pills he was going to give me. Instead, Jeff told him to watch how he wrapped my ankle so that he could do it. Kyron watched attentively and then surprisingly he tried it himself, getting it right on the first attempt. Jeff gave him the pills for the pain and Kyron held onto them as if it was dope and I was a fiend that had to be kept away from it. Jeff said goodbye to me as Kyron walked him to the door.

TRAE

After I kept circling the block trying to find my wife and couldn't, I drove over to Kaylin's. I sat in the truck I had rented for at least thirty minutes trying to get my head right before getting out and ringing the bell. Angel and Jahara both came to the door.

"Hi, Uncle Trae. Where are the kids? In California?" Jahara asked me as if she wasn't a kid herself.

I stepped inside and scooped up my niece. "They're in Florida," I told her.

"Florida? Who took them there? Auntie Tasha? Mommy, I want to go to Florida."

"No, they went with their Nana." I leaned over and kissed Angel on the cheek. "Where's your husband?"

"Down in the basement. What are you doing up this way? Where's your wife?"

I put Jahara down, "Long story."

"I have time, Trae."

"Have you heard from her today?" I asked her.

"No, I haven't. What is going on between you and my girl? I'm not feelin' this drama between y'all at all."

"Me neither." I needed to talk to my man, not his wife, so I felt Angel standing there.

KAYLIN

I was chillin' in my basement watching an old Chinese flick on my flat screen, when Trae came down the stairs. I was surprised to see him because I didn't even know he was in town.

"What's up man?"

"Just had a fight with Tasha. Now I can't find her. Do you know where your brother lives?"

I looked at him to try and read what he was up to. Me and this fool been to hell and back together. "Dawg, word is bond. That nigga didn't tell me where he rest at. Why? You think she with him?"

"Yeah, she with him," my man mumbled. It was no doubt it hurt him to say that shit. "The nigga done bought her a Jag. I'm tellin' you, the shit done got out of control. I'm not gonna sit around and allow this nigga to continue to disrespect me like this. I need to know where he rest at."

I picked up the phone and tried to call him. Of course he didn't answer. Then I called Kendrick, he didn't answer either. I wasn't lying. I didn't know where my brother lived. He was smart about that. I guess once he started fucking with Tasha he figured he better keep his home address on the low. I did know that he brought a spot right here in the city.

"Somebody gotta know where he lives. Come with me to Kendrick's. I know you know where he lives."

I looked at my man. I did not want to get in the middle of this bullshit. I had already told my brother I was fallin' back, because I didn't see nothing good coming out of this situation. Now, Trae sensed my hesitation.

"Look, I know you don't want to get involved. Just give me the address and I'll go over there by myself. I just want to get Kyron's address."

"What happens if he doesn't give it to you?"

Trae looked at me. He took a seat and crossed his legs. "I don't know, man. Right now, I don't know."

KYRON

I was glad that Shorty was going to be alright and that her ankle wasn't broken. I ran her a nice hot tub of water and poured the solution in the tub for her swollen ankle. I gladly helped her strip out of her clothes and put her in the tub. I looked at her body and licked my lips.

"You hungry?" I asked her.

"Not really." She laid back and relaxed in the tub.

"You can't take these pain pills on an empty stomach. You gotta eat something."

She sighed, "Just fix me some broccoli and cheese soup. And some cantaloupe."

"Cantaloupe?"

"Yes, cantaloupe as in fruit. A part of the melon family."

"Alright smart ass," she smiled at me. I left her in the bathroom to find out where I could get some broccoli and cheese soup and *cantaloupe*. I saw that my brother Kay had been calling me. I wondered what he wanted. I made a mental note to call him later as I called Marlo the doorman to see if he could help a brother out. He said he would take care of me. I then put my focus on giving Tasha a nice bath.

KAYLIN

We got to Kendrick's apartment a little after 8:00. I tried my best to talk Trae out of it but of course he wasn't tryna hear that shit. Hell, I couldn't blame him. If it was my wife I'd be ready for war as well. I only wished that I wasn't in the middle of the bullshit. Why did this have to be so close to home? I was relieved when no one answered the door. But it didn't matter. Trae told me to leave. He was going to camp out until he showed. I'd give it a few days and this shit was going to blow up like the World Trade. Neither one of them muthafuckas could hide forever. Kyron didn't act like he was trying to stop fucking with Tasha and Trae was not going to simply walk away.

Before I left, I saw Trae look at his cell phone and then answer it. By the look on his face I could tell that something was wrong. Real wrong. When he disconnected the call and sat down on the steps, I asked him what was up. I wasn't ready for his reply.

"Somebody killed Tasha's cousin, Stephon. They gunned him down right outside in the parking lot of my fuckin' club."

KYRON

This was definitely my night and I was floating on a cloud. I pampered Tasha until she couldn't be pampered anymore. I bathed her, carried her to the bedroom where I oiled her body and wrapped her ankle up. Then I fed her the cantaloupe she had been craving and she ate a little of the broccoli soup and crackers. I gave her a couple of the painkillers, a massage and now she was fast asleep.

I fixed a couple of pastrami and cheese sandwiches, took a nice hot shower and then rolled a blunt. I sat in the living room listening to CDs and sipping on some *CÎROC* red berry. I was feeling real nice and even nicer once my thoughts wandered to Shorty laying there in my bed. She already told me that ain't going to be no fucking going on and I was fine with that. That was until I got up off the sofa and went into my bedroom. Shorty was laying on her stomach, her foot with the wrapped ankle was on a pillow and she was snoring lightly. She had on one of my button-up pajama shirts and her ass was poked out and legs partly spread. Now, what was a nigga supposed to do? The moonlight creeping through the window had Shorty looking like an angel. The next thing I knew I had stepped out of my sweat pants and was standing there butt naked, admiring that fat ass. Shorty had an ass that you wanted to kiss gently and then part them ass cheeks and lick her crack. I had never done that shit before but I was tempted. I grabbed my jimmy and started stroking, nice and slow. As my dick got a little harder she moaned and her legs spread a little wider. It was as if she knew I was there. Right then and there some pre cum oozed out and there was no turning back if I wanted to. My big man was now in control. I crept onto the bed, careful not to disturb her ankle and put my dick at her opening.

TASHA

My mind was foggy and at first I thought I was dreaming. Was I waking up to a long, hard dick sliding up in me? It was feeling good as shit so I knew at that moment it wasn't a dream. After the cloudiness cleared my head I remembered whose dick was all up in my pussy . . . *Kyron*. I went to move and my ankle said, *I don't think so.*

"Kyron . . . wait . . . baby . . . no," I feebly stated. I had told this nigga that we weren't going to be fucking but this nigga was working my pussy like only a champion could. He reached around and grabbed onto my clit and it was on from there. I was scared to move because of my ankle, but I was able to raise my ass a little and this nigga just went in deeper. He was getting his fuck on, I could feel it and it was feeling good as hell. Trae swears on pregnant pussy. He says its juicer, sweeter, hotter and mine is to kill for. Now Kyron was getting a taste and I knew that he was going to be gone. The only sounds was us moaning and his dick sliding in and out of my wet gushy. He was going faster on my clit and the sensation was heightening. I bit down into the pillow and that's when he popped those words out the side of his mouth.

"Marry me, Tasha. Marry me, Shorty."

"What?" I needed to make sure I heard him right as he started cumming.

ELEVEN

ONI

Ever since that bitch Jaz threatened me I had my plan in full motion. What I had planned for her was easy, but getting Faheem to be a little friendlier, now that was hard. However, I finally did manage to get him to at least let me come into their home. Of course that was when I knew Jaz wasn't there. I never told him about our conversation on the porch that evening. I made it seem as though I was very happy with the current arrangement and the way his *wife* was receiving our son. I even got a few smiles from him when I dropped our son off a few times. He wanted to be a father to Lil' Faheem and the only way to do that was to have them spend as much time as possible together. And of course, that meant more time seeing me.

FAHEEM

Shit, I have to admit, things seemed to be getting back to normal. And the fact that a son was added to my family made my life whole. I wanted to hate Oni but ever since I stepped to that ass she had been acting like she had some sense and she was kissing my ass every chance she got. The thing that got her some cool points was when I was riding with my son and he said, "Mommy said you are a good strong man and I should be just like you." The pride he had on his face was priceless. That was the moment I decided to cut her a little slack. Not too much, just a little. I even let her come inside a few times while Lil' Faheem got his stuff together. I have to admit the years were not hard on her at all. She still looked as good as the day I met her, and the fact that she was doing good raising our son added to her beauty.

ONI

I noticed Faheem looking at me and my stomach started to knot and my coochie started to tingle. He walked over to where I was standing and the closer he got with each step, the more I began to tense up. My hands started sweating and I wanted to say something but my throat felt dry as sandpaper. The intensity in his stare always fucked me up. When he got right up on me, the smell of his cologne got my nipples hard and I could feel the chill bumps covering my arms. Yeah, Faheem is all of that.

"I admire what you are doing with our son," he said as he sat Faheem's bags on the counter. They had just come back from doing the father-son thing. He then brushed against me and my heart sank.

"Can I have something to drink?" he asked, already heading for the refrigerator.

"You can have anything you want," I said a little above a whisper. I didn't want him to hear that but it came out anyway.

He turned around and looked at me. "Daddy still got it like that?" he asked as he moved back to where I was standing.

"You know better than anybody that I always wanted to be yours Faheem and nothing will ever change that," I responded, feeling like a school girl getting some attention from the High School jock. I turned away from him and began to go through Faheem's bags. I had to use my nervous energy somehow.

He came and stood behind me. Placing his mouth to my ear and said, "What's mine is always mine."

He was so close to me I could feel his heartbeat. My breathing picked up. I closed my eyes as his hands slid slowly up my arms. The phone rang and I almost jumped out my skin.

"Saved by the bell," Faheem said real slick. "Answer your phone. I'll catch you later." He said as he made his way to the door. I wanted to yell out, "No wait!" But it was too late and he was gone. And once again I was left with that familiar pain in my heart and wetness between my legs.

JAZ

I loved Fridays. I only had my seven a.m. class, which I was running late for, and then a lab. Fridays were my easiest day of the week. I looked out of my rearview mirror and saw the flashing lights. *Damn.* I was only doing twenty-seven. I pulled over and waited. Hopefully I'll be able to talk him out of the ticket and not be too late for my class. The big tall teddy bear of an officer moved swiftly as he approached my car.

"Can I see your license and registration please?"

"Was I going that fast, officer?"

"License and registration." He said as he yanked on the back door. "Unlock it."

"Excuse me?"

"Unlock the doors. What's that in the back?"

I quickly unlocked the doors. He opened it, reached inside and then got on his walkie talkie and called in the stop. I then heard him request backup.

"Get the paper work and then get out of the car," he said with venom in his voice.

Well *damn. You ain't got to be all nasty about it. Ain't like I just killed somebody.* I reached into the glove compartment for the registration and insurance card and retrieved my license from my wallet. As soon as I slammed the glove compartment shut, the officer was all in my face. He took the documents from me and went back into the unmarked car. There I was standing on the side of the damn road. About ten minutes later two more unmarked cars and two regular squad cars pulled up. That's when I called Faheem.

FAHEEM

It wasn't even 7:30 in the morning and someone was banging on my front door as if they were the po-po. I had just dropped my daughter off at camp. My cell phone was ringing and it was Jaz.

"Baby, what's up?"

"I got pulled over for speeding and now these muthafuckas done called for backup," she told me.

"What?"

"That's what I'm saying. They got me surrounded and shit, like I killed somebody."

"Hold on, baby. Some crazy muthafucka is bangin' on my door." I eased the curtain aside to look out of the window. It had to be about thirty muthafuckas in front of and around my house. "Jaz, you said you just got pulled over?"

"Yes and the muthafuckas called for backup."

"Well the muthafuckas are here now. What the fuck is going on?"

"I don't know. Where's Kaeerah?"

"She's at camp."

I opened the door before the punks broke the glass.

"We have a search warrant for the premises. Where is Jasmine Mujahid? Do you live here?"

"Yes, I live here. I'm her husband. I need to see the warrant and you need to tell me what this is in reference to? "

"The manufacturing and sale of methamphetamine. Come on now; don't act like you don't know. Crank, crystal meth, speed. I know your memory isn't that short. Your wife makes it." This midget muthafucka then shoved the warrant in my face.

"Jaz, what the fuck is going on?" I turned my attention back to the phone.

"I don't know."

"Well, these muthafuckas are here looking for you because you supposed to be manufacturing and selling meth," I barked.

"What? Baby, I don't know what the fuck is going on."

"You damn sure better not because you either playin' stupid or you actually are. Hang up. Let me call my attorney and get to the bottom of this shit." I hung up and dialed my attorney Steve Sadow. I always had to keep somebody in the pocket, because you never knew and it was better to be prepared and Steve was that muthafucka to have when it comes to cases. He cost a grip but the way I saw it, if he could get T.I. down from about thirty years to a one and a day, he wasn't to be fucked with. As I watched these muthafuckas go through my shit I thought about my weed. *Fuck.* I had at least an ounce left. Steve's secretary Melissa answered. I told her to have him get to my house yesterday.

Since these bastards weren't here for me they didn't handcuff me. They just asked me to have a seat at the kitchen table.

JAZ

Oh my God. This was not happening to me . . . again. The only reason I wasn't freaking out was because I knew that this time I was innocent. That officer had to plant that shit on me when he told me to unlock the door. "Damn it!" I yelled out as I paced back and forth in a got damned cell. I've been clean as a whistle. *Who the fuck is behind this?* I tapped my forehead against the steel bars. After looking like a mental patient for about ten minutes. It came to me.

Oni.

I had to grin. This ho was fuckin' brilliant. She went all out on this one and what better way to get me out of the picture than to use my past. I don't know how she pulled it off but the bitch played on how the last time I got busted she almost had Faheem on lock. But it didn't go down then and it damn sure ain't gonna go down now.

ONI

I was ecstatic. My plan was carried out. Hell, I knew the charges would probably not stick, but I didn't care. Jaz had that history and Faheem abhorred it. Just the fact of what the charges was would start the war. Let's see the bitch wiggle her way out of this one. But the icing on the cake was when Faheem called *me* to come pick up his daughter. I wanted to scream. But of course I waited until after he hung up.

FAHEEM

I was getting ready to go see about bailing Jaz out when she called and said that she was on her way home and Steve was bringing her. I had already arranged for Oni to swing by and pick up Kaeerah so her and Faheem could hang out. I didn't allow her inside and didn't mention to her what had happened. I sat on the front porch waiting for Jaz to get home. I left the house exactly the way the goon squad tore it up. I wanted Jaz to see what her little side hobby cost us. She did this same shit before and it's obvious that she can't help herself. A hustler is a hustler, regardless of their environment. The muthafuckas definitely were not there for me, especially since they left my ounce of weed right where it was. They were looking for a fucking meth lab and everything that goes with it.

Steve and Jaz pulled up into our driveway a little after six. I got off the porch and went down to Steve's Bentley. Dude was loud with it. Fuck a recession, he was gettin' money. He got out and came around to where I was. Jaz got out to. She put her arms around my waist and held onto me. Steve shook my hand and told me he had to run to his next appointment, and that he had to go back down to the courthouse in the morning to get all the details and he would swing back by to see me as soon as he did. He gave me the few papers that he had and then he bounced.

JAZ

I was so glad to be home in my husband's arms. But I noticed how stiff and standoffish he was. As soon as the attorney pulled off I said, "Baby, this is crazy. I mean of all people why did they choose me to plant meth into *my* car. And where is Kaeerah?"

"I called Oni to—"

"Wait a minute. You called that sneaky, conniving bitch to come pick up *our* daughter? Why Faheem?" I looked at him as if he was crazy.

"Because I didn't want her here with the house looking like it does and I didn't want her to hear us arguing."

"Us arguing? What the fuck are we arguing about? We are not arguing." What the fuck was wrong with this nigga? "Go get my daughter from that bitch's house. Now Faheem! Because if I go, I'm probably going to whip her ass. If my intuition serves me right that bitch is behind this shit."

"Jaz, do you hear yourself? You saying Oni planted meth, your favorite pastime, in the back of your car and got a search warrant handed down to us? C'mon, Jaz!"

No this nigga did not! "Faheem. Are you serious? Listen to *yourself*. Are you saying that you don't believe me?" I pushed him. "I dare you to say that shit, Faheem. Tell me that shit to my face. I fuckin' dare you." Spittle was flying out of my mouth.

"What did I tell you would happen if I ever found out you fuckin' with that shit again?"

I looked at that nigga like he had two heads.

"Jaz, you not only jeopardizing your freedom, but mine as well. We have a daughter and we have assets. What the fuck are you thinking? Who are you doing this for this time? And why?"

"Doing this for? Hold the fuck up. You don't believe *me*? Your wife?"

"Word is bond, Jaz, if you can't let that shit go, you gotta get the fuck out of here."

I was so angry I couldn't form a damn sentence. The tears started streaming down my face. I could not believe that my husband, the love of my life, would believe that I would backslide like that and not tell him. What was that bitch telling him? Better yet, what was she doing to him? Was he seeing her behind my back?

"So what? You fuckin' ole girl again? Is this what this is about? You want to fight with me so that you could run off and be with your little ex-jump-off, now baby momma? Just admit to that shit Faheem and at least I'll feel better. Because right now, with you calling me a liar, I am two seconds from telling you to go fuck yourself. And that's my word."

"Jaz, this shit ain't about me. Don't try to flip the script. This ain't about her either. This is about *you* gettin' busted with that shit and having them muthafuckas all up in our house."

"This *is* about her. This shit don't seem a little suspicious to you? You honestly don't think she could have anything to do with this?" His silence said it all. I chuckled then said, "You spent all that time in the streets and you can't peep game when you see it? Stupid ass!"

Faheem turned his back to me and was on his way into the house. I was right on the nigga's heels. He stopped dead in his tracks when he got to the front door and turned around. "So what's up? You going to admit it or what? If I don't get the fuckin' truth you ain't coming up in here."

"There ain't shit to admit. I told you already that the shit ain't mine. But I guess she back sucking your dick so good your judgment is all fucked up. You always been a sucka for a bomb blow job."

He turned and looked at me with squinted eyes. "Or maybe *you* been sucking my dick so good that my judgment is fucked up."

I hauled back and tried to slap the shit out of him but he grabbed my wrist. "You know what? Thanks for showing me your true colors. Just like that, you would let *any damn thing* come between us? When I thought that air couldn't penetrate what we had. You know what? Fuck it! You want me out? Let me get my shit." He wouldn't move. I tried to go around him and he blocked me. "Faheem, let me get my shit," I gritted.

"You not coming in here until I hear you say it."

"Say what? I'm not saying shit. The shit was planted. Your ex-jump-off set this whole thing up. That's my story and I'm sticking to it."

"Then get the fuck off my property."

I could barely get the words out, I was in such shock." Your property? Nigga, this is my property just as much as it's yours. Move out of my way." He pushed me back and I damn near fell down the steps.

He came at me, "Get off the premises, Jaz. I'm not going to tell you again."

"Or what, Faheem? You gonna throw me off? Nigga, you betta let me get my clothes." He pushed me backwards and this time I fell onto the lawn.

"Wait right here. I'll get your shit," he said and left me out on the lawn, sitting right on my ass. I sat there stunned. No this nigga did not just throw me on my ass and put me out of my own damn house.

FAHEEM

I couldn't believe Jaz. She really had me fucked up. I told her ass that after that first time, if she tried her little games again, she would be sure to feel a nigga's wrath.

I went inside, got her some shit out the closet went outside and damn near threw the shit at her. I dared her to try to come in. When I walked back inside of the house I had to roll something up to try to get my head on straight. It felt right. I hope I just did the right thing. I got up to straighten up the first floor which took me damn near an hour and half. Since I was on a roll I hit the upstairs and knocked that out too. I sat on the living room couch for almost an hour trying to clear my head. Just as I was about to go out into the backyard to get my smoke on again, my cell rang. It was Oni telling me she was on her way with Little Faheem and Kaeerah.

"I should be pulling up in front of your house in about ten minutes."

I told her I was here and then went and put my weed stash up and waited for them to show. Exactly ten minutes later she was ringing the bell. I opened the door and the kids ran right past me. Oni was out of breath and struggling with Kaeerah's book bags and Faheem's football gear. I stepped off the porch and met her. I grabbed some of the equipment allowing her to pass by me and to take the rest of the stuff inside. As she passed, the sun hit the back of her dress in the right spot and I could see right through it. The silhouette of her black lace thong had a brother a little curious . . . especially in my frame of mind.

ONI

"They ate already, and Faheem definitely needs a shower, and I think they both need to get to bed early. They got to fussing in the car right before we pulled up," I filled Faheem in as I bent over to place the bags and knee pads on the floor. They had worn me out. I was going through Kaeerah's bag to find the certificate that she got from completing her ballet lessons. "Kaaerah needs to—" I was caught off guard as Faheem came and stood behind me.

He grabbed onto my hips and said, "And what do you need?" I damn near jumped out of my skin as I turned around.

"Why are you always so jumpy whenever I get close to you?" He backed me up against the wall.

"Because . . . you are always fuckin' with my head, Faheem." I had to let him know that I was on to his little head games.

"Whose fuckin' with your head? Me or him?" He looked down at his now hard dick.

"Both of y'all," I managed to say as he slid his hand up the side of my dress. He spun me around and I dutifully placed my hands on the wall. In a matter of seconds he had my dress up over my ass and was admiring my rear view.

"Gotdamn," he mumbled under his breath as he ran his hand across my ass.

It felt like he was getting ready to take it right there in the hall way. Then we heard the kids running down the steps and he quickly pulled my dress down.

"What y'all doing?" our son yelled out.

"I was getting ready to fix something for your mother."

"He damn sure was," I mumbled under my breath.

Then they ran off into the living room. I grabbed my keys

and turned around. I *had* to stroke his dick. And yes, he was still hard as hell. I wanted to suck the life out of him but this time I would be leaving him wanting. Reluctantly, I gave it one more squeeze and said, "I have to get to work." I headed for the door.

"You won't be able to get away from me the next time."

"I hope not," I said as I walked away wanting to hide the big smile that was threatening to show up on my face. It felt like I was back in.

BROWN DOE

I was very nervous. After two months of physical therapy Nurse Wright dropped me off to where I would be staying until I figured out where I really lived. It was a big boarding house called Happy Hands. I was so frustrated because I couldn't figure anything out. How was it that I could read and know stuff but not remember my past? Where I lived? Who my family was? Nurse Wright and Dr. Shalala assured me that it would come, to be patient and to take it one day at a time. Nurse Wright promised that she would visit me every day and bring me some peach cobbler. At least I had something to look forward to.

TWELVE

TRAE

Being the owner of the club, I was questioned extensively by the LA detectives working Stephon's case. Fuck them pigs, even if I did know something I wouldn't tell them shit. I went to Charli's office to see if I could catch up with her, since none of my calls to her phone was being answered and that turned out to be a dead end. I wasn't exactly sure what was going on, but I knew that his death was directly linked to what Tasha did to her. Since finding out about Stephon's death, I had only spoken to Tasha one time. And although I tried my best to steer her away from paranoia about the Li family being connected to Stephon's death that shit was a stalemate, Tasha was no dummy and I knew it. It seemed as though these days I was on a man hunt for everybody. First Tasha, then Marvin and his bullshit, and now Charli. Charli was far from stupid, but that bitch must be stupid-crazy if she thinks I would let her get away with doing anything to my wife. I told myself that if anything happened to Tasha, I would become the Li Organization's worst fucking nightmare.

I looked up at the church from my rental car and watched people stream in. People from all over had come to pay their respects to Stephon. He would've been proud to know that so many had come to see him home. Funerals weren't my thing. My only reason for being here was to catch a glimpse of my baby, Tasha. She looked regal in her all black going into the church. She has no clue as to how bad I wanted to get out of this car, hug her and then beat her ass. I can't front, my blood boils at the thought of her being with that nigga. Despite everything that we are going through, I love her within everything that's in me and I'm never letting her go. While Tasha thinks she's off playing house with Kyron, in actuality she is just buying me time. I was laying my traps and they both were getting ready to fall right in it. It says that sometimes you have to sacrifice a sheep to catch a wolf. Not to mention that I had other business elsewhere. Marvin was back in Kentucky and I needed to pay him a visit. The limo headed to LAX and I was headed for my destination . . . Kentucky.

TASHA

California is the state that Stephon adopted as his own. He loved it here. "This is my town," he would always say, so for that reason my Uncle Bill chose to have Stephon's funeral here in Cali. How can I describe what I feel right now? I guess numb would be the best word. And fear. I'm afraid for me, for Trae, for my sons. Sitting in the front pew with my family, I couldn't help staring at the silver casket with Stephon inside it. What crushed me inside was the strong possibility that I was responsible for his death. As tears fell down my cheek, I thought about the intense phone conversation I had a few days before with Trae . . .

". . . *You know like I know who killed Stephon!*"

"*I don't know anything, Tasha. All this shit has got me feeling like I'm living in the* Twilight Zone. *You and this nigga Kyron fuckin', the baby growing in your stomach and us not knowing who the father is, you running off to be with that nigga. And now Stephon getting murked. Oh, and how could I forget . . . you in a jealous rage, pushing Charli down a flight of stairs. I don't know much about anything right now.*"

"*That's bullshit, Trae, and you know it. Granted, I'll give you all that other shit you just said, but somebody shooting my fuckin' cousin fifteen times—you know damn well who's behind it. Fifteen times made it personal, and you of all people should know that. That was over kill. It sent a message, Trae. And I heard it loud and clear. Charli Li, your little Chinese bitch had Stephon killed.*"

"*Didn't I tell you to watch your fuckin' mouth on the phone? Believe me I'm just as fucked up about Stephon as you are, but we can't go jumping to conclusions. We don't know what else Stephon might've been into. He could've gotten mixed up in some shady shit. You can't—*"

"*Too much of a coincidence, don't you think? I get Stephon to get Ms. China Ho to the club. I push her down some stairs and now he's dead. C'mon, Trae—this was her—them, all day.*"

"*Listen to what you just said. You* got *Stephon to get her there. You* pushed *her down the stairs. You* assaulted *her at our house that day. You,* not *Stephon. So why kill him and not you? It ain't like you or I are hard to find.*"

"*You just told me to watch my fuckin' mouth over the phone. Now listen to you!*"

I hung up on him mainly because it was the truth.

My uncle taking the podium caught my attention as I tried to become absorbed in his every word and not the conversation I had had with Trae.

TRINA

I stood in the back of the church and watched as family member after family member took to the pulpit and shared memories of my cousin Stephon. Stephon's father Bill, my mother's brother, and I never saw eye to eye. So I didn't fuck with him. I always resented him. When the state took me, Tasha and Kevin into custody and made us a part of the system, he never came to get us or try to get us back. He could've took us in, but he didn't and I couldn't bring myself to forget or forgive that sin. The situation with my parents being on drugs, my little brother getting killed at the age of nine and the state taking us into custody, that shit would break the average kid. But me, I've never been the average kid. By the time I was fourteen, I had done a little of everything. Even murder. Yes. Me, I killed someone. Don't let the stilettos and blow jobs fool you. Stephon was the one who found out that Turner, an older drug dealer, had killed my brother Antoine over some drugs that my mother smoked. Nobody, not even Tasha knew it, other than Stephon because he was with me the day I found Turner and killed him. And it was that day, Stephon told me he was going to Law School to be a lawyer, in case I was ever charged with Turner's murder he could defend me. As the memory played back in my mind a sharp pain rippled through my heart as I asked myself where I was when he needed me to defend him?

As the three of us were shuffled from one foster home to the next, Stephon was the only one that kept in touch and did shit for us. And for that, I'm grateful. He always begged me to come to Cali and go into business with him, but I always refused. I told him that I was content with the East Coast dirt, fog and cold winters. For me, it's all about the bricks. My motto was I'ma live and die a Jersey girl. Plus, I told him that I only fucked with the East Coast niggas, those bird flippin', Timberland and North Face rockin' and big dick slingin' niggas. As Biggie Smalls said, money, clothes and bro's that's all a bitch knows. Stephon always laughed me out, said he felt me and from time to time he would throw me a few ends. He was loyal like that. It's crazy but that all seems like it was centuries ago. And now between him and Tasha I am worn down. But look at me! I live on the West Coast but still gettin' that East Coast dick. I guess old habits are hard to break.

Looking back on everything I knew that my life was a mess. Our rough life in the system had hardened me and turned me into a money-hungry, balla chaser. But, I am what I am.

As I listened to my sister Tasha tell the world why she'd miss Stephon, my blood boiled because he shouldn't be dead. He was too young. Just like Antoine. The same uncontrollable rage and hunger for revenge that I felt years ago was back. My cousin was ambushed and executed. And I wanted to know by who and why? But even if I never found out the why, I'd settle for the who, so that I could do exactly what I did for my brother all those years ago. Kill for him.

THIRTEEN

KYRON

At first I thought I lost her by default. The day that Tasha told me she had to go back to California, for some reason, I had a sense of foreboding. I was sure that she'd hook back up with Trae and put an end to our wonderful fuck game leaving me high and dry. I never factored in a death in the family. I had gotten that news from Kendrick. He was teasing me, saying that I was like Jaheim, sitting around and hoping that she'd find her way back to love. I said nigga you got me fucked up. But who would have thought that me, *that nigga*, would be feenin' for my man'z wife? I said nigga you got me fucked up. Definitely not me. But I was and apparently Shorty must've been feenin' for me just as bad. Because as soon as her cousin's funeral was over, she flew back to New York. Right back to me.

I had Shorty up on the kitchen counter fucking the shit out of her. She made a wisecrack about me busting a nut before she got hers, so we had to play a little game of show and tell. I had to *show* her that she ain't got nothing to worry about. And once I got her to come three times, back-to-back, that would *tell* her that I'm that nigga. Now she can barely hold herself up. You couldn't *tell* me shit.

I was deep dick inside of her, had one leg in the crook of my arm, the other one was wrapped around my waist. I wasn't moving. Her pussy was so wet I could feel her juices sliding on my nuts. I was simply waiting for her to say the word and I was going to finish knocking the bottom out. "You want to go again? What?"

"Unh uh," she whispered.

Shorty was done. You could stick a fork in her. But it was too bad. I didn't feel sorry for her. I needed to get mine off so I started workin' it. She moaned my name and dug her fingernails into my shoulder and back. The name calling shit and fingernail digging only turned me on more. It looked like her eyes rolled back into her head. Even though she was damn near out she was ridin' my dick real nice and I had to give her props for that. You talkin' about a chick breakin' me off, her fuck game was sick. I clearly understood why Trae was going all out on his manhunt for his wife. Shorty started ridin' me faster. She was getting ready to cum. Her pussy muscles were clamping around my dick and I couldn't even move my lips to talk. I could only make sounds, that's how good the pussy was. I grabbed onto the corner of the counter because I couldn't feel my knees. Shorty was hollering and gettin' hers off. My superman cape fell to the floor. I couldn't hold it no longer. It felt as if I released buckets of cum.

TASHA

This nigga was a damn beast in the dick department. He was exactly what I needed to get my mind off of Stephon's death, Charli Li and Trae.

"Shorty, marry me," he asked again. And again it was right after he got his nut off. He let my legs down and started kissing me lightly on the neck. "Marry me."

"I'm already married."

"Divorce him."

"I'm trying."

"So what's the problem?"

"It's not that simple."

"Tell me yes and I'll take care of shit. I'll make it simple."

"How Kyron?" I needed to hear this. "I know you don't think that I want something to happen to Trae?"

"Don't worry about how. Just tell me yes."

"Kyron, he is not going to allow this. Trust me."

"No, Shorty. You *trust* me. Is that a yes?"

I took my time answering. But I said what he wanted to hear. "Yes."

MARVIN

I had just stepped out of the shower and was brushing my teeth when I heard what sounded like Aisha yelling out somebody's name. I shrugged it off thinking that I was trippin'. But as soon as I turned the water in the sink off, I heard it again. I heard her say, "Uncle Trae."

I knew he'd find me. Quickly, I crept into my bedroom and dressed in jeans, a wife beater and slip on loafers. Then I grabbed my burner out the top of my closet. Not knowing exactly what Trae had come to my house for made me chamber a round. I put the 9 mm in the small of my back to conceal it.

"Daddy! Daddy! Uncle Trae is here!" Aisha yelled as if all of her favorite characters from *Toy Story 3* was at the door.

Calming my nerves, I walked down the steps to face the man that I believed killed my cousin.

"Daddy, do I have to go to camp today?" Aisha asked as soon as she saw me. She was hugging Trae's waist. "Can I stay here with you and Uncle Trae? Please! Please! Please! "

I gave Trae a head nod and turned to my daughter. "Your bus will be here in a few minutes, baby, what am I supposed to tell all your friends? I'll make sure that you see Uncle Trae after you get out of camp. He might even pick you up. How about that?"

"That would be super. Uncle Trae, you gonna take me to your house, right? I wanna see the Twins!"

"The Twins are in Florida, but they'll be back soon. They miss you. I miss you. Everybody misses you."

"I miss everybody, too. Auntie Tasha, Auntie Angel, Mommy . . . "

"I know, baby. I'll make sure that you see everybody, okay?" My man told my daughter.

"Promise, Uncle Trae?"

"Promise."

I watched Trae bend down and hug Aisha. She held onto him tight as if she knew that she'd never see him again. Then a horn blew outside. Aisha grabbed her book bag and ran out the door.

"You just up and disappeared on us, yo." Trae said as soon as the front door slammed shut. "How was Florida?"

"It's good to see you too," I replied as we stood across from each other.

"You sure look sober. That rehab joint in Florida was a real good look."

"Cut the bullshit, Trae. Just as sure as you're standing in my living room here, you know I never went to no fuckin' rehab in Florida."

"I don't know shit, son. How about you fill me in. Starting with Kyra. Where is she?"

"Straight like that, huh? No, how you doing or nothing?"

"You know I ain't come all the way to West Bumblefuck Kentucky to bullshit. There's a lot of worried people back home, so again, where the fuck is Kyra?" Trae walked over to the bar, grabbed a stool and sat on it.

My mouth opened, but no sound came out. It felt like Trae was staring through my soul. Shit. I felt naked in front of this nigga. At that moment shit started flashing in front of my eyes like I was watching it on High Def. I started seeing scenes of me taking Kyra through all the bullshit once I started getting high again. I saw the day that she first confronted me about the dope she found in my dirty laundry. I saw the day she brought my daughter to the dope house. I saw her with that cop nigga, Rick. I saw her lying in the car with a bullet in her head.

TRAE

All I did was ask this nigga a simple question and now he standing over there looking all spaced out and shit. This nigga must be still getting high. Either way, it won't matter in a little while. I'ma make all his pain and suffering go away.

"Yo, Marv, what the fuck is wrong with you?"

The focus came back to his eyes. Marvin dropped down on the couch and put his head in his hands. "I fucked up. Now I'm lost without Babygirl."

"What the fuck happened, yo? How did you fuck up? Again, where is Kyra?"

"He shot her . . . it happened so fast. I thought they were bullshittin'. I shot one of em' . . . then Fish . . . Fish—"

"Fish? Who the fuck is Fish? Who shot Kyra?"

"I got out of the car to go and talk to Fish . . . after I shot Junie, Mook froze up. He had a gun pressed against Kyra's head. I thought that . . . Fish had killed Mook. Then he shot Kyra."

"Who the fuck is Fish?" I asked again.

"My cousin. He wanted to rob me. He sent Junie and Mook at me. I was slippin . . . the dope had me . . . I couldn't see—"

"Kyra was shot and you did what? You left her?" I asked already knowing the answer.

"She was dead, yo. We were dirty. I wasn't thinking, couldn't think. Lo kept telling me to come on . . . that was the last time I saw her."

"Where's her body, Marvin?"

"I don't know," he replied and closed his eyes.

"You mean to tell me you just left your wife's body there? You didn't even think about giving her a decent burial? What the fuck is wrong with you?"

"Hers wasn't the only one. We left other bodies—"

"Fuck everybody else! I'm talking about Kyra." I was now yelling at this nigga. He was too long to tell me what I came to hear.

"I told you we were dirty. We had to leave before the cops came."

Standing up, I shouted, "Dirty? What you did to Kyra was dirty, muthafucka." I pulled my gun out of my waist. "You deserve more than death," I said as I cocked one in the chamber. "Let me ask you one more thing, what happened to Rick?"

That question opened Marvin's eyes. His eyes locked on my chrome Springfield Armory .45.

"So, it was you who killed Lo? It had to be you. That's the only way that you would know about Rick. So you would kill me over some punk ass cop? Well fuck it. Go ahead nigga because I wanna die. I'm haunted every day by what I did to Kyra, I miss my wife and I'm losing my fucking mind. Go ahead and kill me. Take me out of my misery."

"You running your mouth and you still ain't answering the fuckin' question. What happened to Rick, Marv?"

"We dumped his body. Hopefully that nigga is rotting in hell."

"Hold the fuck up. Y'all took the time to dump Rick's body but left Kyra's? Something ain't adding up right, son."

"I didn't dump the body, Lo did."

"You's a lyin' mothafucka." I walked over to the couch and stood in front of Marvin. "Look me in the eyes and tell me that you don't know where Kyra's body is."

It seemed like every time I mentioned her name, it cut into him like a hot knife sliding through butter. I stood there waiting for an answer. He stared back to see if I would back down but fuck that. I was waiting for this nigga to come off some info that I could use. The next thing I know this nigga breaks down crying. I decided to let him have his moment. After about five minutes he pulled himself together. I tightened the grip on my burner and stood over this pussy with disgust all over my face. I was ready to air his ass out.

He looked up at me and broke the silence.

"Just promise me you'll take care of my daughter, man."

"Marv, you—"

"Say it nigga! Promise me that you'll take care of my daughter!" He was crying like a bitch.

"That goes without saying. Aisha is family. You got my word that she will be well taken care of."

"Thank you. The camp bus will drop Aisha off at two. Don't let her see me . . . tell her I love her more than anything. Can you do that for me?"

I nodded my head.

"Well, what the fuck are you waiting for? Do what you came here to do. I knew you'd come. I knew it. I saw that shit in your eyes. And you know what else? I have a gun on me now. I could've killed you as soon as I came down the stairs. But I chose not to. Why? Because I'm tired Trae. I even sent ole girl's ass back to Mexico. I'm tired of the nightmares, the dreams, the guilt, the pain. You're getting ready to do me a favor."

"I ain't come here to do you no gotdamn favors. Muthafucka this shit is revenge."

"I can respect that so let's do this. When you shoot me—hit me right here." Marvin pointed to the spot in the middle of his forehead. "Close my casket. I want everybody to remember me the way they saw me last. That's my last wish. Go ahead and do it. I'm ready. And I'm sorry about getting the club raided, for whatever it's worth."

"It's fucked up man, that you forced me to end it like this." I raised the gun and honored a dying man's last wish. I emptied the clip into Marvin's face.

FOURTEEN

FAHEEM

I was seated inside of Steve my attorney's office for the second time. Me paying an attorney to get Jaz cleared of any drug charges was déjà vu. He had his investigators focused on getting the tape of the stop and search as well as any evidence that they had against her. Jaz hadn't been home for two days or called in. She hadn't even called to speak to our child. And now it was looking like this was all bullshit. I left Steve's office not feeling too well.

ONI

I was the designated baby-sitter for the afternoon. Faheem had a 3:30 appointment with his attorney, so he asked me to pick up Kaeerah. I did and now I'm cooking dinner in hopes that I could convince him to stay. The children were in the yard playing.

Around 6:00 I heard a car pull into the driveway. My front door was open so Faheem rang the bell, "Can I come in?"

"It's open Faheem."

"Thanks for watching Kaeerah. Tell her to come on so we can go home. I have another stop to make."

"You're not going to put something in your stomach? I fixed you a little sumthin' sumthin'."

"Nah. I'm good. Did Kaeerah eat?"

"Not yet. Everybody was waiting on you. They've been outside playing hard. You know they ain't thinking about no food."

"Well, fix us both a plate and wrap them up."

I did not like the sound of that. Here I was slaving over a hot ass stove so that he could sit down and eat a decent meal. And here he was talking about fix him a plate and wrap it up. I took off my apron, yes, I had on an apron, hung it over the chair and went to go get the kids. I didn't want him to see the disappointment on my face. On top of that he wasn't talking at all about Jaz and what happened. But I should be used to that, he always did keep their business close to the chest.

"Daddy, daddy. I talked to mommy today," Lil' Jaz yelled as she ran to hug her father.

"Dad, can Lil' Jaz spend the night?" Faheem asked his father.

"Your sister got camp tomorrow. You want to come spend the night with her?"

"No, he can't," I quickly interjected. "Not tonight."

"Awww mom," Faheem whined.

"Listen to your mother, Faheem. We talked about that remember? Come here." Faheem told our son. My son went over to his father and they gave each other dap as if they were best boys out on the block.

"I got you dad." He then started whispering to him. Faheem leaned over to hear what he had to say.

"We'll talk about that."

"Okay, dad."

FAHEEM

I started to leave but after little Faheem whispered to me to please eat with him and his mom I couldn't disappoint him.

"Faheem invited me to dinner. Is that alright with you?"

Oni looked at me in surprise. "When I invited you, you said no, but when your son invites you, it's a yes?"

"Can I stay or what?" I asked as I headed for the bathroom to wash my hands.

Oni wasted no time setting the table. She was acting like a kid on Christmas. When I returned, the table was almost ready and the children brushed past me and ran into the bathroom.

As my little man came back swinging water all over the floor he looked up and said, "Daddy, are you and my sister going to stay?"

"Yeah, and I'm hungry."

"Yaay! We get to eat like a family," he sang as he went to his seat. "Come on Kaeerah!"

We all sat down and I said the blessing and we began to eat. I was surprised that Oni remembered my favorite dishes and she had every one of them. A juicy, deep-fried turkey, with home-made mash potatoes and gravy, steamed asparagus with garlic butter and homemade whole wheat rolls. Not to mention the homemade 7-Up pound cake from scratch. Everything was laid out and now I felt like the kid on Christmas day.

"I see that you didn't forget my favorites." I smiled at her. "You had this all planned out."

"I know what you like in your mouth," she said back real seductive.

I started to say something but little Faheem and Kaeerah both was all up in my grill, so I had to let that one slide for now. Oni couldn't conceal it if she wanted to. She was in her glory. The grin wouldn't leave her face as she kept my plate stacked. If Jaz knew what was going down at this very moment, she would whip both of your asses. I smiled at the thought.

After we ate, she served the cake and we talked and laughed with the kids.

"Thanks for the dinner," I said as I rose to my feet.

"No problem, I enjoyed making it for you, plus I knew it would make Faheem's day if he could have the family dinner, he had been bugging me for weeks. Thanks for staying. But I know you don't think you gettin' off that easy?" she said right after the kids had took off running to the backyard.

"What?"

"You either get to *do* the dishes or *do* me." She was now standing so close to me that I could feel her nipples against my chest.

I knew that she was dying for me to tear that ass up, and with Jaz in the doghouse a brotha was tempted. She saw me look over at the sink.

"Don't even try it. If you think you going to do the dishes, you got me fucked up."

I allowed her to back me up into the open pantry. She took my hand and guided it up under her dress and between her thighs. She was wet as hell. Since I was feeling a little generous, I gave her a little play and began to tease her clit.

ONI

Oh my god, my pussy was so hot I thought that I was going to die. I didn't know how desperate I wanted to get fucked until I saw myself backing him up into the closet. All I kept asking myself was, "Is this really going to happen?" While he teased my clit, as only Faheem could, I dug my nails into his shoulder and spread my legs wider. I was grinding onto his fingers as if they were his dick. All I could think was, please don't let those kids come in here, not until he makes me cum at least one time. I took a deep inhale then started to unbutton his pants and feverishly unzipped them and released the dragon.

He lifted me up and placed me on the top of the washing machine, pulled up my shirt and began gently sucking my nipple just the way I liked it. Just when I thought I was going out of my mind he asked me, "You got some Magnums around?"

"What?" My heart fell to my feet.

"You got some protection?"

"Oh my god, Faheem. Please, don't do this to me." I whispered in his ear, damn near begging. I wanted him to fuck me so bad, and no I didn't have any muthafuckin' condoms in the damn house.

"If you don't have any you can talk into the mic."

Even though my pussy was throbbing, I wasn't letting him leave without getting the dick anyway that I could. And I did. I wanted to taste him, suck his dick, blow on his balls and swallow his seeds. So, I wasted no time sliding off of the washing machine, getting down on my knees and giving him nothing but throat. The nigga made me work for it too. Faheem could hold out longer than any nigga I ever been with. His dick game was impeccable. I was jealous of Jaz, the bitch had it made. He made me suck until he knew that my jaws ached and then he exploded in my mouth. He held onto my head until I drank every drop. When I rose up he had a smirk on his face.

"Do me Faheem, please."

He kept that smirk on his face, while not taking his eyes off of me as he fixed his clothes. "I still know what you like in your mouth. And I told you that you wouldn't get away from me the next time," he finally said.

"So what? Are you going to return the favor?" I asked as I looked down at his now soft dick. It was obvious that I wasn't going to get fucked up, but at least he could give me some head.

He left out of the pantry and I was right behind him. He turned around and gave me a big hug and slapped me on the ass. "Lil' Jaz, time to go," he yelled out.

He left me feeling like a fool.

KYRA

I was getting used to this group home thing. Thanks to the coordinator, Jill Bankston, and of course my favorite person, Nurse Wright. It was like one big family and everyone had a part. I did my part by keeping the T.V. Room and Rec Room clean. We had volunteers of all shapes, sizes, backgrounds and colors coming to visit us. They gave life skills classes, financial literacy classes, creative writing classes, child birth classes, you name it they gave it. I busied myself with taking everything. I was hoping that something . . . anything would make me feel whole again and, most of all, trigger my memory.

"Ladies, whoever is interested in the conflict resolution classes, it will start in ten minutes and it will be in the yard," Mrs. Bankston yelled out. "Ms. Brown are you coming?"

"On my way," I told her. I liked Mrs. Bankston because she would always tell me to be happy, enjoy life and be grateful. She would always pray with me and for me. I brushed my teeth and fingered my locks and then headed for the yard.

It was hot outside and the tent was doing very little to guard us from the Arizona sun. There were only two other ladies seated outside in the second row of chairs on the large grassy lawn. I marched up to the first row and took a seat. I was eager to learn, eager to have my memory triggered.

The young lady who I assumed was the instructor was a red headed, petite white girl. As soon as I sat down she turned around and said hello. She glanced at her watch and turned to who I guess was her partner, another petite white girl with blonde hair, who kept looking at me. I smiled at her, trying not to be rude but she kept staring at me. She finally said, "Kyra? Kyra is that you?"

I turned around and looked at the other two ladies in back of me. They kept talking to each other so I assumed she must have been talking to me.

The blonde haired chick came over to me. The scent of her perfume seemed faintly familiar. "Kyra Blackshear. It's me Keli. Keli Lagowitz? We were lab partners for two semesters. What have you done to your hair? I love it! What are you doing here in Arizona? I can't get away from you! You transferred out here, too? Why would you leave California? Well, you're probably wondering why I left." She held up her ring finger. "I married Ian. Remember him? I married my doctor." She and her friend giggled. "Oh my gosh. Listen at me rambling. Same ole Keli, right?"

"Yes, you are rambling." Her friend said. "You didn't even introduce me to your friend. I'm Dana." She held out her hand for me to shake it. "Any friend of Kels is a friend of mine."

"Hello." I didn't know what else to say. She called me Kyra. Nurse Wright called me Brown. My heart began to race.

"Enough about me. Are you volunteering here as well?"

Who was this white girl? She said that she knew me. Lab partner? Kyra? Is that really who I am?

Mrs. Bankston made her way over to where we were and this chick started rambling again. "Jill, why didn't you tell me you had UCLA Alumni here? Me and Kyra were lab partners and we aced lab both times."

Mrs. Bankston pulled or more like yanked the rambling white girl away from me.

"No wait. I want to ask her something. She knows me." I said as I rose from my seat to grab her other arm.

"Don't worry Brown, give me a few minutes and I will bring her right back." Mrs. Bankston said in her usually calm voice. I hesitated at first but then released her arm and sat back down. I watched as they walked away carrying with them all the new revelations that this stranger had just revealed to me.

They went to the back and I watched as they kept looking at me, but I had no clue as to what Mrs. Bankston was so animated about. I reluctantly turned around in my seat.

JAZ

I called my daughter to say good night. After I hung up the phone I grabbed a jacket and decided to go the nearest Waffle House. This would be my fourth night sleeping in a college dorm. It wasn't bad and it wouldn't be my first. During finals I would pull strings to get a room if one was available because it seemed like I studied better on campus. And since I had midterms coming up it was all good. If I went to a hotel I wouldn't do anything but chill as if I was on vacation. I was just thankful that a room was available. Faheem actually did me a favor. At home the priority was be a mommy, wifey and then get the studying done. So thanks nigga. I'll deal with you after my mid-terms.

ONI

The banging at my front door woke me up. I laid there not sure if I was dreaming or not. Then they started ringing the bell. At first I said it had to be one of my brothers. Them niggas didn't know that I knew it but they all had keys. Then I thought about Jaz. The thought of that bitch got me to jump out of my warm bed. I grabbed my robe and stormed down the stairs. I turned the front porch light on and cracked the door.

Boom!

It happened so fast. The door swung open and I went flying back onto the kitchen table and then hit the floor. I swear I was seeing stars and then everything faded to black.

When I awoke I could hear Faheem's voice screaming, "Mommy, Mommy, help me!" That impact knocked the wind out of me but I mustered up the strength to crawl over to the door and try to block the men from taking my baby.

"Why are you doing this? Please, don't take my son!" I cried while grabbing a hold of the leg of the guy who was carrying my son on his shoulder as he made his way to the front door, dragging me along with him as I held on for dear life.

"Get this bitch off of me, man! What the fuck are you doing? You supposed to have my back. You see this bitch don't you?" he yelled at his accomplice.

"Why are you doing this?" I asked them.

"Bitch, you know why. You the same bitch who own the hotel right? Well, you know what we want. We want what's ours. We work for Steele."

"Now let go, bitch," the one holding the gun yelled at me as he tried to pry my hands off of his partner's leg. Once he saw that that wasn't working he pulled my hair and slapped the shit out of me but I still didn't let go. They were going to have to kill my ass before I let anything happen to my baby.

"Man shoot the bitch and stop fucking around."

"Naw, we can't kill her, nigga." That's when he pulled his gun out and hit me in my face. Once again, everything faded to black.

I lay there feeling my face. *What just happened?* Then it hit me like a ton of bricks. *Faheem. My baby.* I turned over onto my stomach, forced myself up on my knees and started crawling. "Faheem." I thought I was screaming his name, but I couldn't hear anything. "Faheem." I crawled up the stairs and when I made it to the top I stood up and rushed to my son's bedroom.

He was gone.

FAHEEM

"Who the fuck is this?" I sat up in my king-sized bed and turned on the lamp. *It had to be Jaz.* Reaching for the phone on my end table, I looked at the caller ID. *Oni.* It was 3:38. "What's up?" I asked her. She was screaming and crying and shit. "Oni, what is the matter? Is Faheem alright?" Panicking, I flung off my silk sheet and jumped to my feet. *What was this bitch up to?* I began pacing in front of my dresser, my heart rate increasing. "Oni. Stop crying and talk to me. What's the matter and is Faheem alright?"

"They . . . took him."

"What did you just say?"

"They got . . . him."

FIFTEEN

TASHA

I was obviously "dick high" when I told this nigga, yes I would marry him. And because of that now I'm sitting here watching him put this big ass rock on my finger.

"Damn this bitch is beautiful," Kyron said and he brought my hand to his lips and kissed the ring.

I had to admit, it was *all* of that, ten carats of some of the most beautiful stones I've seen in a long time. All VVS of course. If I wasn't already married to such a boss ass nigga I would be in awe. But I've seen bigger. But I wouldn't burst dude's bubble. After all, he is a constant reminder that my A-game is still tight, being as though he is ready and willing to wife a bitch after such a short period of time. But I could no longer revel in the moment. I had to let this nigga down easy. I damn sure couldn't marry him. All I could think about was Trae and the fact that I am still married and I must be out of my damned mind to think that he is going to just sit back and allow this bullshit to continue.

Kyron picked up on my mood. "What's the matter? You don't like it? I can take it back and get something else."

"Of course I like it. But you and I both know, it will never happen."

"Let me worry about that." He kissed me. Kissed me like I belonged to him. "Shorty, chill out. I told you I got this."

"You don't know him like I do, Kyron. Therefore I can't help it. He keeps nagging at the back of my mind. It feels like he is just somewhere plotting and waiting. And like every corner I turn, that nigga is going to be standing there. Plus there is some other shit going on Kyron, and I don't want you to get mixed up in it. The Chinese mafia is watching me."

"I see that I need to get you out of this house. You startin' to hallucinate and shit."

I knew that he was not going to take me seriously. "I am not. It's reality. We are not going to be able to do this Kyron," I slowly began sliding the ring off my finger.

"Yes you are." He took my hand and slid the ring back on my finger. "Look, I told you I'm going to take care of it. Let's just get out and get some fresh air and we'll talk about it when we get back."

I thought about it. "Well, you have been holding me as a sex slave. That is illegal you know. When can I get my freedom papers, massah?"

He looked me dead in my eyes and said, "Never. The pussy is too good. Your shit is addictive, Shorty." He stood up and then pulled me up off the sofa. His hands slid down to my ass and he started caressing my cheeks and gently kissing my neck.

I closed my eyes. "Kyron, I want you to listen to me." He

pulled me closer and I could feel him, he was already hard. "Are you listening to me?"

"I'm listening, Shorty."

His dick pressed up against my pussy was feeling real nice. "Let's just enjoy these stolen moments for as long as we can. We can't make this permanent. Too many things are working against us. I did something in California and . . . it got my cousin killed. They are probably going to come after me next. I'm not hallucinating, Kyron. This is real. And if the Chinese mob doesn't kill us, Trae will for sure."

"Are you finished?"

I nodded.

We started kissing. He took my hand and placed it on his dick. Shit, he didn't need to do that. I already felt how hard it was. He went to unzip my jeans but I grabbed his hand.

"Just let me get up in it for a few minutes."

I giggled, "I don't think so. That few minutes will turn into an hour and I'm hungry, Kyron."

"Five minutes then." He unzipped my jeans and began to take them off. I gave a weak protest but the nigga already had one of my legs out of my jeans. His sweat pants were down over his ass. He laid me down onto the sofa, spread my thighs and moved my thong to the side. He slid in and I wrapped my legs around his waist. I still had on one shoe but I didn't care, the dick was feeling that good. When I felt my juices trickle down my thighs, I knew it was over for Mr. I-only-need-five-minutes. He grunted and started fucking me hard and fast and I think it was about three minutes when he started cumming. I allowed him to pull himself together before I placed both hands on top his head and led him down to Miss Kitty.

"I thought you was ready to go eat?" he teased me as he slid a couple of fingers inside me and started licking my clit. When he found my g-spot, he ate the pussy and tickled my spot just right. I was no better than him. In less than three minutes, I was cumming and it felt like I would never stop. I love me a nigga who eats and swallows everything on the menu.

KYRON

I had to figure out how I was going to keep Shorty here with me for as long as possible. After I fucked her right quick and ate her pussy like a pro, she lay on the sofa spent. I left her there to go to the bathroom and to touch base with Kendrick. I hadn't heard from the nigga in a few days so I called him.

"What's up, nigga?"

"Waitin' to hear from you. Anything up? If not, I'ma head out for a couple of days," he told me.

"Nah, ain't nothin' poppin', we good? Why you bouncin'? You duckin' Trae out?" I couldn't help but to laugh at the thought.

"Man, that nigga straight buggin'. And I don't know how I got in the middle of y'alls bullshit." Now he was laughing.

"So what you sayin'? You gotta stop fuckin' with me now?"

"That's exactly what I'm saying. But for real, yo, watch your back and I'll hit you up in a couple of days. One."

"No doubt." I hung up.

TASHA

I finally pulled myself together, went into the bathroom to freshen up with that "I've just been fucked" glide in my stride. Kyron disappeared somewhere around the apartment, most likely to make some calls. Since he had been stuck in the house pampering and spoiling me for the past few days, whatever it is that he does he had been handling over the phone. Now he was posted at the front door waiting on me.

"Shorty, you decided what you want to eat?" He asked me.

I wasn't a meat eater but I had been craving for a big, fat juicy burger. "I want a burger!"

Kyron gave me a quizzical look. "A burger? We ain't got to go out for that, I can hook you up a burger."

I punched him in the arm. "No, I want a real burger. If I'm going to break my no meat diet, it has to be worth my while. Who knows? Maybe I'll eat a burger and then wrap my lips around a big, fat, juicy steak."

"Damn, Shorty. You are hungry."

"Yes, I am. Now let's go." I was anxious to get outside for the first time in four days. I was glad that the swelling of my ankle had gone down and I could walk normally. I wasn't ready for stilettos yet, and wouldn't be for at least a week or two.

On the elevator Kyron stood behind me and pulled me close. He whispered into my ear, "What did you want to wrap your lips around?"

Damn. I should have known that he wasn't going to let that fly. I saw where this was going and was wondering when he was going to bring it up. "A big . . . fat . . . juicy . . . steak!" I teased him.

"I got something big . . . fat . . . and juicy that you can wrap your lips around and I promise it'll beat a steak anytime."

"Ummmm," I moaned. "I know you do." I could tell by the way he hesitated that he wasn't expecting that response.

"So what a nigga gotta do to test out your head game?"

"I have to be sure that the nigga is *the one.*"

"How do I know if I'm *the one?*"

"Oh, you'll know it."

"So, it's like that?"

I didn't respond and I knew he was sharp enough to let it go. The only dick I was sucking was my husband's! It felt like when it came to sucking dick, Trae had me brainwashed or some shit like that. We stepped off of the elevator hand in hand. I was on my way to suck on a juicy burger.

TRAE

"Uncle Trae, whose airplane is this?" Aisha asked, animated as she sat strapped in the G5's leather bucket seats.

"It's my plane, baby," I replied and looked into her smiling face. "Why? You like my plane?"

"Yeah! It's different from all the other ones. It's smaller but it's fly. Where are all the people? Don't they get to ride on your plane, too?"

"No passengers, baby. Only people that I want to ride. People like you."

Aisha giggled at that remark. "Are we going to Florida to get the Twins and Caliph?"

"Not today. But soon. Right now I'm taking you to California. Aunt Marva will be glad to see you. Then we'll go and get Auntie Tasha, okay?"

"Okay. But, Uncle Trae, why didn't my daddy come out to the bus to get me? Why did he let me leave without saying goodbye?"

It was at that moment that my heart began to ache for Aisha.

She would have to live the rest of her life without her mother and father and never really know what happened to them. There was no way in the world I could ever let her find out the truth about her father's death.

"Your daddy told me to tell you goodbye and that he loves you. He said that he had to go somewhere important but he'd see you later."

I hated having to lie to my niece. But what other options did I have?

After killing Marvin, I cleared the house and got rid of any traces of my being there. Then I puffed a few jays and waited for Aisha's bus. While I was waiting I got thinking how it still didn't sit right with me that Kaylin claimed to have no idea where Kyron lay his head. It nagged at me, but I really couldn't blame him. After all, Kyron was his brother. As soon as I got Aisha settled, I was flying back to New York to get my wife. It was time for this whole game to end. It was overdue.

TASHA

We ended up at Dallas BBQ's in the Bronx. I ordered a double crispy onion cheeseburger and a spinach steak salad. I was going all out. Kyron ordered like he was pregnant too. He ordered Barb-que beef ribs, crispy shrimp and a chicken Caesar salad. We had virgin piña coladas in three different flavors. All we could do was look and laugh when our waitress sat all of our dishes down before us. We both ate and drank until we could eat and drink no more.

I excused myself to go to the restroom. My bladder felt as if it was about to burst. I zoomed into the first stall I saw open and went for it. Only to see after it was too late that I had no tissue.

"Shit!" I mumbled. "Can someone pass me some tissue please?" I heard bitches out there talking and laughing but no one passed me any tissue. "Helllooo, can someone please pass me some tissue?"

"Girl, bitches can be so petty," I heard somebody say. "Here you go." She passed me some tissue under the stall.

"Thank you. I appreciate it. I can't believe them bitches wouldn't pass me any fuckin' tissue. Like they had to put a quarter in the machine and fuckin' pay for it."

"I know. Bitches are a trip and there's still one out here that act like she got a stick up her ass."

"The ho better be gone when I come out of this stall," I threatened and I meant that shit.

"You want me to hold her?" I heard my new friend say. She didn't sound like a New Yorker. That explained why I got some help from her. Them New York bitches are just plain rude.

Then I heard another voice say, loud and clear. "I know y'all bitches ain't talkin' about me. I don't work in this restroom," the woman stated in true New Yorker form, and I heard her leave out of the bathroom.

"Only in New York," my new friend laughed.

Then I took one step out of the stall and stopped. That fuckin' meat I just ate had me. "Oh shit." I had to turn around and hurl into the toilet bowl. "Oh God. Oh my God," I groaned.

My new friend came over to the stall. "Here's a couple of wet paper towels." I turned around and grabbed them and patted my face. I was actually sweating.

"Thank you. Thank you so much." I appreciated that shit.

"No problem. But I was all caught up in your shit, I didn't do what I came in here to do and that's use the bathroom." She rushed into one of the stalls.

"You got tissue in there?" I teased her.

"Yeah, I got some."

When she came out the stall I was brushing my teeth. I saw ole girl out the corner of my eye checking me out from head to toe.

"Are you okay? Was it something you ate out there?" She asked me.

"I wish that's all it was. I'm five weeks pregnant."

"Oh!" She squealed. She was acting like she was the one pregnant. "Congratulations! Is this your first one? Are you excited?"

Excited? If she only knew the half of it. "Girl, this is baby number four."

"Four?" She gasped. "Oh shit."

"My sentiments exactly. I have three boys, that includes a set of twins."

"Twins?"

"Yes, twins. What about you?"

"I have three also. Two girls and a boy."

"Let me see your little ones and I'll let you see mine." I pulled out my diamond studded Goldvish cell phone. Kyron hated when I carried it. He said it was way too flashy. But hell, it was mine. The chick's eyes almost popped out of her head. She was so intrigued by the diamonds she was barely looking at the pictures.

"These are my twins, Shaheem and Kareem. And this is my baby, Caliph." I cooed. I couldn't help myself. These were my babies.

"I can tell that's your baby. He looks just like you. And the twins must look just like their father. All you did was carry them."

She hit everything right on the head. "I know." I beamed with pride. "The twins *belong* to their father. They look just like him and act just like him."

"Are you serious? Let me show you my little ones." My new friend slowly pulled out her BlackBerry and showed me her pictures.

"Awww, they are adorable. Now they all look like you. I wish I had a girl."

She pointed to my stomach. "That could be your daughter right there."

"Girl please, I don't even know if I'ma keep this one."

She gasped. "For real?"

"Girl, it's a long story."

"Well, it's your body. It's your choice and I damn sure ain't the one to judge."

"Girl, you cool as hell. What is your name?"

She started laughing, "I'm Nina. And yours?"

"I'm Tasha. And if you are ever in California, look me up. Better yet, give me your phone. She handed over her BlackBerry. "I'ma put my number in it for you. Promise you'll look me up."

"Hell yeah. As a matter of fact, I'm looking forward to it. California here I come!" We both started laughing.

KYRON

Shorty was taking forever. I got up to go take a leak and to see if she was alright. When I came out of the bathroom there was another cat coming my way. He looked like he was on the same mission as myself. I banged on the door. "Shorty, you alright in there?" I yelled out.

"Be right out." I heard her say. *What the fuck? They having a party in there.* I stepped to the side.

Then dude cracked the door. "Nina, what's up?"

"Here I come."

He looked at me and said, "Man, they in there socializing."

"I see. They been in there for almost a half hour," I said to dude.

He was checking me out. And finally the bathroom door came open and both ladies stepped out.

"Shorty, you aiight?"

"I threw up," she whined.

I figured that something was wrong because she was taking so long. Then she looked over at the girl she was hanging in the bathroom with and said, "Nina here was making sure I was alright. Nina, this is Kyron. Kyron, this is Nina." She then looked at the cat that was standing next to me. She squinted. When they locked gazes she gasped as if she had just seen a ghost. Her hand flew over her mouth as she slowly backed up into the bathroom.

Dude followed her.

On instinct I was right behind him.

"Shorty, what's the matter?" I eased my hand over my burner.

Shorty wouldn't say anything which was getting me spooked. I went around this nigga and stood between him and Tasha. I placed my hand up to his chest and pushed him back. "Man step out for a minute. Let me talk to my Shorty," I told him.

This nigga had the audacity to slap my arm away. "Hold up my man. What the fuck is you doin' with this nigga?" He asked

my Shorty. He tried to step around me but I was keeping Tasha
blocked. *What the fuck? Is this an old flame?*

"I'm not going to ask you again. Step out of the bathroom, yo!"
I gritted. I turned to Tasha. "Shorty, who is this nigga?"

"I'm just a friend of the family," he said, obviously trying to
put me to sleep. But I wasn't falling for the bullshit. "Tasha, tell
him."

Tasha remained behind me. I shoved his ass back again. His
girl grabbed his arm and pulled him out of the bathroom.

I turned around and faced Tasha, who was visibly shaken.
"Who is that nigga, Shorty? You used to fuck with him or something?"

"He's dead. A dead cop," she mumbled.

"A dead cop? What the fuck are you talking about?" I grabbed
her by the shoulders but she was still mumbling some shit I
didn't understand. "Let me get you the fuck outta here so you
can tell me what the fuck is going on." I grabbed her hand and
took her out of the bathroom.

I practically knocked this mystery nigga over who was pacing
back and forth. "Tasha let me explain." He was following behind
us, pissing me off.

"You need to back the fuck up, son. Can't you see she don't
want to be bothered?" I raised my shirt to show this nigga that
I was holding heat.

"Don't show that if you don't plan on using it."

I stopped dead in my tracks. "Oh, I'll use it, muthafucka." I
stepped towards him and Tasha grabbed my arm and pulled me
away.

He must have thought about it because he raised his two
hands in the form of surrender. "I don't want no trouble, man.

It's all good. I come in peace. I told you, I'm just a friend of the family. *Trae* was like a brother to me and I was just wondering what the fuck are you doing with his wife?"

So that's what this is all about. "Don't worry about what the fuck I'm doing and who I'm doing it with. You don't know me muthafucka." I wanted to handle this nigga but I felt Tasha tighten her grip. I turned and looked at her and she was apparently fucked up over this shit. I saw that I needed to get Shorty away from this nigga. She was actually looking sick.

SIXTEEN

ONI

I am freaking the fuck out. Niggas keep telling me to calm down. How the fuck can I calm down when my baby is gone? Two muthafuckas coming up in your house in the middle of the night and snatching your child is not shit to be calm about. After I was able to pull myself up off the floor once the kidnappers left, my first call was to my three brothers. My next call took me about 15 minutes to build up the nerve to make. But I got it together and called Faheem. It was his son as well as mine and I didn't have the right to leave him in the blind about his son's abduction.

Big Mike, my oldest brother, who is Ronnie's daddy, Damon and Wali, they all got to my house back-to-back. They were all visibly disturbed and ready to do major damage to somebody. My nephew, Ronnie the cop, arrived last with some nurse broad that he was fucking. He got her to check out my head and face. Once that was done, Ronnie sent her on her way. I brought everybody up to speed on what happened.

"Slow down, Nene, and start from the beginning," Damon ordered.

"We were upstairs asleep. The banging on the door woke me up. I heard banging and the bell ringing. My first thought was, it was one of y'all and something was wrong, but I remembered that you all have keys. My next thought was there was that bitch Jaz coming to start some—"

"Jaz? Who the fuck is Jaz?" Wali interrupted.

"That's little Faheem's stepmother," Damon volunteered. He was the only one who knew about the whole situation with me and Faheem. "But that's a story for another time. Let's stick to the situation at hand. Go ahead Ne."

"I went to the door and cracked it. The next thing I knew, I flew backwards. When I woke up, I heard my baby yelling. I saw them—"

"Them?"

"Yeah, there was two of them."

"Can you describe them?" My nephew Ronnie asked.

I shook my head. "It all happened so fast. I was on the floor, dizzy and crawling around. I grabbed one dude's leg. He was the one holding Faheem over his shoulder." Just thinking about that moment caused me to break down. But I quickly regained my composure. "I begged them not to take my son. I asked them why. 'Bitch, you know why', the one with Faheem said. He then said, 'don't you own a hotel?' Then he said, 'We want what's ours. We work for Steele.'

"Then what?" Wali inquired.

"Then nothing. They left with Faheem and I called y'all . . . and Faheem."

"Why did you call him?" Ronnie asked with his face twisted up. "He ain't a part of—"

"Faheem is his son. No matter how any of us feel about that, it's a reality. Besides, he'll find out eventually, don't you think?" As soon as I got those words out my mouth, we heard another car skid into the driveway.

My nephew got up and went to the window. "Well, this must be him now."

"You shouldn't have called him, Ne. This is family business and you know the rules, sis. What goes on in the family stays in the family," my oldest brother added.

"Mike, Faheem is now a part of this family because of his son, whether we like it or not. And I'd rather he find out about it from me instead of the police or newspapers if this gets out. God forbid it does."

"I'm ready to rock and roll. Y'all know what we gotta do," Damon snapped.

"Everybody just chill for a minute," Wali stated calmly. "But Mike is right, Nene. Your baby daddy don't need to know what we into. Hell, my own wife don't even know."

Everybody's head turned at the same time and stared at Wali. "What?"

"Stupid ass nigga. Your nosy ass wife knows everything about everything and then some," Big Mike said. "Somebody get the door and let that man in."

FAHEEM

I pulled into Oni's driveway, not knowing what to expect or find out. The driveway was full. I got out, went to the other side, swooped up Lil' Jaz in a blanket and headed for the door. Some big ass nigga was standing there holding it open for me. When

I stepped inside I recognized two of the cats as her brothers. We met back in Jersey. I had never seen the older dude before. I went straight to business. Fuck all the formalities.

"Oni, what's going on? What do you mean they got my son?"

She began crying uncontrollably. "I'm so sorry Faheem. Please . . . don't let this come between us."

"Oni, the only thing between us is my son. You crying ain't telling me shit. Are you going to tell me what's going on or not?"

"They took him. They have our son. I'm so sorry Faheem."

My knees buckled. "Hold the fuck up. What do you mean *they* took our son? Who is they? And where is he?" I wanted to blow her fucking head off. "Somebody better start bumpin' their fuckin' gums." I looked around at all of the sullen faces and knew this was bad.

Her brother Damon stood up. "Why don't you take the baby upstairs, Oni. I'll fill Faheem in."

"Tell him everything, Damon. I want him to know it all. That's the least we can do."

"Somebody better tell me something. And if they took my son, then where is the muthafuckin' police? Why y'all muthafuckas sittin' here so damn calm?" I was slowly but surely losing it.

Oni grabbed up Lil' Jaz and I turned to Damon. He was the only one who seemed to want to talk. "So what's up? Where's my son?"

"Look, sit down so we can fill you in." Damon was getting upset.

"Nigga I don't want to sit down. I want to know where the fuck is my son. Talk muthafucka." And talk he did. For the next fifteen minutes. By the time he finished, you best believe I was sitting down.

KYRA

Mrs. Bankston came and took me into her office and sat me down. She said she had just called Nurse Wright and she was on her way over. The valley girl chick was seated next to Mrs. Bankston.

"Ms. Brown, we may have some good news for you. I want you to listen closely to what Keli here is about to tell you."

Keli scooted her chair in front of me. She took my hand. "The name you are going by, that is not your name. Your name is Kyra. Kyra Blackshear. You were a medical student at UCLA. You are married. Don't remember his name, Michael, Marvin or something. But if I saw him, I would know him and you guys have a daughter. Her name is Aisha and a couple of times you even brought her up to the school," she paused and smiled. "I remember all this about you because we took two semesters together." The look on her face said that she felt sorry for me.

My head was starting to hurt as I was trying to force the memories forward but nothing was coming up.

"Kyra, do you remember anything she just said? Any familiarities at all?" Mrs. Bankston cut in.

Did I remember anything? I was trying to digest what she had just told me. Did this chick just sit here and tell me that I had a family? A husband and a daughter? She said I had a name. My name is Kyra. I could feel the tears welling up in my eyes.

"How sure are you?" I asked Keli.

"Kyra, I recognized you as soon as I got past the hair. You always wore it short. Very short. Trust me, you don't forget lab partners, two semesters back to back and especially not with Professor Jurr. So, I'm sure. One hundred and ninety percent sure."

This time I allowed what she had just told me to sink in. I

wanted so badly to remember. I wanted to remember my husband and my daughter. My life. I couldn't take it anymore. She had my head reeling. I pulled my hand away from her. I needed to get away from these people who were telling me all about me. I stood up, knocking the chair backwards. I hurried out of the office and rushed to my room.

NURSE WRIGHT

I tapped lightly on Kyra's door, well prepared. Mrs. Bankston and Keli had filled me in. All I could say was, "thank you Jesus." My Savior may not come when you want Him to, but when He does, He's right on time. I opened the door to her room. She was laying across her bunk crying lightly.

"Kyra, can I come in? It's me, Nurse Wright." She jumped up and rushed to the door. I stepped in and she hugged me, crying into my chest.

"Why can't I remember anything, Nurse Wright? Where is my daughter now? And if I have a husband, why didn't he come looking for me?" She sobbed.

"Baby, it's going to be alright," I soothed her. "Now get yourself together and don't shed any more tears. The only tears I want to see are tears of joy. Don't worry because like Dr. Shalala said you will wake up one day and may remember everything in bits and pieces or all at once. But I hope that when your memory hits you it will be like the truck that smashed the roadrunner into that brick wall." She started laughing through her tears. I teased her about that because when I saw her always watching cartoons I got worried. And when I asked her why, she said she liked the roadrunner and Wile E. Coyote because it reminded her to never give up.

"This is all too much, Nurse Wright. I'm thinking all kinds of things."

"Baby, it's alright. Relax. Once you relax we can get to the next step."

She took a few deep breaths and began to calm down. "I'm relaxed. What is the next step?" There was no doubt that she was eager.

"We have to go down to the police station and file a report. They will follow up with Keli's story, contact the college, your husband, you know, let them know where you are." I felt her shudder and I could tell that she was petrified. "It will be fine. I'll be there for you, alright?"

It took her a minute but she finally said, "Alright."

"Then let's do this."

FAHEEM

You could hear a pin drop after Oni told me how they were into everything from trafficking to kidnapping to guns and dope. I told Oni to bring me my daughter so that I could get the fuck outta there before I added four more bodies to my resume. Plus I needed to clear my head so that I could figure out how I was going to handle this. Them muthafuckas were greasy, they were punks and none of them had ever bodied a muthafucka. And as soon as my son returned, I was getting full custody. The fucked up thing was that after talking to them I felt like shit because Jaz was more than likely telling the truth about Oni's skank ass. And what did I do? Put my baby out on the streets. And to think I almost gave this bitch some dick.

Damn.

JAZ

It was 6:12 a.m. but I was up studying when my cell rang. It was Faheem, so I let it go to voicemail. That nigga better not ever say another word to me, not in this lifetime. I looked at the text messages and of course his was right there on top. URGENT. CALL ME. If it wasn't for my daughter I would not have bothered to call him back.

"Is my daughter alright?" I asked as soon as he picked up the phone.

"*Our* daughter is fine. My son has been taken."

I thought about what he said and was sure that I misunderstood him. "What did you just say?" I could have sworn that my husband, my rock, was all choked up.

"My son, Jaz. His mom is into some shit and they took my son right out of his bed while he was sleeping."

I was up, on my feet and putting on my clothes. Despite the fact that I was furious with him, we were talking about a child. His child and my daughter's brother whose life was now in jeopardy. "I'll be right there."

ONI

"Steele or Stone, if my son has one strand of hair on his head harmed, I'ma"—Big Mike had snatched the phone from out of my hand. No sooner than Faheem had stormed out, we got the call from the camp who burst into my house and snatched up my son.

"Steele, if there's a problem we bring it to the table and discuss it. I don't even know what all of this is about. But I do know, you wouldn't like it if I burst into your home and pulled some bullshit like that. This shit is unnecessary. Let's meet, give me my nephew and then we can handle this shit like real niggas."

"Put him on speakerphone, Mike." I needed to hear the entire conversation. "Tell him I need to hear my son's voice. Let me talk to him, I need to know he's alright." My brother waved me off and turned his back to me. Soon after the call was disconnected.

He turned to us and said, "They want what belongs to them and they gave us forty-eight hours."

JAZ

I was sitting there in shock at what Faheem had just shared with me. Now he was on the phone talking to Oni. Here I was thinking that this bitch was running a legitimate business and here they were moving weight and robbing the drug dealers that came through their hotels.

Faheem hung up the phone looking stressed as hell. I felt sorry for him. Here he had just came into his son's life and now this. It hadn't even been a good couple of months.

Faheem hung up the phone and said, "I have to make a run. I'll be right back." He reached behind his waist and pulled out his Nine. "Take this. And if some muthafuckas come banging on the door, you shoot first and let God sort it out later." He put the Nine in my hand and headed for the door. When he came downstairs, he headed straight for the front door and I was right on his heels.

"Did she say who the people were?"

"No, only that they were the people who took my son."

"So what about the police? No one is going to call them?"

"I haven't figured it out yet, Jaz. It's going to be hard to call the police and say my son was kidnapped because his momma stole money and drugs from the dealer. Like I said, let me clear my head and then I'll know if I'm going to call my people or just handle the shit myself. Now lock me out."

I did. I stood there with my back against the door, looking stupid. I felt like I was on a movie set. This shit seemed so surreal.

FAHEEM

I left Jaz at the house, drove around for about an hour to clear my head and then headed back over to Oni's. I was like, damn, just when I thought I was out, I get pulled back in. Hell, I probably will end up having to relocate. I had already made up my mind to do what I had to do with or without these niggas. We was talking about my son. I had sworn to myself, if something happened to him, his mother was going to pay.

Oni let me in the house and as soon as she shut the door, she started that crying bullshit. "Pull yourself together. Crying ain't going to do shit to get my son back. You should of thought about that when you made your moves."

"I know that, but I can't help it." Since she saw that she wasn't getting any sympathy from me she turned around and I followed her into the kitchen.

Her three brothers and nephew were sitting at the kitchen table as if they was actually coming up with a plan.

"Look, I'm here to get as much info from y'all as possible. I just want to get my son back. I need to know who these niggas are and where they set up at. But I was also wondering since y'all dealt with them before, will they accept what y'all took back and call it a day? Or will they want war?"

"Man fuck them niggas!" her nephew spat.

"What the fuck is wrong with you? They got my son and you talking about fuck them?" I yelled.

"I didn't mean it like that. Shit, that's our nephew and we want him back too. I was just saying, don't let them dictate what moves we make. I am a cop. I can make some things happen."

I cocked my head to the side. Did this nigga just say out of his mouth that he's a cop? He picked up on my reaction.

"My auntie didn't tell you I was the law?" He looked over at Oni.

"Nah, she didn't. But since you are supposed to have some connections then simply give these people what they want, get my son back and let's call it a day."

"We can't. We talking about five hundred thirty thou and it was 100 kilos. We can't," Oni said. "The kilos have been sold and the money divided amongst us. I put all my share into some rental properties. It would take me months to liquidate."

"Can't? Can't? Bitch, we talkin' about my son." I banged my fist on the table. "I don't give a fuck! Somebody better start diggin' some money up, right the fuck now." You could have heard a pin drop if it wasn't for me breathing all hard. I needed these bama muthafuckas to see and understand that I was ready to take it out of their asses. "Let me ask y'all a question. Do you think it matters to this nigga about the keys? Can we just pay him for the 100 keys or is he on some bullshit saying he wants the drugs back and not the money?"

"Faheem, wait. Listen. We do have a plan," Oni said. She paused waiting to see if I was going to say something.

"Impress me, shit. Something y'all muthafuckas have yet to do. Speak."

"We was talking about it before you got here. The cat Steele is a youngin' on the come-up, but we can get him out the way. We need you. I need you to set everything up. All you have to do is listen and my brothers will tell you everything you have to do," Oni said.

I couldn't believe this bitch. She spittin' this bullshit plan to me as if this ain't her son too. What mother would put their own flesh and blood on the table. I see why I chose Jaz over her. I should have made the bitch choke to death on my dick.

After she finished flapping her gums about this bullshit that they want me to do, I looked around at these crazy muthafuckas as if they had just sprouted ten heads. Here they were ready to take a chance with my son's life as they used him as a pawn. I was livid and they saw that.

"Our plan, it will work. I know this dude, Faheem," Damon said. Just hear me out and I'll tell you why we have to do it like this. And I'll tell you why it will work."

JAZ

Someone kept calling the house phone and hanging up. I got my baby up, we went into the garage and jumped into the car and headed over to Oni's.

When I pulled up, I saw all of the cars in the driveway so I called Faheem. "Baby, I'm outside. Someone kept calling and hanging up so I didn't want to be there by myself. It could be nothing but I wasn't taking any chances."

"I'll be right there."

As soon as he came to the car I asked him, "Is everything alright? Who does all of those cars belong to?"

"Her brothers. I told you the whole damn family is involved in this bullshit." Faheem grabbed my hand and led me into the kitchen.

"This is my wife. She said somebody kept calling the house and hanging up. Oni, you think these niggas been following you?"

"I don't think so. If they have, I've underestimated them," the bitch had the nerve to say. I swear I wanted to spit in her face.

"Daddy, can I go and play with Faheem?" Lil' Jaz asked me. Everybody got quiet.

"Your brother is sleeping over at a friend's. I'll take you into the living room. You want to watch TV or play a video game?" Oni quickly said, obviously doing what she did best . . . lie and deceive. I did not want this shiesty ass bitch touching my child, but since Faheem was in war mode I gave her Lil' Jaz.

Faheem pulled a chair out for me and I sat down at the roundtable. I looked around at who was in the crowded room. When I focused on the brotha sitting in the corner, I did a double take. It was the detective who planted that shit in my car. The next thing you know I was up on my feet.

"You bitch!" I balled my fist and punched the shit out of Oni. The glass of liquid she had just put to her lips hit the floor, shattering.

Everybody was up and over to where we were in a flash. Her brother started to grab me but Faheem looked at him then said, "Don't get fucked up." Then he turned his attention to me, grabbing me by my neck.

"Jaz, now is not the time for this bullshit. What the fuck is wrong with you?"

I couldn't even speak. "Get my daughter, Faheem. Now. And as long as you fuckin' with this bitch, you will not have any contact with me or Kaeerah. Go get my daughter!" I screamed. I was about to go postal in that bitch as I shoved Faheem off of me.

"Jaz, what is—"

I cut him off. "I told you this skank ass ho was behind this shit. Hell, she probably set this whole kidnapping thing up, Faheem. I told you she ain't shit! Just go get me my daughter."

"What the fuck are you talking about?"

I pointed at the detective. "That's the nigga who planted the crank in my car and arrested me. So fuck you, fuck her and fuck all of y'all crazy muthafuckas. And fuck it, I'll get my own daughter, so I can get away from all of y'all sick fucks!" I was heated. I stormed to the living room and snatched my daughter off the couch. The poor thing didn't know what was going on. "That bitch got you blinded. Let me get outta her before I catch a case for real. And Faheem, you know I will. I won't give a fuck about going to prison."

"Hold up Jaz," Faheem jumped in front of me, trying to block me from leaving. The phone started ringing and his attention was briefly diverted so I used that moment to push him out of the way. I was outta there and rushing to the car. As me and my daughter got in I could hear Faheem going off on Oni and her trying to explain but I didn't give a fuck. But I did hope that they get their son back because not her, not Faheem will ever see my child again. It was officially over.

ONI

Shit just hit the fan for real. I was busted. Faheem stormed out after Jaz, while all three of my brothers were staring at me.

"Oni, don't tell me you did that shit. And you got Ronnie here to help you? You didn't even check with us before you pulled some stupid shit like that. And why? 'Cause you want that nigga back? That is so stupid." Big Mike was obviously disgusted with me.

"You was supposed to call a sit down before you made a move like that, Oni. You know the rules," Damon spat.

Mike looked at his son. "And you? You gonna jeopardize your whole career over some bullshit baby mama drama? You should of have sense enough to come to me before you even moved on this bullshit."

"Pops, my career is already on the line. I fucks with y'all remember?"

"Son, listen to me. I can keep you apart from this. But anything outside of this, that's on you."

"Now we got to deal with two crises," Wali said and he smacked the back of Ronnie's head.

SEVENTEEN

TASHA

I just saw Rick. My heart was pounding faster than roaches scurrying away from the kitchen light. I saw King Rick. It was him in the flesh. He was here in the city. He was alive. Alive and well. And what was spooking me even more was that the chick he was with reminded me of Kyra. Kyron was buggin' because he swore up and down that it was somebody I used to fuck with.

"Kyron, you heard what he said. He wanted to know what you were doing with his boy's wife."

"That's what he said?"

"Yes, that's what he said." He picked up that I was getting a little disturbed by his questions so he changed the subject.

"So, the nigga is a cop?"

"Yeah. He lived right down the street from us and he was a detective, a dirty one. But he loved him some Trae." I smiled as a few old memories ran through my mind. Kyron gave me a dirty look so I snapped out of it and kept on going. "I believe they did some things together, I just don't know to what extent. Him and my girl Kyra started messing around when Marvin started back getting high. We think Marvin is the one who deaded him . . . well, we thought he was dead. Trae even went to his funeral, which was obviously a staged one. That's why I'm trippin'. We hadn't seen him since. The nigga was supposed to be dead." I had to call Trae.

"Well, the muthafucka was out of line."

"And what would you have been pulling a gun out in a crowded restaurant?" I asked Kyron.

"Vindicated."

TRAE

I corrupted my mission and got my niece back to California safe and sound. The boys were still in Florida, so I had to call my Aunt Marva over to ask her to house sit and keep an eye on her for me. I wanted to surprise everybody, so I told my aunt not to tell anyone that she was here. I quickly got her settled and was out. I needed to get back to New York to go pick up my sons and to bring Tasha back home.

When I arrived in New York and had yet to catch Kendrick or Kyron, which only pissed me off more, I was forced to resort to some of my old tactics.

I set my plan in motion and then picked up my sons and headed back to Cali to drop them off, only to turn around and head back to New York. Yeah, lately I had become a flying muthafucka. Our private plane had become my new apartment. I'd been on and off that muthafucka for almost a week straight. I was showering, sleeping, the whole nine yards.

When I arrived back into the city, I went to my apartment and set the trap.

TASHA

We had just come back from getting a whole pizza from Famous Ray's. Its delicious aroma smelled up the car and my stomach was growling. I couldn't wait anymore. I opened the box and tore off a slice.

"Shorty, we about to go inside," Kyron said as he looked at me as if he couldn't believe that I was eating pizza in his ride.

Obviously this was his first time being around a hungry, spoiled, pregnant woman so I went easy on him. "I know, but my stomach is growling. Can't you hear it? And plus there's nothing like hot pizza right out the box." I looked at him as I took a big bite of my slice of pizza with extra cheese. The oil from the cheese was dripping down my chin but I didn't care. He turned the car off and we sat there. Me with my pizza and Kyron had rolled himself a blunt. We was sitting there chillin'.

The evening was crisp and clear. When we finished Kyron opened the door and was getting ready to get out, when out of nowhere this nigga comes and pulls the door back and then slammed it on Kyron's leg. "Fuck!" Kyron yelled out. It happened so fast, neither of us saw it coming.

"Get out muthafucka," the dude barked, holding the door with one hand and a .357 in the other. His partner appeared from the shadows holding a double barrel in Kyron's face.

I didn't know what to do. I knew that Kyron had a hammer, but before he could get to it the guy snatched him out the car so fast, patted him down and took it.

"Just let my Shorty go and we can do this."

"Nigga, that ain't your shorty," the dude with the burner said.

"Get out the car, Tasha," Kyron told me right before the dude punched him in the face.

I threw the pizza box down and went to open the door when another dude snatched it open, scaring the shit out of me. "Hold up. You are going to have to come with me." I looked over at Kyron and they had him on the ground whupping his ass. People walking past looked but kept it moving.

"Come on, get the fuck out," Dude glared at me.

I looked at dude closely and he looked to be my height and from the way he was cut up, the nigga lived in the gym or just got out of the pen. When he licked his lips, that's when I really got shook. But I promised myself that I was not going out without a fight. I got out of the car and yelled, "Somebody call the police. I don't know this guy! Help me! Help!"

He grabbed my arm and snatched my Louie. "Shut the fuck up!"

"If you want the bag, keep it. There is money there and you can have it all."

"Do I look like I came out here to rob you? Now look, I'm supposed to bring you back in one piece but if you don't cooperate, just like ya boy over there, you gonna get fucked up, too."

A limo pulled up and dude shoved me towards it. The back door flew open and I was pushed inside. When the door shut, I was sandwiched between two more fresh outta prison looking niggas. I turned back to look for Kyron but they were gone.

"You can stop shaking, we are not here to hurt you," the dude who was already in the limo said. I didn't even realize that I was shaking like a leaf.

"Then where are you taking me?" No one said a word. "What

are they going to do to him?" The new guy smiled. His partner made a call and simply said, "We got her and we are on our way."

After we got into Jersey, I soon noticed several signs saying Teterboro Airport. Teterboro is a small airport for many private jet holders. That's when it all clicked . . . *Trae*. Then I thought about Kyron. My stomach knotted up and my hands started sweating. They probably killed his ass. The limo pulled up to the third hangar. For real, I didn't want to get out of the car. As a matter of fact I had made up my mind that I wasn't going to get out and if I could, I would make a run for it.

Both of my escorts got out. The quiet one closed his door. The other one said, "This is your stop, Mrs. Macklin." So this lame knew my name all along. I kindly sat glued to the seat. "Yo, this is your stop. You need to get out."

I still didn't move.

"Deuce, she ain't gettin' out," he yelled to his partner.

The other door flew open. "Mrs. Macklin, just so you know, we have specific instructions to drag you off if necessary. So what's it going to be?"

I crossed my legs and sat back into the seat, making my stance obvious. "Tell my husband if he wants me, to come and get me. Why does he have to get y'all to do all of his dirty work?"

Deuce closed his door and came around to where his partner was. His partner grabbed my ankles and yanked me towards him. I swung at his face. Somebody gripped my arms. "Get the fuck off of me. Let me go!" I screamed.

The quiet one pulled a gun on me and said, "Dead or alive makes me no difference."

The look in his eyes said *Tasha get the fuck out*. I slid to the door and made my exit.

"Oh, so now you ready to walk on your own?" the one who took my purse said as he grabbed my arm yanking the rest of the way.

"Y'all better get the fuck off of me," I threatened.

"Jimil, let her go man." They both turned me loose. The one named Deuce held out my Louie.

"There's your ride right there. Go ahead up the stairs. Nice doing business with you," smartass Jimil said.

"Fuck you." I snatched my bag from him and headed for my ride in the sky. Each step I took weighed me down more than the previous one.

TRAE

I fixed my stare on the portrait of the waterfall in hopes of not losing my composure. I was refusing to believe that my marriage had evolved into this spectacle and just how off the chain Tasha had gotten. As far as Kyron was concerned, whatever happens happens. But at least nobody can say that I didn't give the nigga ample warnings.

TASHA

I stepped onto the plane and the stewardess Maggie greeted me. "Mrs. Macklin, good to see you again. Let me take you to your seat. Mr. Macklin is waiting on you."

I didn't say anything, even though she was still talking. I had completely blocked her out. I was focused on preparing myself for *Mr. Macklin.* He was seated, looking calm as ever, legs crossed as if he was posing for the cover of *GQ* magazine. He gave the appearance of not having a care in the world. Of course he had that smirk on his face that said, "I told you I would find your ass and drag you back home." He motioned for me to sit down across from him.

The captain made an announcement to buckle up and prepare for departure. Maggie came by and asked if we would like anything to drink before takeoff. Trae told her no.

I sat there occasionally stealing glances at my husband. Of course, he did not take his gaze away from me and didn't open his mouth during the whole time we were ascending up into the air. When the fasten seat belt sign turned off, I got up to go to the restroom. As soon as I closed the door I went to the toilet and threw up. I wasn't sure if it was from fear, the flying or from the delicious slice of greasy pizza I had just gobbled down.

I made it to the sink and checked out my surroundings. I loved this bathroom. It reminded me of an upscale nightclub. It had a plush, butter soft leather sofa, a marble vanity table and all of the amenities you could think of, except for toothbrushes and toothpaste. I hit the call button for Maggie. I hoped that there was some mouth utensils somewhere around. In the meantime I would just hang out in here as long as I could.

I sat on the sofa, tilted my head back and closed my eyes. Once again my thoughts turned to Kyron. I was wondering if he was dead or alive. If he was dead what would I do? If he was still alive what would he do next?"

The bathroom door flew open and instead of it being Maggie, in waltzed Trae. "What are you doing?" he asked me.

"What did you do to him, Trae?"

I swear he looked like he turned into the devil. The whites of his eyes turned red, his nose flared and his face was contorted. He looked at me as if I had lost my mind. "Come again?"

"What did you do to him?"

"Ask me about the next nigga again and I promise you, I'm gonna lace your jawpiece."

"Trae, I just asked you a simple question. You can't give me a simple answer? What. Did. You. Do. To. Him?" My dumb ass obviously forgot who I was talking to and what he promised to do to me. Because the next thing you know he had punched me dead in the jaw, keeping his promise. My bottom lip started bleeding after I bit it and this nigga had the nerve to put his ear to my mouth. Yeah, this nigga has officially lost his muthafuckin' mind.

"Now what was it that you asked me?" When I didn't answer he yelled, "Speak up! I can't hear you."

TRAE

After that little incident, all I heard from my wife was some sniffles. I didn't want to hit her, but damn. How the fuck was she gonna ask me about the nigga who she was fuckin' on the side? I admit, if she would have fucked any other nigga I'm sure I would have been able to deal a little bit better, but she fucked a nigga who was supposed to be like family. She really had me fucked up.

"What do you want from me, Trae?" She asked through sniffles.

"You want to ask me about the welfare of the next nigga?" I wasn't ready to leave that shit alone. I was mad insulted.

She shook her head no.

"Good. Now that we got that out the way, clean off your

lip, come out here and sit down and I'll tell you what I want from you."

I left her in the bathroom and went to sit down. I saw that Maggie had left a tray of beverages and snacks on the table next to us. I needed to clear my head so I sparked up what was left of my spliff, hit it a couple of times and put it out. My wife finally decided to join me. She took the seat across from me looking like she lost her best friend.

I got right down to it. "Tasha, you know what I want. I don't even have to tell you. Why the fuck you think I'm chasing you from coast to coast? Because I ain't got shit else to do? I want my wife back. I want my family back together. If you are pregnant, I want to know who the baby belongs to. If it's not mine, I want you to get rid of it and stop fuckin' around like you ain't got no damned sense. That's what the fuck I want."

TASHA

No this nigga did not hit me . . . again and turn around and give me this long ass list of demands of what he wants. "Trae, what about what I want? I wanted you to stop fucking that Asian bitch. I wanted you to not bring home an STD. I wanted you to never put your hands on me. I wanted you to not break my heart into itty bitty pieces . . . like you promised me you never would." I had begun raising my voice.

His suave ass took a sip of whatever was in his glass. I swear I *wanted* to scream, "Fuck you!"

And while I'm at it, I am going to say, "Fuck all of you haters!" I'm sitting here thinking about how my life has turned into a

DVD series of Maury's first second and third seasons. Yeah, I've been fucked on the hood of a car by a certified thug nigga. And yeah, I have a fly ass, gangsta ass nut case for a husband. Yeah, I don't know who I'm pregnant by and for real, at this point, I honestly don't give a fuck. Why? Because my shit is still on point. I checked my Twitter account and all of these haters was on there tweetin' about . . . you guessed it . . . ME! So fuck this next ho emailing my girl Wahida talking about I'm a chicken head, I'm this, I'm that. NO! What I am is full of *Thug Matrimony, Every Thug Needs a Lady* and me and my girls all have *Thugs and we are the Women Who Love Them.* So the next time you out in cyber space flappin' ya gums, get it right. If you want a happy ending I suggest you go pick up a Harlequin romance. Wahida's shit is for the big dawgs, the street thugs and the bitches.

TRAE

I'm sitting here sipping on a shot of Jack Daniel's looking at and listening to my wife rant. I had to admit, that I must be fucked up in the head because I was more in love with her ass now than I was the day we met. This shit was making no kind of sense. And it was fucking me up because I didn't want to forgive her. She was glowing and the thought of the baby not being mine . . . words can't describe. I sat my beverage down and slid to the edge of the seat.

"Baby, I never told you I was perfect. I can't take none of that shit back. If I could, I swear on my cousin Shaheem's grave that I would. I would take it all back in a heartbeat."

"Trae, please." She sucked her teeth and gave me the hand.

I did a double take and took the hand in my face in mine.

I looked at this big ass rock on her finger and counted to four. Fuck ten. I couldn't get that far. "Tasha, what is this?"

"A ring, Trae." Her voice was trembling.

"I can see that. But it damned sure ain't the one I put on your finger. What the fuck?"

"Ain't nothing, Trae. Nothing at all." She turned away from me and tears began to flow down her cheeks. The devil was telling me to break her fuckin' finger off. The angel said, "No. Don't do that. Count all the way to ten this time." And miraculously I managed to do so. It wasn't easy. He then told me to simply take the ring off. The devil said, "Yeah, and flush that bitch down the toilet of the friendly skies." I slid it off of her finger, went into the bathroom and flushed it.

I came back and sat down. I started laughing. "You turned that nigga completely out, got his nose wide open. He actually proposed to you? Damn, girl. You really put it on the nigga. Just like you did to me. I ain't gonna lie, I'm jealous as fuck. Wait. Wait. Hold up. I bet you know what did it. That pregnant pussy. That's what took him over the edge. Oh, yeah. Ain't no turning back after a nigga hit that pregnant pussy. Your shit will bring the strongest nigga to his knees. I should know, right? I mean look at my ass. I can't turn back. I can't let you go." I was talking to myself more so than to Tasha.

"Trae, shut up!" She screamed at me. I guess she didn't want to hear what I was saying. "You started this shit, so now what?"

"You want your top lip to match your bottom?"

She sat back and crossed her arms and shook her head.

"Now back to your question. First things first baby girl. We gonna get the pregnancy test and that needle DNA thing. If you are not carrying my seed, we are getting an abortion."

TASHA

"We are not getting an abortion, Trae and that's my final answer. So where does that leave us?"

"So, what are you telling me? You think I'ma just sit back and give you a free pass to ride off into the sunset with this nigga? I don't think so."

"I'm not getting an abortion."

The next thing you know, this nigga snatched me up and started dragging me, to where I had no clue. That was until we came to a door and we were at the top of some stairs. Down below, I guess was where they kept the luggage and everything else. He dragged my ass down the steps. But when I saw the emergency exit, I panicked and started kicking and screaming. The closer we got to the emergency exit the more terrified I became.

"Trae, stop! Why are you doing this?" I screamed.

"You want to be with that nigga? Well, you can join him in hell. You think the Li Organization is going to kill you anyway, right? Well, I'll do them a favor . . . and that's my *final answer*."

He was trying to get the emergency door open but was having a hard time holding onto me and pushing the door open at the same time. I was frantically trying to break away from him. I couldn't believe this nigga was about to throw me off a plane. When he started kicking on the emergency door, I pissed on myself.

"Please, Trae don't do this," I begged. I had to get him out of the zone. It was now or never. "What if it's our baby? What if it's your baby?" He kept kicking. "Okay, okay, please. I'll get the abortion. I'll get the abortion. First thing in the morning I'll get the abortion." That did it. I got through. He stopped kicking at the door and looked down at me. "I'll get it, baby. I'll get it, I assured him."

The door at the top of the stairs opened and the pilot rushed down the stairs. "Mr. Macklin! Oh god . . . please. Calm down. Mr. Macklin, please . . . come back upstairs."

Trae dropped me to the floor I sat there trying to gain my composure as I watched him walk towards the steps.

"I'll get the fuckin' abortion!" I screamed after him.

Trae stopped, looked down at me, turned around, walked past the pilot and went up the stairs.

I had never been so scared and so embarrassed in my whole life. The pilot and Maggie helped me up and practically carried me up the stairs. I had pissed on myself and there was nothing that they or I could do about that. I didn't have any clothes and neither did anyone else. The pilot went to talk to Trae and Maggie took me to the ladies room. I told her thanks but wouldn't let her in.

"Are you sure you'll be alright?"

"I'm sure, thanks." I closed the bathroom door and locked it. I sat my pissy ass down on the plush butter soft sofa and didn't come out until the plane landed.

I was not about to lose my life over Kyron who was probably dead anyway. I was ready to get the abortion.

TRAE

I knocked on the bathroom door and when Tasha opened it, I handed her the pocketbook or whatever they called it. Of course I went all through it. Her ring was in there and I took her hand and placed it where it belonged. She was stiff as a zombie. Her hair was all messed up, the whole nine. Hell, if somebody tried to shove me off a plane, way up in the air, I guess I'd be a little shook too. I didn't say anything.

The limo took us to the house and it was a long quiet ride. Kaylin had called me several times. I guess it was to question me about Kyron. The nigga must have been alive. Good for him.

TASHA

When we pulled up to the house, Trae let me in and then he left. I went straight to the bathroom on the first floor, took off my pissy jeans, tossed them into the trash and jumped in the shower and cried.

The only thing I had to look forward to was seeing my kids who I was anxious to see. I hadn't seen them in a couple of weeks, however it seemed like months. I had meant to ask Trae if they were coming back from Florida this week, but after his little stunt I couldn't even think straight. I took my time in the shower, and collected my thoughts. I could no longer lie to myself, Trae scared the shit out of me. The game was over. Our family was more important.

I stepped out of the shower and dried off. I wrapped the towel around me and went upstairs. I heard a little peoples cough and it sounded like my baby, Caliph. That could only mean that my boys were home and Aunt Marva was most likely in the mother-in-law suite. I went into the kids' bedroom and turned on the lamp.

"My babies. My babies are home." I was so thankful to Trae for that as my eyes swelled with tears. I missed them so much. I didn't know who to kiss first, but then, there was a fourth body.

What the hell? I was a little scared to pull the comforter back. I counted the bodies again. "One. Two. Three . . . four." I knew I wasn't crazy.

A little arm raised up and the voice said, "Move over, Caliph."

"Oh, my God!" I knew that voice. But how could it be? I went over to the bed and pulled the cover back. "Aisha! Aisha! Wake up baby! Oh my God!" I screamed, probably waking up the entire neighborhood. I forgot about my drama for the time being.

My niece was back.

EIGHTEEN

NINA

I stood there watching my man pack his bag. No. I didn't want him to go to LA. Why? Because ever since I met this chick in the bathroom of a Dallas BBQ restaurant in New York, I noticed a slight change of attitude. Then when he started calling the number she stored in my phone and couldn't get through, he got fed up. And now he was on his way.

RICK

I'm laughing to myself as I'm packing my bag. Nina's standing here watching me acting like I ain't never coming back. I told her I'm going to check on a few things and I'll only be gone for a few days.

It's buggin' me out because I had a change of heart. I told myself to let sleeping dogs lie. Don't go back. Not even to visit. I was blessed to walk away once . . . alive. It was close though.

I was blessed to walk away from Atlanta. I hated it down there. That's two times I was blessed to walk away with a clean slate. However, I'm still a detective at heart and I've been one for almost seventeen years. I have learned to listen to my gut. But for whatever reason, this time is not a gut instinct. It's more like a pulling or a nagging. I'm being pulled to LA and the harder I fight it the stronger it gets. Obviously Nina is feeling it but doesn't know what it is, so she can only react by telling me not to go.

FAHEEM

Jaz was going through the house like a maniac, packing all hers and Kaeerah's shit. She was pissing me off. "Jaz, where the fuck do you think you are going?"

"Why should I believe you? You didn't believe me. You kicked me out of the house remember? And all because of that bitch. So the only question that comes to my mind is, 'Did you fuck her?'"

"Jaz, dead that. You know I ain't fuck her and you know that I didn't put you out because of her."

"I told you the bitch set me up and you didn't believe me. What the fuck does that say about our relationship? No, better yet, how do you think I felt sitting out on the gotdamn grass while you scolded me like a child, Faheem? Me and you are better than that. You let that bullshit just come between us. Like I'm some fuckin' hood-booger and not your soulmate. I'm not putting up with that shit. No. I'm out of here just like you said."

"No! You ain't goin' no fuckin' where!" I yelled as I started going crazy, throwing her shit back in closets and dressers.

Kaeerah, our little Jaz came into the bedroom. "Why are y'all fighting?"

Me and Jaz looked at each other.

"Y'all don't love each other anymore?" she asked in her innocent voice. This pierced through my heart. I walked over, and picked her up. I looked into her little eyes and explained. "Because daddy made a big mistake. I messed up and now your mother is mad at me and wants to move out. I love your mother very much and I don't want her to move out. I want for all of us to stay here. Tell your mother to stay here."

"Mom, don't be mad at daddy because he's sorry. And don't leave. We don't want you to leave. We all belong here." My daughter came over to where I was and began to help me unpack Jaz's stuff.

JAZ

Oh he's good. That was a very low and dirty little trick to get our daughter in on this shit. If it wasn't for Kaeerah, I swear to God, I would have left my husband for good. She came into our bedroom at the right time. I meant it. I was out. They unpacked all of my stuff while I sat outside on the front porch trying to cool off. When they finished Faheem came outside to join me.

"When this crisis is over with your son, I am out of here."

"Jaz, I'll be man enough to admit that as soon as that shit went down, I tripped. So you mean to tell me that you're going to hold that against me? Because of that one mistake you're going to leave me?"

"Faheem, my mind is made up."

He grabbed my hand. "There is nothing I can do or say to make you change your mind?"

"No."

"You are overreacting, you know that right?"

"You overreacted when you threw me out and without a second thought. Oh yeah, that's right, I sucked your dick so good your mind was all fucked up. Ain't that how you put it?" I had to remind him of what he said to me.

"I didn't mean that shit. In the heat of the moment I was pissed at you and I did regret it after the fact. That's no excuse. But having that shit happen all over again after what we went through before came back to haunt me and it fucked my head up. I was fuming and I couldn't see straight, let alone think straight. Cut me some slack Jaz, damn."

"Cut you some slack? Sometimes you can be really selfish, Faheem. Let's look at the reality of this situation, here we are fighting over some bitch you fucked while mad at me. Then let's look at the fact that she has a child the same age as ours, which tells me you was fucking me and this bitch raw at the same time. Hell, I'm still dealing with that shit. I know that bitch still wants you, and when shit didn't go her way she gets me arrested. Now all of a sudden your son is missing and I'm right here for you like always. I have always supported you Faheem, but when I needed you, you turned your back on me."

Faheem sat there silent, I guess he was trying to digest my point.

"Baby you right. And when this shit is over I'm going to make it up to you. I promise."

I heard him but I didn't even bother to respond, I just changed the subject. "So what about Lil' Faheem?" I knew it was no longer about me and him right now. I couldn't imagine what it would be like if my daughter was missing.

"I need you to go stay with Angel or Tasha while I do me. Can you do that for me? I won't be able to concentrate worrying about if you two are safe or not."

I thought about what he said and it wasn't sitting right with me. "It don't smell right to me Faheem. First off, them mutha-fuckas over there are too damn calm. They acting like this is all a formality."

"That's because they giving me the impression that they parlé with these muthafuckas all of the time," Faheem said.

"You need to call Sadow, like yesterday. If something goes wrong Faheem, you need be one step ahead of the game."

KYRA

Me and Nurse Wright stood in the hallway of the police station. I had accepted that my name is Kyra Blackshear. I am a registered student at UCLA. I was working on my Masters. From what I understood, we now had to get a court order to subpoena my records from the university. They were being real hard asses. My school records had vital information, references and contact numbers or so they claimed. I didn't want to get my hopes up. The detective assigned to my case was also doing a California, DMV search. They said being a University student, I most likely had a license. It was ironic that I was no longer in a rush to get all of this information. Because once I got it, what would I do with it? They said that since we are living in the information age, everything is on line and they would have me back home in no time. There was no turning back now.

ONI

I was lying in bed, gazing at myself through the mirrored ceiling when I decided to call Faheem to come over so that we could talk.

"About what?"

"What I did to Jaz."

"Oni, why would you pull some shit like that?"

"Faheem, I apologize. It was very immature of me," I told the truth . . . well part of it.

"Yeah, it was fucked up and if you thought it was going to get us closer, it only pulled us farther apart." Faheem stated matter of factly. It felt like he rammed a stake into my heart.

"Did you use to fuck this nigga who took my son?" he asked me, catching me totally off guard. "You had to. Shit is too informal for you to have not."

I didn't say anything.

"Did you?"

"Yeah."

"Ain't this some shit!"

NINETEEN

ANGEL

I rose from my bed and I looked at the clock wondering who was calling me so damn early.

"Angel, I miss you. My true partner in crime."

When I caught Tasha's voice I had to smile.

"You want to go catch a baller tonight? " she was teasing and giggling but I could still hear the stress and sorrow in her voice.

"Bitch, we ain't twenty-one no more. So act like it."

"Girl, I wish we was. I wish I could turn back the hands of time. I swear I would do it right this time."

"Sorry that we couldn't make it to Stephon's funeral. We did send some flower arrangements."

"I saw them and thank you."

"I called you for days trying see how you were doing but I couldn't reach you. What happened?"

"I'll have to tell you that in person." I could hear the lump forming in her throat and decided to let that go but not all of the other bullshit she was caught up in. "So why are you calling me at 5:30 in the morning? Where are you? Trae hasn't killed you yet? What the fuck is going on, Tasha? "

"Well, he found me and no, he didn't kill me but he tried and now I'm back home."

"Well he should have. What is all this drama I'm hearing about?"

"Listen smartass, the story about my cousin is a long one. I'll tell you about that later. But you ain't going to believe this. Get Jaz on the phone." Tasha's mood went from shit to sugar and she now sounded like she was bubbling over.

"Bitch, are you serious? It's 5:30 in the morning, Tasha."

"Trust me. Get her on the phone."

I dialed Jaz's house phone and clicked Tasha in.

"Yeah," Jaz answered.

"Damn, why you answer the phone like that?" Angel snapped.

"Because somebody keeps calling and hanging up. Girl, we got some drama down here that is making my head spin. You are not going to believe this."

"Well hold that thought because you are going to want to hear this," Tasha said.

"Hey, Tasha. I was getting ready to call both of y'all. Which one of y'all want to put up with me and Kaeerah?"

"Girl, listen to me first!" Tasha snapped. "Now guess what? Guess who's at my house?" Tasha was fully animated.

"Who?" I asked.

"Come here. Say hi to your Auntie Jaz and Angel."

We could hear fumbling in the background and then a little voice said, "Hi Auntie Jaz. Hi Auntie Angel. I miss y'all."

I sat up in the bed. Tasha jumped back on the phone. "Did

you hear her? Did you catch your niece's voice? She is so big and she looks so much like Kyra it's scary. Y'all got to see her."

"That was Aisha?" Jaz asked.

"Aisha, y'all! Aisha is back!" Tasha screamed.

"Oh my God!" I screamed too. Shit everybody else was screaming and my ass woke Kaylin up.

"Red!" Kaylin barked. "What the fuck, yo?"

"Baby, Aisha is at Tasha's house," I slapped him on the back.

"Angel," he growled.

I lowered my voice and got out of the bed.

"How did she get to your house?" Jaz took the words right out of my mouth.

"Trae made it happen and that's all I can tell you. She was here when I got here." Tasha admitted. "I need to talk to the both of you. I need to see y'all. Please come out here within the next few days. I really need it. Each and every one of us need our asses kicked for allowing us to go this long without getting together."

"I can't even argue with that," Jaz said. "Me and Kaeerah will be on the first thing smoking."

"Oh goody!" Tasha screeched. "I can't wait. Call me as soon as you are on your way."

"Tasha, what is Aisha saying? Is she talking about her mother? Where is Marvin? How did Trae get her? I swear that nigga is the truth." I was anxious to know while at the same time scheming on how I can take a quick run out to Cali. I needed to see and talk to Tasha and especially my niece.

"She is not saying anything. I didn't give her a chance to. As soon as I saw her I called y'all. Oh shit!" Tasha screeched as if she was in pain.

"What's the matter with you?" I wanted to know.

"What happened?" Jaz asked.

"I just had a sharp pain in my stomach. Shit. It felt like a cramp. Make sure y'all call me later. I need to lay my ass down. Y'all don't have a clue what I've just been through. Let me go. Love you guys." She hung up.

"Damn, Jaz. I forgot that our girl is supposed to be pregnant."

"Yeah, and it don't sound like she's alright. We do need to get up there. And I got some shit to tell y'all. They took Faheem's son."

TRAE

Even though it was the wee hours of the morning, I didn't care. Shit, when do dope fiends actually go to sleep? The last time I stopped by Marvin's favorite get high partner's crib, she was nowhere to be found. I hoped I would find her ass this time. She was my last hope. I was hoping that somebody had told her where Kyra's body may be. I was obsessed with finding out. We all needed that closure.

As I pulled onto the block and stopped, two niggas were coming out of Mimi's house. I deaded the engine and got out. All of the lights were on inside and the front door was cracked. I knocked on it.

"What y'all niggas forget?" Mimi's raspy voice asked. "Ain't no refunds. And what the fuck y'all knockin' for? The door is open."

I stepped inside and Mimi was sitting at the kitchen table. "Girl, you live in Compton. Not Beverly Hills. Talkin' about the door is open," I teased her.

"When it's your time to go, it's time to go. Ain't nobody but junkies coming up in here." She looked up at me and then lit her cancer stick. "Well come on in and grab a seat. Why you just standing there? I heard you been by here and Blue told me you been down there."

"How you doin', Miss Mimi?" I asked, looking around at her nasty house.

"Reason I ain't been around when you came lookin' was because I was in the hospital."

"Oh, yeah. How come?" I grabbed a chair and got comfortable.

"Kidney trouble. Was surprised it wasn't more than that. An old dope fiend like myself. You want sumthin' to drink?" She stood up.

"Nah, I'm good."

"I got some bottled water in here," she insisted.

Mimi was tall, skinny, and black. She had big eyes that bulged. She had a red scarf tied around her head. I watched as she sat a bottle of water down in front of me and took her seat.

"Got a call today from some people down in Kentucky. They say that the police done found Blue in his house dead. They say he been shot to death. If I wasn't a God minded person, I'd think that Blue paid somebody to kill him."

What Mimi said caught me by surprise, "Why do you say that?"

"Blue never quite got over Kyra getting shot, knowing she came here to save him that day. He said he couldn't face her. The guilt was too much. That's why he took the baby and left. The night all the shit happened, I was the one who called the ambulance. When they pulled up out front, they put Mook and Fish in body bags. Yes, they did. Zipped 'em right on up. Junie survived his wound to the stomach, but somebody killed him not too long ago. Blue never admitted it, but everybody knows that he killed that boy. Now that girl—Kyra—unh uh. Nope. They didn't put her in one of them body bags."

My heart raced, "Are you sure?"

"Positive. I stood out front and watched everything. The medics loaded her into the ambulance and hauled her away. I told Blue that."

"I don't believe that."

"I swear on my own daddy."

"And you told Blue that?"

"I sho' did."

"Well if you right, then where is she? She just up and disappeared. That shit don't sit right with me. Why would he leave her for dead if she wasn't and he knew it?"

"I told you. He couldn't and he refused to face her." She took a pull off her Newport and blew out smoke rings. "So you got the little girl?"

"Yeah, we got her."

"That's good. My gut told me you had her. The child needs a stable home. Now Isis and her momma is making arrangements to have the body shipped here to Compton to bury it. At least that's the last thing I heard and that's what they think. But you know his brothers in Jersey ain't goin' for that. They want to bury him up that way. So we'll see how it all plays out. Black people always fight over the wrong bullshit."

I allowed my thoughts to drift. I wanted to question Marv again but it was too late, he was gone. I sat at Mimi's kitchen table for a good half hour just thinking about all of the hustlin' and sacrificing we did to move out here, and for what? All it did was fuck everybody up. I stood up. It was time for me to go.

"You leavin' so soon?"

"Yeah. I've imposed enough."

"Well don't be a stranger. Trae, he did love that girl. And just so you know it, Blue always had nothing but good to say about you."

"Wish I could say the same about him."

KYRON

The last thing I remember is three niggas whipping my ass and they probably would have killed me if them white ladies hadn't started screaming.

I opened my eyes and thought that I was seeing things. Mari was standing there.

"Where . . ."

"You're in the hospital, Kyron."

"What are you doing here? You hate me that much that you wildin' out and sent muthafuckas out to kill me?" I asked her.

"Don't flatter yourself. I'm only here because the police called me. They found my number in your wallet. If you are so done with me, why are you holding onto my number?"

I raised my arm and it was stiff and heavy. It felt like my head was bandaged up but I wasn't sure because at the same time I couldn't feel my body.

"Kyron, you haven't been out of prison a good six months and look at you."

"Did you call anybody?"

"No, not yet."

"Good. I don't want anybody to know I'm up here but Kendrick. I'ma give you his number."

"Kyron, who did this to you?"

"Why? What's the damage? I can't even feel my body."

"Fractured skull, broken arm and broken rib cage. But you'll live. Who did this?"

"Take down this number." I rattled off Kendrick's number. "Call him and tell him where I am."

She grabbed her cell phone and called Kendrick. When she hung up she said, "I know you fucked up right now, so I'm not going to throw salt in your wounds. However—"

"Oh shit. Here comes the *however*."

"Don't think for a second that I don't know about that bitch you been running around with. I'ma give you a pass for this one only because I know how niggas act when they first get out of prison and have access to some new pussy. Y'all act like y'all don't have no damned sense. But I'm telling you Kyron, stay focused. We got too much money on the fucking table for you to be acting like a fucking fool." She went over to the chair and sat down.

TRAE

Daybreak was on its way in when I stepped into my house. Tasha hadn't even been home for a day and I already could feel the difference. We were going to make this right. I felt it.

I stopped at the kids' bedroom. They were sound asleep. I went to the guestroom and it was empty. That made me feel good because that meant Tasha was in our bed. When I stepped into the bedroom, she reached over and turned on the lamp. I sat on the edge of the bed.

Tasha had a funny look on her face. "What's the matter?"

"I had a sharp pain and then I went to the bathroom, I saw that I was spotting." She said as she sat up.

I looked at her to see if she was disappointed, angry or what, but saw nothing, except for a swollen bottom lip. "I'll take you to the doctor whenever you're ready. How are you feeling now?" I asked her.

"No more sharp pains."

"I ain't going to front, I'm hoping that you lose the baby so that I won't have to live with subjecting you to a fuckin' butcher. But if you don't lose it, fuck it. You know what you gots to do." Just thinking about it was getting me all amped up.

Tasha got quiet. I thought she was going to respond to what I said but instead she changed the subject. "Thanks for bringing Aisha home. I owe you for that. Kyra wouldn't have wanted it no other way."

"You know I'll do *anything* for you. Come on downstairs. Let me cook us some breakfast," I told her.

TRINA

When Kendrick got the call I knew it had something to do with Kyron. He jumped up and started getting dressed. Just like that, his whole mood changed.

"What's the matter? It's Kyron isn't it?"

"He's in the hospital."

"What?" I threw the covers off of myself. "What happened? Was that my sister?" I was now fumbling around looking for my clothes.

"No, it was his ex."

"Then where is my sister?" My stomach knotted up just thinking about it.

"I don't know. Hurry up and get dressed. We about to go find out."

I quickly started putting on my clothes. I grabbed my cell

and called my sister. Of course she didn't answer. "If something happened to my sister Kendrick . . . I swear I'ma—"

Kendrick chuckled. "You gonna do what Trina? You ain't no street nigga. Shut the fuck up and get dressed."

No this nigga did not just call himself checkin' me. He don't know me like that. "That's my sister, Kendrick."

"And that's my cousin, Trina. So chill the fuck out and we about to go see what happened."

We arrived at New York-Presbyterian in forty minutes. Kendrick broke every traffic law known to man. Then when we got there they had the nerve to tell us to come back, visiting hours were at noon. We snuck upstairs and slipped into his room. Some model looking chick was sitting next to his bed, thumbing through a magazine. I have to admit that bitch was bad.

She looked up. "Kendrick." She said dryly.

"Mari."

"I didn't want to leave him here by himself, even though he wanted me too. I wasn't going to leave until you got here. Tell him to call me when he's ready to come home." She stood up, looked at me dirty, grabbed her purse and said to Kendrick, "You too huh?" She had a smirk on her face, shook her head and walked out.

"She gone man?" Kyron asked, startling both of us. His head was all bandaged up and his arm was in a brace.

"Nigga, yeah she gone. Why you playin'? I thought your ass was in a coma," Kendrick spat but was sounding relieved.

"I had to act like I was in one just to keep her from grillin' me. Sit me up. I'm tired of laying here on my back. I need to get the fuck outta here."

"What the fuck happened, yo? Don't tell me Trae did this," Kendrick said.

"What's up Trina?" He asked me as I raised the head of the bed. I guess he could see the desperation on my face.

"Where was my sister when all of this happened? Is she alright?" As bad as Kyron looked, I could imagine what my sister would look like. I don't know about the two of them, but I saw Trae's hand in all of this. I know they didn't think that he was going to take that shit laying down. If I wasn't before, I knew now that I was on his shit list.

"She should be. Trae sent his henchmen to take me out and to take her home. I haven't talked to her since. Yeah. Them mutha-fuckas would have killed me if this group of white ladies hadn't started screaming and shit. They was wildin' out," Kyron said. By the look in his eyes it was as if he was replaying the incident in his mind.

"Well nigga, I guess you can say, today is your lucky day," Kendrick told him.

"Sheeit, everyday is my lucky day."

"Whatever, nigga," Kendrick said.

"I still won't be able to relax until I'm sure that she's alright. Call her for me," Kyron told me.

"I just did. She didn't answer."

"Use this hospital phone right here. She don't know that number."

I called her cell phone again and she didn't answer. So I dialed her house phone and had the call on speaker.

TASHA

Trae had pulled out the waffle iron and was cooking a breakfast of homemade waffles, turkey sausage and cheese eggs. He was fixing my plate when the phone rang. New York Presbyterian on the caller ID threw me off guard, so I answered it.

"Hello."

"Tasha, it's me. Are you alright? Why didn't you call me, girl? What happened?" It was my sister.

"Trina, I'm okay." Trae turned and gave me this look. I hit the speakerphone button because I didn't want any drama. Everything was going to be out in the open.

"Kyron is in the hospital all bandaged up. Me and Kendrick are up here now. He wants to talk to you."

"Trina, stay out of the middle of this shit. Whatever was going on between me and Kyron is over. I won't be talking to him anymore. I—"

Trae cut me off. "Is that nigga listening? Let me get in his ear," Trae spat.

"Shorty, you alright? Where are you?" Kyron was acting as if Trae didn't exist.

"She's home nigga, where she belongs. I guess that ass whipping didn't send the right message. Tasha, tell this nigga who you want to be with."

"Kyron, it's over. I'm staying with my husband."

"Naw baby, that ain't clear enough. Tell this nigga that he was just a revenge fuck and that you were just having some fun and using his ass, trickin' him out for his money."

"Kyron, you were just a revenge fuck which I told you from day one."

"Kyron, you there nigga?" Trae was fucking with him in the background. "You sound like you don't believe her. You want to know how to tell that it wasn't serious?"

"The only thing I can tell is your wife been having fun

slidin' on my dick like she more single than married," Kyron spat.

"Yeah, nigga but did she suck it?"

"This some bullshit," I heard Kendrick say.

Kyron got quiet.

"If you could tell me right now that she sucked your dick, then you could have her. I would just walk away. But she didn't did she?" When Kyron didn't respond, he said, "I'ma take your silence as a no. Nigga, I know my wife. The only dick knocking them tonsils back is my big black one. So stop calling my wife. Leave us the fuck alone and be glad that out of respect for your moms and brother, I let your ass live. Oh, and the baby that you was all excited about, after I cook my wife breakfast, feed her and get my dick sucked, I'ma kill that muthafucka. So go plant one in ya own bitch."

I took a deep breath. Now this was the hard part because Kyron wanted this baby so bad. "Kyron, I am getting an abortion this morning."

"Hang up the phone, Tasha."

TWENTY

TASHA

After we hung up with Kyron, Trae did exactly as he promised. Even though shit was awkward, he cooked me a wonderful breakfast, fed me and then asked me to give him some head, lips swollen and all . . . and I did. It reminded me of old times and it felt good.

I then called my doctor and made an appointment for that afternoon. No sooner than I got off the line with her I caught another sharp pain. And then another one. I was doubled over. Trae found me balled up next to the dresser and called an ambulance. Sure enough I had a miscarriage. True to his word, Trae killed that baby.

FAHEEM

I dropped Jaz and Kaeerah off at the airport and then scooped up Wali. I had to get the skinny on this Steele nigga before my peeps from up North showed up. Wali was instrumental in setting up the meeting and I couldn't wait to be done with his good for nothing ass. I swear Oni and her brothers all are a bunch of simple muthafuckas. They don't know their asses from their elbows. I still can't figure out how they were getting away with all of the shit they were into.

They definitely wouldn't have been getting over like this on no up north niggas. The only way they could be of any use to the situation was to give me 411 on this Steele cat and put the money up. I took care of the keys and I'm making them muthafuckas pay for it. I was also able to get all of the firepower that we needed. I couldn't trust them. If I was going to go down it would be from my doing. I had to make a call to up North, but I was gettin' ready to get this shit poppin'. The only thing left for me to do was wait.

JAZ

Faheem dropped us off at the airport. When I heard that his family from up North was coming, I began to pray. The only time he called on them was when it was time for war. Before the flight I sent Tasha a text telling her that me and Kaeerah was on our way and she sent me a text back saying that she was in the hospital. She had a miscarriage and she didn't know how long they were going to keep her. I then sent Angel a text and she said that she was on her way as well and that she had some info on Kyra. I was dying to hear about it.

KYRA

I was on pins and needles. I was now standing in front of the house that was supposed to be mine. It had a *For Sale* sign sticking up out of the lawn, listing the real estate contact. I wrote down the number and stood there.

"Excuse me lady. Do you want me to take you somewhere else?" The cabbie asked me.

"Yes. Give me a minute." I walked around to the backyard in hopes of remembering something. I couldn't. Nothing looked familiar.

"Are you ready?" The impatient driver asked me. I guess he saw that I was looking at the neighbor's house.

"I'm ready."

We headed for the address that was listed as my contact in case of emergency, Tasha Macklin. I said a quick prayer, asking that if her house was for sale, that I would have the strength to handle it. Because if it was, I'd be shit out of luck and the only thing left to do would be to call Nurse Wright. She didn't want me to come out here by myself but I insisted. I felt that I had to start somewhere. If I was going to reclaim my life, I had to do it on my own. I was hoping that I had the right address because it was taking forever for us to get there.

"Excuse me," I said to the cabbie. "Are you going the right way?"

"Yes ma'am, I am. According to the GPS system we are one and a half miles away."

I sat back in the seat. I rubbed my stomach, trying to slow down the butterflies, but it wasn't working. I peeked up at his GPS and saw that we were close. We made a left turn and the houses were gorgeous.

"O.J. used to live in this neighborhood."

I guess the cabbie called himself a guide, giving me a tour at the last minute. But I didn't care about no O.J. I had my fingers crossed hoping that a *For Sale* sign was no where to be found.

The cab slowed down. Thank God there was no For Sale sign posted. Toys were tossed around on the freshly manicured lawn but it was quiet.

"Thank you." I told the cabbie and paid him his fare.

"Do you want me to wait?"

"No. I think I'll be alright here."

"Well just in case, here's my card if you need me to come back."

I took it from him, got my stuff and got out. I was sick of riding. That uncomfortable plane ride. The long cab drive. I was hungry and was ready to relax. I waited until the cabbie pulled off and was out of sight before I trudged up the walkway, getting more excited with each step I took. I reached the front door and sat my bags down. I rang the doorbell. I rang it again and again and again. No one answered.

FAHEEM

We had just pulled up to an abandoned club not too far from Chandler Road. I immediately went into war mode. I looked over at my cousins G and Snell and said, "Our main objective is my son's safety. I don't want no cowboy shit when we get in there."

"C'mon, nigga. You know we got you Fah. That's why you got us down here," my cousin G said. "Once little man is safe if them niggas flinch we killing everything moving."

I checked my gun, popped the locks and we rolled out. Oni's punk ass brother was in the Lexus behind us. The *only* reason I let dude roll with us was because they wouldn't meet with us unless at least one of them muthafuckas who stole from them was present. I gave him the signal, he deaded his engine, got out and met me at the trunk of my ride. I took the dope out, checked it over, zipped it up in the duffels and slammed the trunk shut. I had one bag and gave Snell the other one. We headed to the back door, looking around the deserted street for witnesses in case shit got ugly.

There was two niggas standing guard. They gritted at us, let us in and followed us. The slim nigga led the way while the other, who looked like a linebacker, took up the rear. My adrenaline was charged up. I wanted to just start busting niggas right then and there. But I knew I had to be cool until I got my little man out of harm's way.

When we got to the back this fag ass nigga Steele was sitting in a high-back leather chair like he was a fucking don or some shit. The image of him toking a cigar vexed me as much as the smoke that clouded the room. I wanted to hawk and spit on this skinny, dread-headed muthafucka.

"Aiight, we here. I got your shit, now where is my son?"

"Who the fuck is you?" Steele spit, mean mugging me as if I gave a fuck.

"Usually I'm a niggas worst fucking nightmare but today I come in peace. I just want what belongs to me and in exchange I'm giving you what belongs to you," I said as I patted the duffle bag I was holding and nodded to the one Snell had.

"Let me see what y'all working with."

"Let me see my son." Fuck the bullshit.

The nigga took a minute to size up the situation, then he nodded at his boy. There was a door behind him and when he opened it a chick came out with my son, who was blindfolded and had his hands taped together. It took everything within my power to not lose control.

"Aiight, you see him, now let me see my shit."

My nostrils flared up. I took a deep breath then unzipped the bag so that he could see the dope. Snell did the same thing.

"Pass it over here."

"Nah, nigga same time." Who the fuck this nigga think I am? I ain't new to this shit. And just as we were getting ready to make the exchange I hear Wali's punk ass yell out.

"Y'all niggas foul as hell. Who the fuck steals little kids?"

Steele rose to his feet yelling, "Muthafucka you and that bitch violated my shit. I was happy never meeting you muthafuckas. You know how much money y'all cost me? Sheeit you lucky I let all of y'all live, nigga."

"Fuck you nigga!" Wali spat back. Now the whole room was beyond tensed up. My cousin G grabbed Wali in an attempt to try and calm him down.

But when I heard my son crying, "Daddy! Daddy!" I lost it.

"Hold the fuck up. Wali shut the fuck up!" I yelled at the top of my voice. I must have made the muthafuckin' walls shake because niggas got real calm, real quick.

"Now look, I ain't got no beef with you man. I ain't got shit to do with what they took from you. If you want to kill they ass when it's over you got my blessing. Shit I'll probably help you. But the only thing I'm concerned with is my son. If it wasn't for him I wouldn't give a fuck what happened to them muthafuckas."

Steele stood there taking in what I was saying.

"Yeah, aiight. Pass me the bag. And y'all release his son."

They took the blindfold off and pushed him towards me. I then went to pass the bag across the table. Once I got Lil' Faheem in my arms, Wali passed the bag of money. But when he reached in his pocket all hell broke loose. All I heard was,

"The nigga pulling a gun!" That's when bullets started flying. I felt one hit me in my shoulder and I flew back but not before grabbing my gat and letting off a few shots. Once I hit the ground I covered my little man with my body and I could see niggas falling all around us.

When the smoke cleared I was hit and I rolled off of Faheem over onto my back. The pain in my shoulder wouldn't let me move. I stared up at the ceiling for a minute. "You alright, lil' man?" I felt for his hand as I looked around again to see who was standing and who wasn't. Wali's ass was down which was cool with me because I was putting that nigga in a box myself for opening his mouth.

"Fah, you aiight nigga?" I heard Snell ask and he got up and came over to where I was.

"Did we dead all of them muthafuckas?"

"Steele and that pussy who was standing behind the chair got away with the bags."

"Damn! We gotta get out of here. I'm hit in my shoulder. Help me up so I can get little man in the car." When I looked at my son my worst fear had surfaced. He was bleeding from a hole in his head and his body was limp. "Faheem. Faheem. Get up. Daddy's here and he's not going to let anyone else take you away from him." I started calling him and shaking his arm. I tilted his head back and tried to give him mouth to mouth but it was too late.

"He gone, Fah. We got to get the fuck outta here." G said and put his hand on my shoulder.

"Get the fuck off me!" Tears came to my eyes as I tried one more time to give him life. But there was none there. I grabbed him in my arms and just held him tight.

"Fah this place is going to be crawling in a minute. He gone, Fah. We got to get the fuck outta here. Let me take him." My cousin tried to convince me once again.

But I was fucked up. I just wanted to feel the last warmth left in his body. Vomit threatened to spill out of me. I knew right then and there I would never be the same. It's over for Oni and her entire damn family. The only thing I could think about was how the streets was a muthafucka. Just as a nigga hung up his gats they go and touch my seed. I am vowing to *Justify My Thug* in blood.

RICK

I didn't realize how much I missed LA. I sucked in as much of the LA air that I could. Being here had me feeling rejuvenated. I used to run this city. I called Nina and told her that I wished I would have brought her with me and that we gotta talk about moving out here.

My ex-wife wasn't home, and being a detective, I know how much people are creatures of habit. She was the definition of habit. The bitch kept a tight and rigid schedule. And sure enough, I went to her house and she didn't answer the door. I went around back for the spare key and it was in the same spot, down in the flower pot.

I went inside and did a walkthrough. Surprisingly, I didn't get nostalgic. Most likely because she made sure it never felt like home to me in the first damn place. Everything that I knew of was gone. Everything was new. It looked like she had stripped the damn place. Stripped it of me.

When I went to her bedroom, I went straight to the closet to see what kind of man she had stuck her claws into. Whoever he was, I felt sorry for the muthafucka. But to my surprise the closet was full of nothing but women's clothes. I looked down at the shoes and it was the same scenario, all women's stuff.

I walked over to the dresser and she still had the picture of me and her at her sister's wedding. The rest of the pictures were of her and a dark-skinned sister with a mole on her chin. In some of the pictures they were hugged up, in others they were out to dinner, or in the backyard . . . my wife had turned to dyking. Ain't that some shit!

I left her bedroom and went downstairs to pour a drink. Hell, I ended up having two. I thought about how when I passed Trae's house I was scared to stop. Me. Muthafuckin' King Rick was scared of something. Why? I didn't know. Well I knew but I didn't want to accept it. It's not like I did them dirty and left on bad terms. The truth was I wasn't sure how he would treat me since I was responsible for Kyra's death . . . in a way. Hell, Tasha wouldn't even talk to me and I know she knew it was me who was calling her. Fuck it! I'm stopping by there. Hopefully they will hear me out, if not at least I can say that I tried. But either way, it felt so good to be back in LA, the City of Angels. I got in my rental, looked at where I used to live and smiled.

"Rick? Is that you?" Mrs. Singer, my old neighbor startled me.

I didn't even bother answering. I started the car and headed down the block. There was someone sitting on Trae's porch. She had her head in her lap, a little chick. *It can't be.* I parked and got out. The young lady looked up and then stood up.

"Excuse me. Do you live here?" She asked me.

Her voice went right through me. My heartbeat started racing. My mouth turned dry. I rushed up the porch. I stood there face to face with . . . her. I wanted to turn my back towards her and stop my tears but I couldn't. I couldn't take my eyes off of her.

"Do you live here?" she asked again.

I wanted to open my mouth to answer but . . . *how could this be?*

Finally I asked her, "Kyra is that you?" She cracked a smile. "You don't remember me?" I asked her.

"You know me?" she asked.

We stood there staring at each other for a good ten minutes. I didn't want to believe it was her. It couldn't be. The dreads was telling me it wasn't her. But the scar. I could see the scar. She was shot. That's when I knew. My eyes again welled up with tears.

She reached out and wiped them with her thumbs. I kissed her hand. She was trembling.

"Rick? Rick?"

She kept saying my name. Tears were rolling down her cheeks. She hugged herself as she backed up. "Rick. Your name is Rick. I remember you."

And then she fainted.

TWENTY-ONE

KAYLIN

Just when I thought I left the game behind the shit keeps coming back to haunt me. The last thing I wanted was to get in the middle of Trae and Kyron's nonsense. I'm now a legitimate business man and all of this hood shit is beneath me. I'm going to make one last attempt to clean up this mess between the two of them and then I'm done with them both.

I pulled up in front of Trae's apartment in the city and he was coming out the door with a blunt in his mouth. He hopped in the car and did his usual, reclined the seat all the way back. I pulled off thinking to myself that if these muthafuckas don't get their shit together, heads are gonna roll.

TRAE

As I reclined the seat all I could think was if I get up here and this nigga say one wrong thing he is going from the hospital bed to the morgue.

Kaylin was silent the whole ride. Shit, I didn't know why he was all fucked up, since it was *my* wife who was running around like a fucking chicken-head fuckin' with *his* brother. Keeping it 100, he should be lucky that we are only on our way to the hospital and not to a closed casket funeral.

KYRON

I opened my eyes and these two niggas was standing at the end of the bed with rocks in their jaws, faces tighter than a bitch on Botox. Looking at their faces I had to laugh. It was painful because it felt as if someone was digging a jackhammer through my skull, but I couldn't help myself, they looked funny as hell.

"Look, I ain't got all day so I'm going to make this quick. This whole situation is sloppy. People are talking, and talking loud," Kaylin said as he looked back and forth between me and Trae before he continued.

"I got a message from the dons. They said to make sure that the both of you understand it when they say, if y'all can't handle business they know someone who will handle it for you. They shouldn't be contacting me or us about this petty bullshit. And I'm no longer going to be the middle man for y'all two ignorant muthafuckas. I got my own family to worry about. So now, we need to lay all of our cards on the table. Speak now or don't say shit later."

I was sitting here listening to my little brother lecture me and this nigga. Trae's ass was standing there looking at me all square and shit. But before I could say anything he took Kay up on his offer.

"Looking at this nigga laying here in the hospital I think I said enough."

Then I mustered up the strength to bang on the side of my bed. That was as close that I could get for a clap, since I only had one hand operating.

"Big bruh, your speech, that was some beautiful Hollywood shit right there." I continued to bang on the side of the bed. "Y'all niggas can't be serious standing here sounding like two bitches." I pointed at Trae, "This nigga crying over some pussy." Then I pointed at Kay, "And baby bruh, you just flat out got soft on a nigga. Your bitch must carry your dick around in her purse. Keith Sweat ass bitches. I ain't want to believe it. I thought we had the game on lock. Niggas was telling me y'all was all wifed up and shit, crying about getting out the game. Get out? We used to fuck the shit outta New York, raw. I gave y'all the muthafuckin' keys to this city."

I turned my attention back to Trae. "And this nigga over here moved to Hollywood and grew a vagina." After I said that these two niggas looked at me like they didn't know who I was.

"You—"

Kaylin tried to interject but I shot that shit down. "Shut the fuck up nigga I'm talking. You said lay the cards on the table, and I got a whole muthafuckin' deck. I put y'all on, do a bid for y'all pussies and get outta jail thinking we gonna be out here making this paper, but y'all niggas ain't hungry no more."

"Hungry? Nigga we ate. It's time to live now."

"Let me finish nigga. Never in my whole life would I have thought that some nigga would try to kill me over some ass, and my own brother don't even got my fucking back."

"Man, what you talking about ass? That was this nigga's wife who you was fuckin' around with," Kaylin yelled back.

"So! We ain't in the game to love these hos. You suppose to hit it and pass it to the left. I ain't love that ho, it was just something to do."

I could see Trae's fist ball up tight, but I wasn't fazed. I laughed in his face before continuing to lay out my cards. "I don't believe this shit. Y'all use to be some killas, robbing niggas, selling more dope than the Pope pray on Sundays. Now these bitches got y'all in robes and house shoes. Y'all use to cook coke on the stove now y'all heating up baby bottles, rushing home at 4:00 to watch soap operas. Y'all done got the game fucked up."

"I am now convinced, that you are out of your got damn mind," my brother said to me.

"Man I'm perfectly sane, it's y'all niggas that crazier than a muthafucka. Scary ass, pussy whipped, walking through the mall holding your bitch's purse ass, niggas. Never thought in a million years."

I had to laugh at the thought. "This is some bullshit, asking me why I fucked his wife. Why the fuck you think? 'Cause I can. And as far as the Dons, don't worry about me and them. I can handle myself. But after this I ain't ridin' with y'all niggas no more. Get the fuck outta here."

I know these two niggas wanted to take my head but they ain't crazy they just walked out the room. I know they could hear me laughing harder with every step they took.

THE END

Kaylin and Trae stood in dead silence, waiting on the elevator. Kaylin was still trying to wrap his mind around the things his brother had said. He began to question his loyalty to his brother and to the streets, "Damn, am I really getting soft?" he asked himself while trying to justify his recent endeavors to become completely legit and walk away from "the game."

"Fuck this shit! I'm done; I'm out . . . I'm cutting all ties to the streets," Kaylin said to himself.

—Ding—

The sound of the elevator broke the eerie silence that filled the hall, the elevator doors opened and Kaylin stepped inside but Trae did not. He stood there with the smell of revenge seeping through his pores. Kaylin glanced over his shoulder as if he smelled him and his lust for revenge that was obviously seeping out.

With his back still turned to his partner in crime Kaylin said, "The game is over, when you get tired of playing."

Trae shook his head and said, "You said you wanted out the

game, well this is the best time to bounce because shit just got real."

The elevator doors closed, leaving Trae behind.

In the dimly lit hallway Trae removed the ski mask from the side pocket of his pants and put it on top of his bald head wearing it as a skully. He then placed a pair of black leather gloves over his hands and turned his reversible blue hoodie inside out revealing the black inside. He had planned for the worst and was glad he came prepared.

Making his way down the hall and not looking anyone directly in the eye, he dipped into a sleeping patient's room, grabbing the bouquet of flowers off of the table. The three on duty nurses were distracted by an elderly patient going into cardiac arrest giving him the window of opportunity that he needed.

He walked into Kyron's room, undetected with flowers in hand, closed the door and placed the flowers on the table.

Kyron's eyes popped open.

Trae pulled out his S30v steel blade pocket knife and pushed the curtains back.

Trae plunged the blade deep into his throat, turned it and pulled it out.

TRAE

"What you got to say now, nigga? Talk shit now muthafucka!" He held down Kyron with his one hand, watching life slip away from the brother of his best friend.

Kyron reached for his throat with his free hand unable to breathe properly. His silence was golden.

I stood there until this grimy muthafucka took his last breath all the while thinking to myself: out of all the lives I took, and all the shit I did, not until this very moment had any of it felt justified. I knew that now I was no longer a retired hustler. I had just reentered the game.

Reading Group Discussion Questions

1. How do you think Kaylin handled the whole Trae/Tasha/Kyron fiasco?
2. How should Jaz have dealt with Oni after her initial contact with Faheem?
3. Should Faheem have made passes at Oni?
4. What were your thoughts when Trae fucked Charli again?
5. Do you think Trae overreacted on the plane? Or was he just passed his boiling point?
6. If you were Tasha, would you have given Trae head after he punched you in the mouth?
7. Did Tasha seem too nonchalant about Stephon's death?
8. Was Tasha wrong for continuing to fuck with Kyron? Should she or could she have quit while she was ahead?
9. Do you think Rick should get back with Kyra or stay with Nina?
10. Did Faheem overreact when he threw Jaz out? If so, why? If not, why?

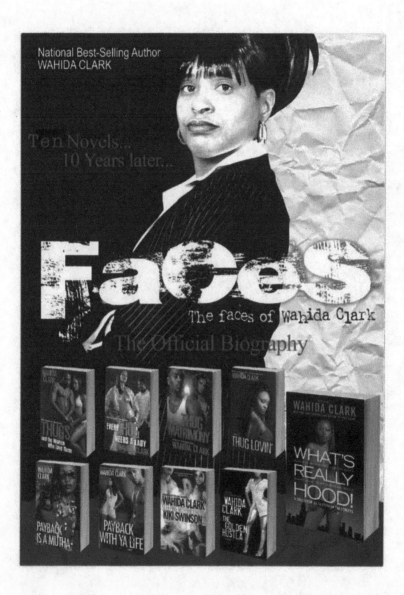